WHO KILLED
THE HUSBAND?

AN AMOS LEE MAPPIN MYSTERY

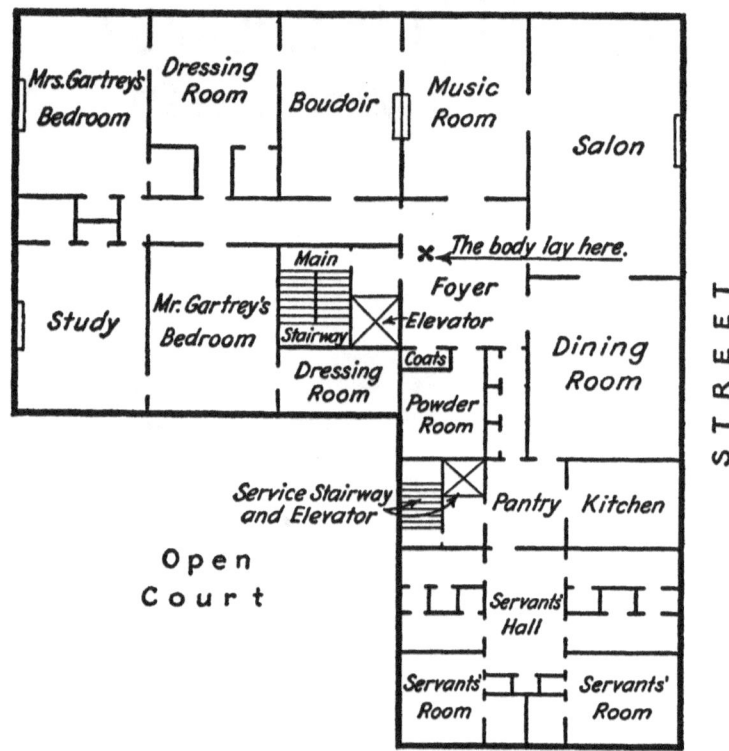

FIFTH AVENUE

Mrs. Gartrey's Bedroom

Dressing Room

Boudoir

Music Room

Salon

Study

Mr. Gartrey's Bedroom

Main Stairway

Dressing Room

The body lay here.

Foyer

Elevator

Coats

Powder Room

Dining Room

Service Stairway and Elevator

Pantry

Kitchen

Open Court

Servants' Hall

Servants' Room

Servants' Room

STREET

A SKETCH PLAN OF THE GARTREY APARTMENT
WHERE ALL THE EXCITEMENT TOOK PLACE

WHO KILLED
THE HUSBAND?
AN AMOS LEE MAPPIN MYSTERY

HULBERT FOOTNER

COACHWHIP PUBLICATIONS

Greenville, Ohio

CONTENTS

CHAPTER ONE

MR. AMOS LEE MAPPIN WAS BREAKFASTING by the fire in the immense living room of his apartment. With the steam heat, a fire was not in the least necessary, but he enjoyed it. The date was November 4th. During the pleasant fall days it was Lee's habit to turn off the steam, open the windows and toast himself in front of the cheerful blaze. "I am a primitive creature," he would say, which was one of his innocent affectations. Nothing could have been farther from the truth.

He was wearing a crimson damask dressing gown with a blue silk scarf around his throat and blue morocco slippers. His taste in dress ran to such flamboyant effects but, conscious that they sat rather comically on his little, roly-poly figure, he sported them only in the privacy of the home. He nibbled his grilled kidney and sipped his coffee in great peace of mind. His big book, "The Psychology of Murder," was progressing well. He was revolving the day's work in his mind while he ate, and occasionally put down his knife and fork to make a note in his little pocketbook.

Since he had become famous, somebody was always trying to engage his services in this case or that. Being as fastidious as a cat, he hated to soil his paws with the actual investigation of crime; his job, as he told himself over and over, was to study crime in the privacy of the library a long time after it had been committed. So he refused all offers, however tempting the fee; he didn't need the money; nevertheless, every now and then such pressure was brought upon him that he was forced to take a case. When he had solved the mystery he always drew a sigh of relief and vowed that it should be the last. At the moment there was no important criminal case to agitate the public mind and he envisioned a long succession of serene days to be devoted to his philosophical treatise.

His servant, Jermyn, tall, lean, leathery and correct, entered bringing the *Herald Tribune*, which he placed folded upon the table beside the breakfast tray. Jermyn did not speak, but he had been working for Mr. Mappin for a long time, and his master could read him like a printed page. It was evident from Jermyn's overcasual air that there was something in the morning's paper that he considered it important his master should see. He left the room.

Opening the paper, Mr. Mappin saw at once what it was. Jules Gartrey, the prominent banker, president of the famous Hasbrouck firm, had been found shot dead in his apartment and the police were looking for young Alastair Yohe, society's pet photographer. Mrs. Gartrey, whom they called "the most beautiful woman in New York," was said to be "prostrated." Mr. Mappin threw the paper aside pettishly. The vulgarest of crimes! He was annoyed that Jermyn should have supposed he would be interested. Of course, it would cause a terrific sensation because of the conspicuousness of the principals. Mappin hated empty sensationalism. He disdained to read the details.

Putting it out of mind, he finished eating and went out on the balcony to bask in the morning sun while he smoked a cigarette. The East River sparkled far below; it was pleasant to think of the fascinating, baffling problems of human conduct that formed the subject matter of his book. Not this commonplace killing. Afterwards he went to his room to dress. For the street he affected a modified early nineteenth-century style. With his bald head, his polished glasses, his round belly under a white waistcoat, his neat legs encased in tightish pants, he looked like Mr. Pickwick as Cruikshank drew him, and gloried in it. He couldn't go all the way with Mr. Pickwick's costume; that would have made him too conspicuous. He hated to be stared at.

When he arrived at his office on Murray Hill the heads of both his assistants, blonde Fanny Parran and brunette Judy Bowles, were bent over newspapers, and that annoyed him afresh. No need to ask what they were reading. The girls were so absorbed that their greeting was perfunctory; "'Morning, Pop," they said without looking up. He went on into his private office.

Presently Fanny came in bearing the newspaper. "Have you read this?" she asked.

"The headlines," he answered.

"This is the biggest case since Cain killed Abel!" said Fanny solemnly. "Fancy, Jules Gartrey shot in his own house!"

"Humph!" snorted Mr. Mappin. "Husband comes home unexpectedly; finds a younger man there; probably attacks him and gets shot for his pains. It happens every day somewhere."

"Not to the Jules Gartreys of this world," said Fanny. "We've got to get in this case, Pop."

"Get in it!" cried Mr. Mappin, now thoroughly exasperated. "For heaven's sake, what is there in it for us?"

"Useless for you to talk that way," said Fanny coolly. "A man as prominent as you simply can't be left out of a case as big as this. You'll see."

"All the police have got to do is catch the killer."

She shook her head. "Not so simple as all that. There's a lot that's unexplained. Sure, Al Yohe and Mrs. Gartrey have been running around together, but that doesn't prove anything. You're thinking in the terms of mellerdrammer, Pop. Modern people don't act like that—not *that* lot, anyhow. There's something back of it. . . . Do you know Al Yohe?" she asked suddenly.

"Haven't that pleasure," said Lee stiffly. "I've seen him, of course. Couldn't very well avoid it."

"He's not the type," said Fanny. "If he was caught by a husband he would laugh."

"You seem to know him pretty well!"

"Oh, I've met him at the Sourabaya; it's his job to greet everybody who comes there. If you were to judge by what the newspapers say, he is just a common sort of Casanova who goes around rolling his eyes at women and trying to hypnotize them. But that's not the truth, Pop. He's an American boy, full of jokes, laughing all the time. It's true that women fall for him right and left—Mrs. Gartrey is mad about him; I've seen it—but that's because he tells them the truth about themselves. No woman can resist it, Pop—not when the man is so darned good-looking."

With that she left him. Lee was sufficiently impressed by her earnestness to pick up the newspaper and read the Gartrey story from beginning to end. It was meager as to fact and voluminous in innuendo.

The Gartreys lived in a magnificent apartment on Fifth Avenue overlooking the Park. Gartrey had had two wives before marrying the present Mrs. Gartrey, one dead, one divorced, and this one was thirty years younger than her husband. Alastair Yohe had called at three o'clock on the previous afternoon and was still there when the husband came home half an hour or so later. This was earlier than his usual hour, the house elevator boy testified. Gartrey had let himself in with a key instead of ringing; consequently nobody was aware of his return until the shot was heard. He was found lying in the entrance foyer, shot through the temple. The butler, Robert Hawkins, found him.

Oddly enough, the gun was lying on the floor near by. But the absence of powder burns in the dead man's flesh precluded the idea of suicide. There were no fingerprints on the gun. Mr. Gartrey was still holding his latchkey between thumb and forefinger, proving that he must have been shot down at the moment of entering. There could be no question of the killer's having acted in self-defense. Mr. Gartrey was not armed. The elevator boy and the boys on duty in the hall of the apartment house, all testified that, saving Alastair Yohe, no other person had been taken to the Gartrey apartment previous to the shooting.

The stories told by the inmates of the apartment were contradictory. Mrs. Gartrey, upon the advice of her husband's principal business associate, George Coler, talked fully to the police. Both she and her maid Eliza Young asserted that Mr. Yohe had taken his departure five minutes or more before the shot was heard. The maid added that she had opened the front door for him herself. Both women, of course, were anxious to divert any suspicion of scandal and were obviously desirous of clearing the young man. The maid's story was seriously damaged by the front elevator boy, who swore that he had not taken Mr. Yohe down in his car. Whereupon the maid pointed out that Yohe had several other friends in the apartment house and might have gone to call on one of them by the stairs. After the murder, so many people came and went that the elevator boy could give no account of them.

However, the maid's story was altogether destroyed by the butler, Hawkins, who testified very reluctantly that immediately after the shot was fired Mr. Yohe had come back into the rear entry of the apartment and had left by the service door. He had not said anything. He looked very disturbed. The other servants were in their rooms and had not seen him. The boy on the service elevator testified that he had not carried Yohe down, but there was a service stairway. The maid Eliza intimated that the butler had a grudge against Mr. Yohe and was lying. The most damning fact, however, was that Yohe had run away. The police promised an arrest within twenty-four hours.

Having digested the facts, Lee skimmed over the columns and columns of fluff that were considered due the occasion. In the minds of the newspaper writers, Yohe was already convicted of murder. They played up the romance of his career for all there was in it. The poor boy who had come to New York with nothing to recommend him but a certain skill in camera portraiture, plus remarkable good looks and charm of manner. It had been sufficient. Within five years he found himself publicity agent, official photographer and all-round hurrah boy at La Sourabaya, the smartest and most popular night club of the time. Al Yohe had made the place what it was. Not to be a friend of Al's was to argue yourself unknown around town.

In this short space of time, Yohe had become one of the most conspicuous social figures in New York. Men and women alike courted him—millionaires, actresses, authors, even scientists—not for himself but for the publicity that his wicked camera commanded. Not only was he the lord of La Sourabaya (the Oriental proprietors kept themselves discreetly in the background); gifts

were showered on him by the smartest shops in town; he was never
expected to pay for anything anywhere; he was besieged with invi-
tations to the best houses. In respect to his amatory adventures,
the writers had to be a little more careful.

They managed, however, to convey very clearly that Don Juan
of Sevila was a piker compared to Al Yohe of New York.

In order to build up Al, it was necessary to suggest that the
unfortunate Jules Gartrey was an unpleasant sort of man, hard and
unrelenting, unpopular alike in business and society. All the lush
adjectives in the reportorial vocabulary were used in referring to
Agnes Gartrey's beauty. The newspaper story actually managed to
suggest, without laying itself open to libel, that she had had lovers
before Al Yohe. The name of Rulon Innes, a well-known glamour
boy, was brought in.

Lee Mappin tossed the newspaper aside. "Vicious!" he muttered; "this attempt to make a hero out of a common murderer!"

Fanny, who had been watching him through the open door out
of the tail of her eye, came in with the morning's mail. "Well, what
do you think of it, Pop?" she asked casually.

"I think no different from what I did before," he answered
sharply. "Certainly there's nothing in the newspaper that would
induce a sensible man to change his opinion."

"You're wrong, Pop. Al Yohe is not the type."

"So you said before. How can you possibly know? Murderers
belong to no type. All kinds of people commit murder when the
provocation is strong enough."

"That's just it," said Fanny. "There is no reason in the world
why Al should have killed Mr. Gartrey."

"*Please*, Fanny," said Lee with heavy self-control, "don't let me
hear you falling into the vulgar habit of referring to a criminal as
if he were an intimate friend. Call him Yohe."

Fanny smiled with great sweetness. "All right, Pop, dear. . . .
Look, somebody obviously was lying in wait for Mr. Gartrey. That,
at least would be impossible for a man like Al . . . Yohe."

"I don't know," said Lee, "and neither do you. Al . . ."

"Yohe," whispered Fanny wickedly.

"Al Yohe was how old? Twenty-five. Twenty-five is too soon for a comely young face to reveal the real character of its wearer. Only the old *look* wicked."

"There were no fingerprints on the gun," said Fanny. "Yet they all say, that is, Mrs. Gartrey, Eliza Young, the elevator boy, even the lying butler, that Al Yohe's hands were bare."

"He had gloves in his pocket," said Lee. "It takes no time at all to pull on a loose glove and pull it off again."

CHAPTER TWO

DURING THE FOLLOWING THREE DAYS, the sensation caused by the murder of Jules Gartrey rose to monstrous proportions. Extra editions of the newspapers were issued every half hour; nothing else could be talked about. Great crowds stood dumbly in the street gazing up at the windows of the Gartrey apartment and midtown Fifth Avenue was choked in front of the Stieff Building where Al Yohe lived. They even stood all day long packed front and rear at Police Headquarters, on the chance that Yohe might be brought in. Disgraceful scenes attended the funeral of Mr. Gartrey. To avoid the crowds, he was carried to his country place in Westchester and buried from there. Word of it got around, and thousands besieged the place. Finding the gates locked, they swarmed over the fence and trampled down all the shrubbery and flowers.

Mrs. Gartrey remained in close seclusion, but was not, however, averse to being interviewed. She had a case to put before the world, and she presented it with skill, though nobody believed a word of her story. She had frequently met Mr. Yohe in society, she said, but he was not in any sense a close friend. It was the first time he had come to her house except when there was a party. She had sent for him to discuss the plans for a ball that was to be held at the Waldorf-Astoria in December in aid of Polish Relief. St. Bartholomew's Guild, of which she was secretary, was getting up the affair. At a meeting of the Guild it had been decided to ask Mr. Yohe to manage the ball because he was such a good organizer. In sending for him to talk the matter over, she was merely acting for

14

the Guild. He was out of the apartment a good five minutes before Mr. Gartrey came home. "My husband," said Mrs. Gartrey, "like all successful men, had bitter enemies. There were people who believed that they had lost money through him." She could not, however, furnish the police with names.

Mrs. Gartrey promptly discharged the butler, Robert Hawkins, whose story did not agree with hers. Hawkins could have made a small fortune by selling stories of the Gartrey household to the newspapers, but he proved to be a man of very unusual decency; he moved into a modest furnished room and declined to add a word to his first statement. When the pestering of the reporters became unbearable, he quietly left town without advertising his new address.

The maid, Eliza Young, loyally supported her mistress' story. She, of course, could let herself go more than the grand and dignified Mrs. Gartrey. Eliza was always available for an interview, and proved to be a passionate partisan of Alastair Yohe's. This reacted against him. A plain woman, no longer young, Eliza's lot in life had been singularly unexciting and, as was natural, all this notoriety began to go to her head. She talked too much. It was obvious to those who read her statements with attention that she was better acquainted with Yohe than would have been possible if he had made only one visit to the Gartrey home.

On the third day, Alan Barry Deane, a rich young man about town who lived on the second floor of the house where the Gartreys had an apartment, came forward to say that shortly before four o'clock on Monday (the afternoon of the murder), Alastair Yohe had called on him with the object of persuading him to serve on the floor committee of the Polish Relief Ball. He had consented to serve on the committee. They had talked together for a few minutes and had then gone out to discover the cause of the excitement that was filling the house. Deane said he did not know what became of Yohe after that, but insisted that up until then Yohe had appeared quite his usual self. This story, which was calculated to destroy that of the butler, was not, however, generally believed. The public felt that Deane had delayed too long before telling it, and that he was merely trying to recommend himself to the beautiful Agnes Gartrey.

Various new pieces of evidence were brought out. Upon the news of Gartrey's death, the securities of all the companies he was interested in had broken sharply. There was a heavy short interest which had taken the opportunity to cover at an enormous profit. The police had not been able to trace this interest to its source. It came out, moreover, that Gartrey's life had been threatened mysteriously and that about a month before, he had asked for police protection. About the same time he had taken out a permit and purchased a gun. Apparently he believed the threatened danger had passed, for at the time of his murder the gun was lying in a drawer of his bureau. The police at the same time were endeavoring to trace ownership of the gun found on the scene from which one shot had been fired. When they established that this gun had been sold to Alastair Yohe during the previous year, it was admitted that the case against Yohe was complete.

Meanwhile, that much-wanted young man succeeded in keeping out of the hands of the police. Though he had thousands of "friends," though he was the most be-photographed young man in the country, and his smiling, handsome face must have been familiar to every reader of newspapers from the Atlantic to the Pacific, he was not found. Trainmen, bus conductors, airplane stewardesses, ticket agents everywhere were looking for him. There were innumerable clues which came to nothing. Arrests were made by the local police of Philadelphia, Hanover, New Hampshire, Milledgeville, Georgia, and as far away as Fargo, North Dakota, and New York detectives sent out to bring him in, only to find themselves fooled. A bitter note crept into the communiques issued from Headquarters. It was obvious that somebody must be concealing the wanted man. Each day the police promised results within twenty-four hours.

It turned out that Yohe had proceeded directly from the scene of the murder to his own small bachelor apartment in the Stieff Building near the Plaza. The elevator man testified that he had looked "very upset." After a few minutes he had gone out again with a different suit on and was swallowed up by the unknown. He kept no personal servant. A maid employed by the management of the building said significantly that Mr. Yohe seldom slept at home. The public loved it. Upon searching his rooms the police had found nothing that pertained to the case. He was a discreet young man; he left no scrap of writing from any of the many women with whom his name had been connected. There were thousands of photographs of the great, the near-great and the would-be-great, some of which had a great potential value. They were so unflattering that the subjects might have been willing to pay anything to keep them out of print. But it was never charged that Yohe had taken money for such a purpose. A few of the photographs found their way into the newspapers, affording the town a series of laughs. The Commissioner of Police then cracked down on the press and impounded the lot.

These three days were full of little irritations for Lee Mappin. He was not allowed to forget the vulgar affair for long and his work suffered. Even the discreet, the correct Jermyn permitted himself to suggest that his master ought to take a hand in the case. At the office little Fanny Parran, usually so sensible, displayed a prejudice on behalf of the handsome young murderer as passionate and unreasonable as that of Eliza Young in the press. When the police finally identified the murder gun as Yohe's, Lee fetched a sigh of relief. Now, please God, they'll leave me alone! he thought.

When he got to the office there was no sign of grief or disappointment in Fanny's pretty face, no change of any sort. When she brought in the mail she said with a beguiling air—Lee had never seen her looking sweeter:

"Pop, why don't you talk to Inspector Loasby about the Gartrey case?"

"What is there to talk about?" said Lee, keeping a careful hold on his rising temper. "I am not a bloodhound. It is no part of my job to track down fugitives from justice."

"Of course not, Pop. That's not what I had in mind. Everybody in the world believes that Al Yohe is guilty. In the interests of justice you ought to examine the evidence that the police have against him and point out the flaws in it."

"My dear girl, have you the face to pretend you still believe that man to be innocent?"

"I'm not your dear girl when you talk to me like a stuffy school-master," said Fanny with spirit. "And I am *not* pretending."

"After the police have established that Gartrey was shot with Yohe's gun!"

"How can you be so wrongheaded?" cried Fanny. "That is the best proof of Al's innocence that has come out! Can you conceive of a man so stupid as to leave his gun at the scene of the killing? That gun was planted there!"

"Maybe so," cried Lee waving his hands. "It's no business of mine. I'm sick of hearing the fellow's name! If he's innocent why does he choose to live like a hunted creature? Let him come back like a man and face the music, and if he needs help I'll help him!"

"Now, Pop," said Fanny soothingly, "honestly, after taking everything into consideration, would you come back if you were in his place?"

Lee disdained to answer.

"If he came back there would be a hundred thousand yelling people around Police Headquarters. And what would the authorities do? Rush him to trial in order to quiet the mob; obtain a snap verdict—no jury would dare go against the mob—and rush him to execution. Would that be justice?"

"I cannot fight for a man in hiding," said Lee.

Fanny gave him a level look. "Well, I'm disappointed in you," she said, marching out.

Lee was left to nurse an unreasonable feeling of soreness and frustration. Fanny was not to be drawn into any further discussion and he was forced to argue it out with himself. Very unsatisfactory. He was satisfied that his attitude was the correct one, but how could you convince a woman when she wouldn't listen?

He spent a part of the afternoon in dictating to Judy. She was of an entirely different character from Fanny, more serene and placid, not so liable to fly off the handle, in a word more feminine, Lee told himself. Judy was of the tall and statuesque type with big brown eyes and hair like a raven's wing. Lee's eyes dwelt with pleasure on her graceful, bent head.

"You are very beautiful," he said.

"Thanks, Pop," she said calmly. She had heard it so often before. And went on all in the same breath: "Pop, why are you so prejudiced against poor Al Yohe?"

It was like a dash of cold water on Lee. "You too!" he said in the same tone that Caesar must have used to Brutus.

"Well, you are not usually so influenced by the newspapers," Judy went on. "How often have you told us that we should think for ourselves."

"Fanny's been getting at you!" said Lee.

"Of course we've talked the case over," said Judy; "how could we avoid it? But I don't take all my ideas from Fanny. I have a mind of my own, I hope."

"Will you please tell me what sources of information you possess besides the newspapers?" asked Lee.

His sarcasm never touched her. "None," she said in her calm and gentle manner. "I read the newspapers and form my own conclusions."

"And what are they, may I ask?"

"Why can't you talk about it reasonably, Pop? Why do you get sore whenever Al's name is mentioned? According to your own rule, that proves your case is weak."

It did not make Lee feel any less sore to have his own words turned against him.

Judy went on in her calm way: "It all sounds too cut and dried, Pop. Something important is omitted. They say that Mr. Gartrey came home unexpectedly and surprised them. They also say that the shot was not fired in the heat of passion but that Al was laying for him. They can't have it both ways, Pop. If he came home before he was expected, how could Al have been laying for him at the door?"

Lee looked at her in surprise. "That's rather neatly argued," he said.

Judy blushed with pleasure. "You think I'm beautiful but dumb," she said.

"That's not so," insisted Lee, "or I couldn't afford to keep you here."

Judy made haste to follow up her advantage. "That woman is certainly lying, Pop!"

"Why, she's Al's only friend!" In spite of himself Lee was falling into the habit of referring thus familiarly to the celebrity.

"If she's really his friend she's a fool," said Judy. "She's not going the right way about it to clear him. I often have to lie myself and I can tell when another woman is lying."

"What is your idea of what really happened, my dear?" asked Lee quite mildly.

Judy spread out her hands. "Ah, I haven't any," she said. "That's where we must depend on you, Pop. If you delved into the case you would find out the truth about it."

Lee said judicially: "In the apartment at the time of the shooting were Mrs. Gartrey and Al Yohe; Hawkins, the butler; Eliza Young, the lady's maid, and four other maids. There is a second manservant but he was out on an errand. How could it have been any of these excepting Yohe? How could I even start an investigation without having an opportunity to hear Yohe's own story?"

"That's so," said Judy rising. "It hadn't occurred to me." She went out thoughtfully. A moment later he saw her in deep confabulation with Fanny.

A man from the *World-Telegram* came in to see him. He was followed by a *Daily News* reporter and a whole group of others, including redheaded Tom Cottar from the *Herald Tribune*. Tom had been sweet on Fanny Parran for a long time. Lee noted that her greeting today was somewhat cool. Tom was a prime favorite with Lee, and the others, knowing it, let Tom do the talking.

"Mr. Mappin, we want an opinion from you on the Gartrey case."

"Now, Tom," warned Lee, "you know that I have made it a rule not to discuss a crime before it comes to trial."

"You don't need to express an opinion as to Al Yohe's guilt," said Tom. "That's established. Just discuss the case generally. Tell us what it suggests to you from a social point of view, or any such tripe."

"Tripe?" said Lee, running up his eyebrows.

"You know what I mean," said Tom, grinning. "This case has reached such proportions that the public is demanding an expression of views from their favorite criminologist."

"Poppycock!" said Lee. "The truth is, the public is ravenous for news about the case; you haven't any for them today and so you come to me for a filler."

"Well, you have never let us down yet," said Tom cajolingly.

"I'm going to now. I have nothing to say."

"Now, Mr. Mappin . . ."

"By Gad! if I'm pestered any further about this damned case I'll leave town!" cried Lee.

"Pestered?" asked the *Daily News* man, scenting a story. "By whom?"

"By all of you! Not another word!"

When they saw that he meant it, they filed out. Lee detained Tom. "I want to speak to you about a personal matter."

Tom looked at him inquiringly.

"Who tipped you off to come to me today?" asked Lee.

Tom shrugged innocently—too innocently. "The assignment came to me in the usual way."

"Tom, there appears to be a kind of conspiracy afoot with the object of forcing me into this case. You and I must make a stand against it."

Tom, after glancing uneasily over his shoulder, mutely put out a hand.

Lee grasped it. "What's behind it, Tom?"

"I'm with you, Pop," mumbled Tom, "but I can't say anything when she's just outside the door."

Lee glanced at his watch. "I'll be leaving here in half an hour. Meet me in the Vanderbilt bar at five-ten."

"Okay, Pop."

Sitting at a little table in the Vanderbilt bar with Scotch and soda before them, Lee and Tom compared notes. Said Tom:

"This guy is as guilty as hell, Lee. That was nothing in my life until Fanny felt that she had received a call to save him. Since then

I have had no peace. She is threatening to ship me because I can't change the policy of the *Herald Tribune* toward the case. Damn him anyhow! By God! how I would like to flatten his Grecian nose with my fist! All handsome men are so-and-sos!" Tom had no pretensions to good looks, though there was a pleasing masculinity about his strongly marked features.

"I sympathize with you," said Lee. "What started Fanny off at this tangent?"

"Don't ask me. She is mysterious."

"Is it possible she could have seen Al Yohe since the murder?"

"No."

"Before this happened, had you any reason to suppose that Fanny had fallen in love with him?"

"She's not in love with him," said Tom coolly. "I would know how to deal with that. This is worse, Pop. God help a man when his girl embarks on a moral crusade! He is helpless!"

"Well, we've got to stand out against this foolishness until it blows over," said Lee firmly. "To give in to it would only be to make ourselves ridiculous!"

They shook hands on it again.

CHAPTER THREE

LEE WAS ENGAGED to dine this night with the Curt Wintergrenns. He had been looking forward to the occasion because Carol Wintergrenn had snapped up a French refugee chef who was a master of his profession. This was his first performance and he would certainly be on his mettle. Lee loved masterly cooking. However, when he reflected that the table talk would inevitably concentrate on the Gartrey case, his heart sank. He called up Mrs. Wintergrenn to beg off.

She wouldn't hear of it. "Lee!" she screamed. "At the eleventh hour! The dinner of the season! I am depending on you to hold it together; to give the affair a cachet! How could I replace you now? My party will be ruined. I don't believe you've got a headache. Tell me the real reason you want to stay away."

Answered Lee: "You're entitled to the truth, my darling. I am so fed up with this nasty Gartrey affair that it nauseates me. I know, people being what they are, nothing else will be talked about to-night, and I can't face it."

"Is that all?" she said in a voice of relief. "Well, I haven't been giving dinners for ten years for nothing. You sit beside me and I shall keep the conversation in my own hands. I promise you you shan't be annoyed."

So Lee agreed to be there.

Unfortunately for Carol Wintergrenn's promise, there were two men at her table whose names had been connected with the Gartrey case, George Coler and Rulon Innes, and she found herself helpless. She would no sooner get the talk steered away from the all-absorbing

23

topic than somebody would ask Coler or Innes a question. The whole table would wait in silence for the answer, and off they would go again. However, Lee did not mind it as much as he had expected; the limelight was beating on the two men in the know, and little Lee was allowed to savor the marvelous *salmi de caneton* in peace.

Coler, who was Gartrey's principal lieutenant in business, was a handsome bachelor in the middle forties with a reputation for wit and *savoir-faire* that caused him to be much in demand for dinners. Lee had never cared for him, simply because he had himself under such perfect control. Lee himself was not accustomed to wearing his heart on his sleeve, and he freely granted the necessity of keeping a guard on yourself in the great world, but such people did not interest him; for him in woman or man it was the native wood-note wild that charmed.

A woman asked: "Mr. Coler, honestly, how is dear Agnes bearing up under the strain?" The affected solicitude did not conceal the purr of satisfaction in her voice. Older and plainer women naturally were delighted to see Agnes Gartrey catching it.

"Magnificently!" said Coler smoothly. "Like all your sex, when faced by something really big, she has risen out of herself."

"Is she in love with Al Yohe?"

"Honestly," said Coler, spreading out his hands, "I don't know. I am the watchdog of her business affairs, not her heart."

"Of course she is!" cried another woman. "Look how she stands up for him!"

"That proves nothing. She has to stand up for him in order to clear her own skirts."

"Strange as it may seem, I think she was attached to her hard-boiled old husband," said Coler. "At least, they got along pretty well together, considering."

"Impossible!" exclaimed all the women together.

"A man thirty years older!"

"If she is in love with Yohe," Coler went on, "so much the worse for her. Even in the unlikely event of his clearing himself, they could never come together now."

Young Rulon Innes, feeling that he had been left out of the conversation long enough, now delivered his opinion authoritatively:

"None of you are being fair to Agnes. Nobody understands her. She has the heart of a child!"

Hearing this, the women kept their lips decorous, but their eyes were frankly derisive. Lee, glancing around the table, enjoyed the comedy.

Innes was a handsome young man in a somewhat luscious style. He was so filled with the consciousness of his beauty that he appeared to be about to choke on it. Lee wondered how a woman could fall for him, yet many had; perhaps it was because he, after Al Yohe, was the fashion.

"*Is* she in love with Al Yohe?" persisted the first woman.

"Nothing to it," said Innes languidly, regarding his fingernails. "Al's methods with women were those of a truck driver. No finesse." He paused to point the contrast between Al and himself. Some of the women bit their lips. "Agnes would never fall for that sort of thing," he went on. "She is too fastidious. . . . Does it not occur to any of you that she may be telling the simple truth?"

Carol Wintergrenn was provoked. "The truth is never simple," she said, "and nobody nowadays ever tells it. . . . For heaven's sake, let us talk about something else."

They paid no attention to her. Everybody at the table had a contribution to make to the Gartrey case and sat bouncing in impatience to get a word in. There was Miss Delphine Harley, the actress, perennially lovely and smiling. She said:

"I must take exception to truck driver. Poor Al's manners were free but never coarse. He despised the sultry innuendo that passes for love-making in the night clubs. Al never 'made love.' He captivated women by making them laugh. His apparent sexlessness was a challenge to us. His naturalness, his honesty were as refreshing as a breeze off the sea."

This produced a little babel of assent and dissent around the table. Miss Harley popped a forkful of the *salmi* into her mouth and murmured: "Delicious!" Rulon Innes laughed a thought too loudly and was heard to say:

"Al Yohe sexless! That's good!"

"Women will know what I mean," said Delphine quietly. "Don't think that I am belittling sex," she went on with her delightful, wicked smile. "Sex is grand! But I must say we women get a little tired of seeing it paraded like a drum major."

There were murmurs of assent from other women. "Perhaps," said Delphine, delicately balancing her fork, "perhaps Al Yohe's pretense of sexlessness was the finest kind of finesse."

Lee went through the motions of clapping his hands. He loved wit in a woman. Delphine Harley was doing something that Fanny and Judy had not been able to accomplish, forcing him a little to reconsider his ideas about the legendary Al.

There was a Senator at the table, who protested throatily: "But, my dear Miss Harley, a murderer!"

"Oh, that's something else again," said Delphine with a shrug.

"Surely you can't have any doubt as to his guilt?"

"I have no opinion at all," said Delphine sweetly. "I leave that to my betters."

"Well, I'll tell you what *I* think," put in the woman who had started the discussion. "It has not been suggested in the newspapers, but I believe that Agnes Gartrey herself is keeping him under cover."

This was received around the table with the silence of astonishment.

"I don't believe he ever left the apartment!" she added triumphantly.

This opened up fascinating possibilities to her hearers.

"Oh, I assure you you are wrong," said George Coler earnestly. "Mrs. Gartrey has discussed the case with me in all its implications. I can state positively that if she knew where he was, she would be the first to produce him."

After the ladies had left the table and the gentlemen were occupied with their cigars and liqueurs, a footman approached Lee Mappin.

"If you please, Mr. Mappin, you're wanted on the telephone, sir."

Lee left the table in some surprise. He could think of no reason why anyone should call him there. The servant led him to a telephone booth at the back of the hall. It was a woman's voice that came over the wire, a voice unknown to Lee.

"Mr. Mappin, please forgive me for disturbing you."

"Who is it?" asked Lee mildly.

"Agnes Gartrey."

Lee felt like a big round O of astonishment. He had never met Mrs. Gartrey, but the quality of the voice, its agitation, assured him that this was certainly she.

"Yes, Mrs. Gartrey?"

The voice became imploring. "Would you come to see me tonight?"

"But I'm dining out, Mrs. Gartrey."

"I know. It doesn't matter how late you are."

"But what can I do for you?"

"Just give me a little advice. Everything I do or say seems to be the wrong thing!"

Curiosity is a powerful motive force. "Very well, Mrs. Gartrey, I will be there as soon as I can get away."

"Oh, thank you so much! Please don't say anything about your visit to me."

"I shall not do so."

When he returned to the dining room Curt Wintergrenn said: "No bad news, I hope, Lee."

"No, indeed, Curt. A bit of routine business, that's all."

"You looked a little disturbed."

Lee laid a hand on his epigastrium. "I partook a little too generously of the *caneton*."

"Have a brandy?"

When they returned to the drawing room Mrs. Wintergrenn was sitting alone at the coffee table and Lee went to her. "Carol, I have had a phone call, I shall have to slip away, my dear."

She looked at him doubtfully. "Don't you like my party? . . . Honestly, Lee, I'm distressed because I couldn't steer the talk better."

"You needn't apologize for that," he said. "I'm positively becoming interested in the case."

"Do me a little favor before you go," begged Carol.

"Anything within my power, my dear."

"While you men were at the table we got to talking about crime. Somebody said that criminals had a snap nowadays because of modern inventions. For instance, a call made from a dial phone cannot be traced. I said that might be, but that you were able to read off a phone number just from hearing it dialed. They all scouted at the idea. Please, Lee, give them a demonstration."

"I hate to do parlor tricks," said Lee.

"I know, but just to bear me out, *please*. Afterwards you can slip out quietly, and I'll make your excuses."

Lee submitted and the whole party adjourned to the hall to make the test.

One went into the booth while Lee, provided with pencil and pad, turned his back on it. As the numbers were dialed, Lee made marks on his pad.

Out of five tries he read off four correctly, and great was the wonder of the beholders.

"There is no magic in it," said Lee; "simply a question of training your ear. Some people pull the dial around quickly, some slowly; you pay no attention to that sound. But the dial always comes clicking back at the same measured rate of speed; that is what you listen for. I can do it without pencil and paper, but there is a danger of forgetting a number before the call is completed. So I make these marks of different lengths corresponding to the passage of the dial, and then I have a record."

"Marvelous!" they cried.

Soon afterwards he made an inconspicuous get-away.

THE GARTREY APARTMENT occupied the entire eighth floor of one of the finest buildings on the avenue. A manservant admitted Lee to a stately foyer. An immense music room opened off on his left and in front of him a salon as big as a museum. Today the very rich have more space in their city apartments than they once had in a whole house. Mrs. Gartrey presently came swimming to meet him in something pink that set off her cunningly dressed chestnut hair. She looked like a girl and was, perhaps, thirty years old. She was beautiful but not so beautiful in the flesh as in her photographs. It was because hers was a beauty of feature rather than expression. The touch of gentleness that makes a woman wholly adorable was lacking. It was clear that she had suffered dreadfully during the past few days, but it had not softened her.

"How good of you!" she murmured.

"I was glad to come if you think I can be of the least use," said Lee.

She led him to a settee by the fireplace. She was alone in the vast room. Lee reflected that rich people were apt to be lonelier than the poor. They sat down.

"Will you have a drink, Mr. Mappin?"

"Thanks, no. I have just come from a too-hospitable house."

A bitter expression crossed her face. "I expect I was well discussed around the table."

He wasn't going to lie to her. "You were," he said candidly.

"What did they say?"

"Oh, come, Mrs. Gartrey, you didn't ask me here to repeat silly gossip. I assure you you did not lack defenders at the table."

She put a handkerchief to her lips. "It's so hard to know where to begin my story!" she murmured.

"Tell me why you chose to send for me instead of somebody else."

"That's easy," she said. "One reads your books; one reads in the newspaper how extraordinarily clever you are in bringing the truth to light in baffling cases. I want you to find out the truth of this case."

Lee waited for more. It was obvious that the woman was suffering intensely, but did she really want the truth? He doubted it.

"You understand," she went on, "I am asking you to accept me for a client. I expect to pay for your services."

Lee waved his hand. That didn't commit him to anything.

Her voice scaled up. "The newspapers are like a pack of dogs, like a pack of dogs yapping at Mr. Yohe's heels!" she cried. "He is innocent of any wrongdoing. He was out of the house before my husband came home. I want you to prove that to the world."

"How can I without his co-operation?" said Lee.

She put a hand over her eyes. "Oh, I know! I know! It was suicidal for him to run away and to stay away. I wish to God I could reach him. I could soon persuade him to come back."

Lee said, to see what kind of reaction he would get: "It has been suggested that you do know where he is."

"That's a lie," she said scornfully. "Would I be suffering this horrible uncertainty? Would I stay here if I knew? This place has become a nightmare to me. Every time I cross the foyer I can see my husband lying there."

"Why do you stay here?"

"Because I think that Al . . . Mr. Yohe may try to get in touch with me here. By telephone. Even the telephone is risky, but he might take a chance. I am listening for it day and night!"

Lee thought: Okay, she does not know where he is.

He said: "Until he does come back, Mrs. Gartrey, I don't see what I can do."

"Oh, you must, you must help me!" she cried, clasping her hands. "Ask me whatever you like and I'll gladly pay it!"

"Believe me, it's not a question of a fee," he said mildly. "I have sufficient for my modest wants. I have no family."

"All you have to do is to come out in his favor," she pleaded. "Then, wherever he is, he would see that he had a friend and a powerful one; that would bring him back."

Lee said firmly: "I can't come out in his favor until I see some reason to doubt his guilt."

"He's innocent!" she wailed. "Who should know that better than I?"

"If Alastair Yohe didn't shoot your husband, who did?" asked Lee bluntly.

"Oh, I don't want to accuse anybody else! I have no proof!"

"If you have even a suspicion it will be safe with me."

"Have you thought of the butler, Robert Hawkins?" she asked in a muffled voice.

"Hm, that's a new lead," said Lee.

"He was in a position to do it," she went on eagerly, "and it would explain why he tried to put it off on Al."

"What motive could Hawkins have had?"

"Personal motive? None! He was only a servant. But my husband had enemies. Men of great wealth. It would have been easy for one of them to get at Hawkins and to pay him, to pay him a great sum, perhaps, to do away with my husband."

"That's a possibility," said Lee. "I will investigate it."

"I understand that Hawkins has disappeared," she said.

"Only from the newspaper reporters. He has given the police his present address."

"Oh, he's a smooth customer," she said bitterly. "Don't be deceived by his snowy hair and his seeming honesty!"

"I am not easily deceived," said Lee mildly.

"He washes his hair with bluing to make it whiter," she said acidly. "My maid told me. It wouldn't do any good for you to talk to him. He would only lie."

"Naturally. I shall endeavor to find out if he has come into any money lately."

Mrs. Gartrey arose. "You must let me give you a check, Mr. Mappin. You shall name the amount yourself!"

Lee held up his hand. "Thank you, no! I have not yet taken the case."

Mrs. Gartrey's eyes never left his face. As they proceeded toward the door, she saw him looking at the masses of expensive flowers that filled the room, and murmured: "People *will* send flowers. And usually the people one doesn't much care for. It is so inconsiderate. Every box that comes administers a fresh stab!"

"Why don't you send them to a hospital?" he asked dryly.

"The senders usually call to extend their condolences. They would be offended if they didn't see their flowers."

Lee passed a huge bouquet of American Beauty roses with stems three feet long. Under the edge of the vase which contained them was caught the edge of a card—presumably the sender's. On it was written: "Deepest sympathy—Rulon."

"Mrs. Gartrey," said Lee, "why don't you address Mr. Yohe through the newspapers? Wherever he is, we may be sure that he reads them."

"How can I?" she murmured distressfully. "In the first shock of this awful happening I was so confused, so distracted, that I made the mistake of telling the police that he was just a casual acquaintance. You know better than that. I can't hide anything from you. But I trust you. You see, if the truth about what I feel came out now, it would only react against him."

There was something very flattering, very affecting in the sight of the famous beauty casting herself on his mercy like this. And she knows it! thought Lee. "I see," he said.

"But Mr. Mappin, I swear to you there has been no wrong-doing!" she protested.

"I accept it," said Lee. He took a pinch of snuff. "I may say, though, that it wouldn't make the slightest difference to me if there had been."

She laid her hand lightly for a moment on his arm. "Ah, you are so kind and understanding!"

"Still," he said, "why can't you put an ad among the public notices that none but he would understand. Haven't you some private way of addressing him that he would recognize?"

She shook her head with an appearance of great sadness. "No! It hadn't gone as far as that, you understand."

CHAPTER FOUR

LEE MAPPIN HAD NOW REACHED the point where he read with care every word in the newspapers appertaining to the Gartrey case. His face turned a little grim next morning when he came upon this item in the *Herald Tribune*:

> Amos Lee Mappin, the well-known author and criminologist, is known to have called on Mrs. Jules Gartrey at her apartment late last night.
>
> What took place during this interview can only be surmised, but it looks as if Mr. Mappin was preparing to enter the case on behalf of the missing Alastair Yohe.

Tipped off the paper herself, thought Lee.

When he reached the office he was a little disturbed to see the glint of a fresh determination in Fanny Parran's blue eye. She did not keep him long in doubt as to what it portended. Bringing in the mail, she said:

"Pop, I've been thinking all night about something you said to Judy yesterday."

"What was that, my dear?"

"You said you couldn't make any move to help Al Yohe unless you could hear his story."

"That's right," said Lee, wondering what on earth was coming next.

"Would you consent to see Al Yohe and let him tell you his story?"

Lee almost bounced out of his chair. "Good God! Fanny, do you realize what you're saying?"

"Perfectly."

"Do you know where he is?"

"No," she said calmly.

"What am I to understand from this extraordinary proposition of yours?"

"Well," she said cautiously, "I've been approached by somebody who knows Al and presumably is able to communicate with him."

"Was it Mrs. Gartrey?" demanded Lee.

Fanny turned pink with anger. "No indeed! I believe that woman is playing a double part and Judy thinks so, too."

"Then who was it?"

Fanny's soft lips hardened. "I won't tell you that, Pop. It's useless for you to ask me."

"My dear girl," said Lee, holding himself in, "don't you understand that for you to have any truck with a fugitive from justice without informing the police, constitutes you an accessory to his crime?"

Fanny was unimpressed. "Surely, I know it. It's one of those things men make such a fuss about that you might think it was important."

"And what is more important?"

"Many things. Justice, honor, good faith—" Fanny touched her breast, "and that something in here which prompts you how to act in a specific case whatever the usual rules may be."

"I am being instructed," said Lee dryly.

"I am only applying what you have taught me," said Fanny firmly.

Though he preserved an appearance of calmness, Lee was growing a little warm. "Those are brave words," he said, "but the plain truth of the matter is that you have become infatuated with this . . ."

Fanny turned pink again. "That's not so, Pop. It's not desire for the man that has got me going, but a desire to see justice done. Why this woman who came to me . . ."

"So it was a woman!"

"She is much closer to Al Yohe than I could ever be—or wish to be. Would I be trying to help her if I wanted him myself?"

Lee shifted ground a little. "Am I to understand that this request for an interview comes from the woman or from Al himself?"

"From Al. He wants nothing in the world so much as a chance to tell you his story."

"Do you know his story?"

"I do not, and neither does the person who came to me. Al will not tell it to anybody but yourself."

"Can't he write it?"

"He dare not trust it to paper."

"But if he told me his story I would have to carry it direct to the police."

"Al does not believe that you would do that after hearing his story, that is, not until you had conducted an investigation of your own. There are certain facts that have to be established. The truth is well hidden and he feels that only you can dig it up. It would be fatal to put it in the hands of the police."

Lee had recovered his good humor. "This is horribly tempting," he said. "My curiosity is at fever heat, but I must stick to the line I have adopted. Unless I play along with the police I might as well go out of business altogether."

"Then I am to send word that you refuse to see Al Yohe?"

"Unless there is a policeman present," said Lee, smiling.

"No good," said Fanny glumly. "He won't give himself up."

"And what's more," said Lee, "for your own sake I must urge you to play along with me. This is a dangerous business you're embarking in, my dear. Let the young fellow be arrested and you may rest assured that I will leave no stone unturned to discover the truth."

She shook her head. "That's your notion of the right thing to do; you must let me have mine. I couldn't betray the girl who trusts me. You can fire me if you like."

Lee was startled. "Bless your heart, I'm not going to fire you! But you mustn't tempt me any further. If I did right I would report this conversation to Inspector Loasby, but I'm going to stretch my conscience that far."

Fanny went out with her chin up.

Presently Lee taxied down to Headquarters. The moment
Loasby caught sight of him he said bitterly:

"I see you've started your own investigation of the Gartrey
case!" The handsome Inspector, owing to his failure to arrest Al
Yohe, had been the target of biting criticism in the press. He was
inordinately sensitive to criticism.

"To a certain extent," said Lee composedly, "but *not* at the
behest of the lovely widow."

"What did she say to you?"

"Wanted to retain me in her interest at a big fee . . ."

"Some men have all the luck!"

"I declined the fee. . . . The only thing she said that interested
me was to suggest that Robert Hawkins was the murderer."

"Don't believe it! Hawkins is the only square shooter in the
whole crooked bunch. What motive could he have had?"

"She suggested that some powerful enemy of Gartrey's had
hired the butler to do away with his master."

Loasby considered this. "Well, it's worth looking into. It puts a
new angle on the case."

"Keep it under your hat for the present," said Lee. "Will you let
me talk to Hawkins before you take any action?"

Loasby glanced at him with suspicion in his eye.

"I have no interest in this matter except to satisfy my own
curiosity," said Lee blandly; "and if I work with anybody it will
only be with you. . . . It won't be the first time."

The Inspector's face cleared. "Sure that's right, Mr. Mappin."
Picking up a phone from his desk, he asked a subordinate for the
address of Robert Hawkins, and when it came, repeated it to Lee.
"147A Orthodox Street, Frankford, Philadelphia. Is known there
under his right name. The landlady is Mrs. Quimby."

Lee made a note of it. "I'll run over to Philadelphia and report
to you on my return."

Loasby said: "Hawkins doesn't know it, but I'm keeping him
under surveillance, just in case anybody should try to bribe him to

make a real disappearance. The story he tells is very unpleasing to Al Yohe's friends."

"Quite," said Lee.

AT THE ADDRESS on Orthodox Street some two hours later, Lee found an old-fashioned rooming house. The door was opened to him by a decent body who looked as if she might belong to the Quaker meeting house across the road.

"Is Mr. Hawkins home?"

"I'll see, sir."

"I won't trouble you to climb the stairs," said Lee. "Just tell me which is his room and I'll go up."

There was nothing about Lee's natty little person to arouse a landlady's suspicions. "Two flights up, sir. Front hall room."

Lee knocked on the door and an agreeable voice bade him come in. The narrow room was shabby, comfortable and clean. The tenant, an elderly man, clean-shaven, was sitting by the window, reading. From old habit, Lee glanced first at the title of his book: *The Life of Andrew Jackson.* Hawkins hastily put the book down and rose, removing his glasses. He was tall and well made; his expression mild and benignant.

"I beg your pardon, sir. I thought it was the maidservant."

English, obviously, an old family servant whose beautiful manners had no trace of obsequiousness. This is very flattering to the masters. Lee could not help but feel drawn to Hawkins. He reminded himself that the perfect butler is the product of art, not of nature. After forty years of butlering, it would be impossible for an observer to tell what was really passing through a butler's mind.

"Do you know me?" asked Lee. "If you do, it will save explanations."

"Your face is familiar, sir, but I can't quite place it."

"Amos Lee Mappin."

The old man's eyes widened in surprise. "Mr. Mappin! Indeed, sir, I know you well by reputation."

"Then you know I'm not a mere curiosity seeker. The New York police furnished me with your address. I want to talk to you about the Gartrey case."

"Please to be seated, Mr. Mappin." He insisted on Lee's taking the comfortable chair by the window; himself remained standing.

"Sit down," urged Lee. "You are not in service now."

Hawkins sat in a plain chair beside the washstand.

"I will assume," said Lee, "that your story as reported in the newspapers was substantially correct. You need not repeat it but just answer my questions. At three o'clock last Monday afternoon Mr. Yohe came to see Mrs. Gartrey and you let him in."

"Yes, sir. I couldn't swear to the exact hour."

"It doesn't matter. Was he expected?"

"Yes, sir. Mrs. Gartrey had told me to bring him direct to her bou . . . her sitting room."

Lee did not miss the slip. "Her boudoir?"

"Yes, sir. That is what we called the room. But I have noticed in the United States that boudoir is taken to mean a bedroom, and I do not wish to convey a misapprehension. It was Mrs. Gartrey's private sitting room where she received her friends."

Lee smiled at the old man's conscientiousness. "I do not misapprehend you, Hawkins. Had he visited her before?"

Hawkins looked distressed. "Yes, sir, I am obliged to tell the truth. Many times, sir."

"Were they lovers?"

The old butler was shocked. "How should I know, sir?"

"Well, what is your opinion? Understand this is just for my information, not for the record."

"If my opinion is of any value to you, sir, I should say no. The young man's bearing was not that of a lover."

"And the lady's?"

"She was infatuated with him, sir. But saving myself, no one would be likely to have perceived it. I have lived a long time and have seen much."

"Is it your opinion, Hawkins, that Mr. Yohe shot Mr. Gartrey?"

"No, indeed, sir!" came the prompt reply. "I cannot conceive of his doing such a thing! It is a great grief to me that I am forced to give what appears to be damaging testimony against Mr. Yohe. Such

a merry young gentleman! Every servant in the house was devoted
to him. He didn't treat us like inferior beings, but as his friends.
He has a good heart, sir."

"Hm!" said Lee, stroking his chin. This was not the sort of
answer he had expected; it didn't fit any of the possible theories.
It annoyed him.

"And your master," he asked dryly, "were you attached to him?"

"I could hardly say that, sir. Mr. Gartrey was a very reticent
man; he never, so to speak, unbent."

"And Mrs. Gartrey?"

"A good mistress, Mr. Mappin; fair, and I may say, liberal. But
hardly to arouse any warmth of feeling, if you know what I mean.
She wouldn't have liked it."

"What were the relations between master and mistress?"

"Always polite, sir."

"Friendly?"

"Not exactly to say friendly, sir, but they never quarreled before
the servants."

"In these situations it is necessary to speak plainly, Hawkins.
Did they sleep together?"

"No, sir."

"Did other gentlemen come to see Mrs. Gartrey?"

"Oh, yes, sir, many gentlemen."

"Hawkins, can you be certain that there was no other gentleman
in the apartment on Monday when Mr. Gartrey was shot?"

"Absolutely, sir. Why, how could he have got in without our
knowing it, or the elevator man, or the boys in the hall downstairs?"

Lee spread out his hands. Realizing that he wasn't getting very
far, he changed his line. "Hawkins, is the Gartrey apartment a
duplex?"

"No, sir; all the rooms are on the same level."

"Where is the boudoir?"

"Facing the avenue in the bedroom wing, sir. There is a door
from the foyer into the bedroom corridor and in the corridor it's
the first door on your right."

"Can you draw me a rough plan?"

"Certainly, sir." Hawkins procured pencil and paper and presently offered the result for Lee's inspection. "In the bedroom wing, you see, sir, there are three rooms on the front. They constitute Mrs. Gartrey's suite; boudoir, dressing room and bedroom. Mr. Gartrey's bedroom and his study are across the corridor."

"Now, to return to Monday," said Lee, "after you had shown Mr. Yohe into the boudoir where did you go?"

"I returned to the pantry, sir. Monday afternoon is my time for polishing the silver. I was not interrupted at it until I heard the muffled shot in the foyer. You see, there was a hallway with a door between."

"What did you do?"

"Well, I wasn't *sure* that it was a shot. No other sounds followed. I listened for a moment or two, then I wiped my hands, took off my baize apron, put on my coat and started for the hall leading to the foyer. Before I reached it, Mr. Yohe appeared in the opening. I said: 'Is there anything wrong, sir?' He didn't answer me. He looked very wild. Perhaps he didn't hear. Crossing the pantry, he went on out to the service door and disappeared through it."

"You made no attempt to stop him?"

"No, sir. I only kept asking what was the matter. I was dumbfounded!"

"What about his hat and coat?"

"Hat on his head, overcoat over his arm, sir."

Lee considered. "Hawkins," he said, "if you stopped to listen, to take off your apron and put on your coat, a minute or so must have passed since the shot was fired."

"Yes, sir."

"What do you suppose Yohe was doing during that minute? He seems to have been in a powerful hurry since he forgot the gun."

"That has occurred to me, sir. It seems as if Mr. Yohe could not have been in the foyer when the shot was fired. Of course, he had to pick up his hat and coat, but that was right at hand. That wouldn't have taken a minute."

"When he came through the door from the foyer, did he have gloves on—or one glove?"

"No, sir, both his hands were bare."

"Could you swear to that?"

"Positively, sir."

"He had gloves with him?"

"Yes, sir. I had seen them in the pocket of his topcoat when I took it. Presumably they were still there."

"Well, that's a point in his favor."

Hawkins looked pleased.

"You then ran into the foyer?" Lee continued.

"Yes, sir. But I lost a minute or two. I first ran after Mr. Yohe, begging him to tell me what was the matter. I followed him out to the service stairs. He ran down the stairs. I went back to the foyer."

"Describe what you saw."

The old man was agitated now. His lip trembled, he paused to pass a handkerchief over his face. Recovering himself, he said: "My master was lying at full length on the floor just inside the entrance door. He was lying partly on his right side and there was a bullet hole in his left temple. He had been killed instantly and he did not bleed much. His latchkey was in his right hand; his hat had rolled away in front of him. The gun lay about two yards from the body."

"On which side?"

"Toward the front of the building; that is to say, near the opening into the music room." Hawkins illustrated on his plan.

"Was it the custom of your master to let himself in without ringing?"

"No, sir. I had never known him to do such a thing. He might open the door with his key, but he always rang outside to summon a servant to take his hat and coat."

"You were the first on the scene. Who next appeared?"

"Mrs. Gartrey and the maid, Eliza Young, sir. Eliza came out of the bedroom corridor and Mrs. Gartrey from the music room."

"The music room?"

"Yes, sir. There is a door between boudoir and music room." Hawkins pointed to it on his plan. "It was really shorter for her because there are two doors to open the other way."

"But why did she allow several minutes to elapse before she appeared at all?"

"How can I answer that, sir?"

"Well, go on."

"There was great confusion, Mr. Mappin. I'm afraid I cannot give you a very clear account. The cook, the kitchen maid and the two housemaids came. They were hysterical. I was the only man in the house . . ."

"And you had your hands full," put in Lee.

"Yes, sir. We employ a second man, John Denman by name, but he had gone to the watchmaker's to have his watch repaired."

"What time did Denman go out?"

"Shortly after three, sir."

"After Mr. Yohe had come?"

"Yes, sir."

"What time did he return?"

"About four-thirty. The police had been in the apartment for some time."

"Hawkins, what is your opinion of this man Denman?"

"Personally, I never cared for the young fellow, sir. Always watching and listening; too sly for my taste. But he did his work all right."

"How did your mistress bear herself, Hawkins?"

"She was shocked, sir. She looked awful."

"Hysterical?"

"Not her, sir. She kept quiet. She had her wits about her."

"Did she approach the body?"

"No, sir. She told me to call a doctor. I said: 'Mr. Gartrey is dead, Madam.' She said: 'Call a doctor anyhow.' I did so. I then asked her if I should notify the police. She said: 'This is not a case for the police; he killed himself.' She indicated the gun. I pointed out to her that he still had the key in his right hand. There is a doctor's office in the building and he came immediately; Mrs. Gartrey's own physician a couple of minutes later."

"Was there any other telephoning done?"

"No, sir, not at that time. News of the shooting had spread through the house and all kinds of people were trying to get into the apartment. I had all I could do to keep them out. A policeman came in off the street and it was him who telephoned to his captain and the captain notified Headquarters. The confusion got worse and worse until Mr. Coler came. He straightened us out."

Lee thought this over, stroking his chin. "Hawkins," he said finally, "I suppose there are many possible hiding places in that big apartment."

"Oh, yes, sir. There is the coat closet in the foyer and there is the powder room, opening off. The rear hall is lined with cupboards which I have not indicated on the plan."

"Was the apartment searched for a possible skulker?"

"No, sir. We couldn't conceive how anybody could have got in without being seen."

Lee said: "According to my recollection the entrance foyer is sparsely furnished. Is there any piece of furniture behind which an assassin could have concealed himself until Mr. Gartrey was well inside the door?"

"No, sir. There is no furniture at all on that side of the foyer."

"Hm!" said Lee. "This is a hard nut that you have given me to crack, Hawkins."

"Yes, sir."

"Is the entrance door a self-closing one?"

"Yes, sir."

Lee's further questioning elicited nothing material from the old man. When Lee finally got up to leave, Hawkins said: "What is your opinion, Mr. Mappin?"

As Hawkins asked the question, Lee became aware that there was another, a sharper personality peeping from behind the benignant facade. But he could not be sure that it was evil.

"I am completely at sea," he said.

"If Mr. Yohe would only come back and clear himself!" sighed the old man.

"So say we all of us!" agreed Lee.

As Lee came down the stairs on his way out, the courteous landlady appeared below to open the door for him. Lee's eyes twinkled behind the polished glasses.

"Mrs. Quimby, do you ever cash checks?" he asked. Naturally, she was astonished. "Why . . . why . . . why for my lodgers, sir, not for strangers."

"Where does Mr. Hawkins bank?"

She was so flustered that she answered without thinking. "At the Girard National, sir."

"Thank you so much," said Lee. "Don't mention to anybody that I asked you."

Out on the sidewalk he glanced at his watch. Being Saturday, the bank would be closed, but there might be somebody on the premises.

He taxied into the city and found a vice president at the Girard National. Lee, introducing himself, stated his errand and the vice president sent for a bookkeeper with his ledger. This man said:

"The account of Robert Hawkins was opened two days ago with a deposit of $2,500. This was a cashier's check from a New York bank. This morning Mr. Hawkins is credited with cash, $5,000, deposited here in the banking house."

Lee's face was like a mask. "Is the teller who took the money available?"

He was presently produced, a slender, pale young man with an expression of anxiety, wondering why he had been sent for from the front office.

"This deposit in cash to the credit of Robert Hawkins," said the vice president, "do you remember who made it?"

"Yes, sir, the circumstances being a little unusual. It was a young gentleman, sir; good-looking, extremely well dressed. I took him for a junior partner in a prominent law firm, or a stockbroker."

"In what form was the money?"

"Tens and twenties, sir."

"Were the numbers taken?" Lee put in.

"No, sir. They were mixed old bills. Just put in with our cash, sir."

"Would you be able to recognize the man who deposited them?"

"Yes, sir. A very handsome young fellow, sir."

"Please say nothing about this for the present."

ON HIS RETURN to New York, Lee reported the result of his mission to Inspector Loasby, and convinced him of the necessity of keeping the discovery to themselves until they could trace the source of Hawkins' bonus.

CHAPTER FIVE

ON SUNDAY MORNINGS Mr. Mappin permitted himself an extra half hour in bed, no more. If he had been up late on Saturday night, he found it refreshing to take a cat nap or a couple of cat naps later in the day. Having finished his breakfast by the fire, he was leaning back thoughtfully smoking a cigarette. Today the dressing gown was orange faced with black; the scarf and slippers scarlet. There was a line between his brows and he was not thinking serenely of his big book. What he termed to himself "that infernal Gartrey case" had driven it out of his head. He admitted, however, that l'affaire Gartrey was not as obvious and common as it had seemed at first. It had become a puzzle.

He heard the distant sound of the doorbell without concern. He kept his home address a secret so far as was possible and it, of course, did not appear in the telephone book. All sorts of nuisances occasionally came to the door, but he could depend on the efficient Jermyn to protect him. He was therefore surprised to see Jermyn enter, wearing an odd expression which suggested that something had turned up which was too much for him.

"What is it?" asked Lee a little sharply.

"If you please, Mr. Mappin, there's . . . there's a young lady calling."

"Good gracious, Jermyn! At nine o'clock on Sunday morning! What's her excuse?"

"She didn't say what she wanted, sir, but she wrote her name on a piece of paper." Jermyn extended the paper.

Taking it, Lee read: "Mrs. Alastair Yohe."

"Jehu, Kingdom come!" he exclaimed. "This is impossible! . . . This is a practical joker, Jermyn, or a newspaper woman in disguise!"

Jermyn shook his head. "No, sir! A very personable young lady, sir, and appears to be in great trouble."

Lee noted that he had twice spoken of her as a lady. Jermyn was never the one to apply the term lightly. Lee was divided in his mind; curiosity was working powerfully; on the other hand, "great trouble" promised the kind of emotional scene that he detested. He said: "You'd better go into the kitchen where you can't be overheard, and call up Inspector Loasby. You'll find him at his home. Tell him who our caller is, and let him take what action seems best."

Jermyn's generally inexpressive face betrayed the keenest distress. "Oh, no, Mr. Mappin! If you please, sir! Oh, Mr. Mappin, you can't go for to do that!"

"Why can't I?"

"She has a baby, sir!"

Lee stared, openmouthed. "A baby, did you say?"

"Yes, sir, a fine, pretty child."

"What's a baby got to do with it?"

"You wouldn't have the heart to turn them over to the police, sir."

"Well . . . well . . ." said Lee pettishly, "you needn't telephone to Loasby. . . . But I won't see her! The baby is just an excuse for sob stuff. No sensible woman would bring a baby! Send them away!"

As Jermyn turned, Lee heard a gentle voice from the door saying:

"*Please*, Mr. Mappin, I won't make a nuisance of myself. I won't stay but five minutes!"

Lee jumped up in great perturbation, drawing his dressing gown around him like a woman caught in her wrapper, and saying: "Really, young lady! Really! This is too much!" He looked around for Jermyn, but Jermyn had slipped incontinently through the dining-room door, leaving him to face the monster alone. Finding himself trapped, Lee looked the intruder straight in the eye.

"I know this is dreadful of me," she was saying imploringly, "but I felt desperate!"

She was a pretty thing, small and young. Lee had not realized that girls so young had babies. The baby looked enormous; he didn't see how such a little woman could possibly have produced it. "Well, as long as you're here you may as well come in," he said gracelessly.

She glided in and, dropping on a chair behind the settee, started nervously to unfasten the baby's jacket and cap. "I'm not preparing to make a stay," she said deprecatingly, "but I'm afraid he might catch cold when we go out again."

Lee, inexperienced with babies, was very ill at ease in the presence of the unfamiliar. He had no idea how old the child might be; he was able to sit up but had clearly not reached the walking or talking stage. She took his cap off and smoothed down the fuzz on his head.

"Hasn't got much more hair than I have," said Lee grimly.

"He will have," she said quickly. "See how thickly it's coming in."

Lee declined to approach. "How old is he?"

"Going on nine months. . . . Weighs eighteen pounds," she added proudly.

"Good Lord, how did you do it!" said Lee.

She blushed. "That's what everybody asks me. I guess the size of the mother doesn't make much difference."

The baby looked around the room with a bland expression. Lee, he ignored in the most insulting fashion, but that pleased Lee; at least, the baby was not going to try to get around him. When she had taken off his outer things, his mother planted him on the rug in front of the fire. It was a rare Bokhara.

"Hadn't you better put something under him?" suggested Lee.

"He has his rubber pants on," his mother said, a little hurt.

Lee blushed. There was a silence. The baby evidently enjoyed the fire for he crowed and bounced two or three times on his fundament. Lee felt softer feelings stealing over him. "What's his name?" he asked.

"Alastair," she said with a lift in her voice, "but we call him Lester."

That name chilled Lee. Spawn of the devil! he thought.

"My name is Charlotte," she added naïvely.

"Have you breakfasted?" Lee asked, with stiff politeness.

"Oh, yes, thank you." Such a pretty little brown-haired girl, sensitive, prone to blush, her face revealing quick changes of expression.

Lee jerked his head toward the little Buddha on the rug. "Isn't there something I can get for him?"

"A soda cracker, perhaps, if you would be so good. He's always hungry."

Lee rang for Jermyn and ordered soda crackers, looking very stern.

Jermyn's face was like wood. When he brought the crackers the young mother offered one to her child. He knew what to do with it. Calmly accepting it, he conveyed it to his mouth and returned his gaze to the fire.

After an awkward period Lee and Mrs. Yohe found themselves talking together naturally enough.

"You know why I am here," she said simply. "It is to beg you to receive my husband. Our happiness, our very lives depend upon it." She nodded toward the child. "And his. He has such a long time to live!"

"I'm afraid it is impossible," said Lee.

"My husband is innocent."

"How do you know?"

"He told me so."

Lee smiled.

Mrs. Yohe blushed, but spoke up with spirit. "I'm not just a fond and foolish little wife. I have no illusions about my husband. He has told me many painful truths, heartbreaking truths, but he has never lied to me."

"But in this case wouldn't he be justified in lying?"

"Certainly. But I know him so well that if he was lying for the first time some change in his voice, in his expression would warn me of it."

"If he's innocent, for heaven's sake why doesn't he face the music?"

"Ah, he's a strange, wild creature, Mr. Mappin. To be confined would kill him."

Lee said nothing. His expression was politely incredulous.

"He has other reasons," she went on. "I don't know what they are, but they seem sufficient to him. I'm not claiming that he is very wise, Mr. Mappin. Like all manly men, he's as stubborn as the devil. Oh, if you would only consent to see him; I am certain he would do whatever you advised. Look, he thinks you have one of the keenest minds of the day. If he were not innocent, would he be so anxious to put himself in your hands?"

Lee smiled. "Very subtle flattery, Mrs. Yohe."

"I'm not trying to flatter you. Oh, if I could only find the right word!"

"Why doesn't he write his story for me? I will guarantee that no eye shall see it but mine."

"He says he can't express himself properly in writing; that his brain seems to freeze when he takes a pen in hand."

"He could call me up on the telephone. If he uses a dial phone the call could not be traced back."

She still shook her head. "There is too much at stake. He must be able to see your face when he tells you. He wants you to question him."

"Here's a proposition," said Lee. "If I consent to hear his story, will he agree to give himself up if I so advise?"

"He would give himself up, I am sure, but he would never bind himself in advance to do so. He doesn't know you, you see, and after all, it is his life which is at stake. He is convinced that it would be fatal if he fell into the hands of the police now. He'd be railroaded, he says."

"That's as far as I can go," said Lee.

Mrs. Yohe squeezed her hands together. "Oh, if he does not succeed, I know what will happen! He will leave Lester and me and start a new life far away. We will never see him again!"

"Abandon you!" exclaimed Lee.

"I don't mean leave us to starve. There is plenty of money. But a man always has that way out, hasn't he? Just to go away."

"The search for him will never be abandoned!" asserted Lee.

"The police aren't very clever, Mr. Mappin. Certainly not clever enough to take my husband unless he allows himself to be taken."

Lee rose and paced back and forth. "Mrs. Yohe, what you have told me about your husband doesn't make me feel any kinder toward him. Even before this happened, he appears to have treated you abominably; A secret marriage! I take it you are forced to live under an assumed name."

She nodded miserably.

"It has cut you off from your own people?"

Another nod—but with firm lips.

"And, of course, you have to do your own housework besides caring for the baby. You couldn't trust a servant."

"I went into it with my eyes open, Mr. Mappin. He did not deceive me. He explained the kind of life he led and that the secrecy would be necessary until he had made a sufficient stake for us to get a fair start away from New York." Her chin went higher. "And I'm not sorry for what I did, either! Even if the worst should happen, even if he leaves us, I shall not be sorry for what I did. And Lester won't reproach me for it, either, when I tell him about it after he grows up."

Lee paced up and down snorting with indignation. "But, my dear child, this is mere infatuation!"

"Infatuation!" she repeated with a scornful shrug. "That's only a word! I don't care what you call it. It is something that comes to only a few women. It has lifted me out of myself! It makes me feel rich!"

Lee could no longer trust himself to speak.

She partly broke down. "Oh, I have said the wrong things!" she mourned. "I wanted to make you understand what a dear he is! how tender and honest and goodhearted! And I have only made you angry! If you could see him and Lester romping together, it would melt your heart! A man who can laugh with a baby can't be a bad man!"

This unhappy scene could have but one conclusion. She finally picked up the baby and started putting on his jacket with trembling fingers while the tears rolled down her soft cheeks. Lee felt like a louse; no good for him to tell himself that he was taking the only possible course. Word of this will be conveyed to Fanny and Judy, he thought, and my life at the office will be a purgatory. He rang for Jermyn. When Jermyn saw the wet cheeks, his eyes reproached his master too. Hell! thought Lee, was ever a well-meaning man put in such a box! As Jermyn showed Mrs. Yohe out, Lee thought: She will go blindly through the streets. If I sent Jermyn after her, she would lead him straight to Yohe. She's un-doubtedly hiding him herself. But, damn it all! I can't do it!

CHAPTER SIX

DURING THE REST OF SUNDAY the relations between Jermyn and his master were a little strained. Lee did not go out and wore his dressing gown all day. It was his custom to sup alone in his apartment on Sunday evenings. Lee was a sociable soul but, as he said, in order to fully appreciate good society, it is necessary for a man to spend certain hours in solitude. Late in the afternoon Jermyn came to him.

"Mr. Mappin, I dislike to ask an extra favor of you, you are always so considerate, but I have had a telephone message from my friend Abbott in Brooklyn—he's the one who came to this country with me—saying that he was ill and out of a place and asking me to come over and see him."

Lee was relieved at the thought of being spared the sight of Jermyn's long face for an hour or two. "Go by all means," he said.

"I'll serve your supper first, sir. Unless you would prefer to eat at the Club."

"I'll eat at home," said Lee. "Not in the humor for company."

"Very good, sir."

When Lee sat down to his supper he said: "You needn't wait, Jermyn. Get yourself a bite to eat and be off with you."

"Very well, sir, I will; and thank you, sir. Just leave everything until I get home, Mr. Mappin."

"On your way out," said Lee, "instruct the men in the hall downstairs that if anybody comes to see me while you're gone, the name is to be telephoned up to me."

53

"Very well, sir."

When he had finished eating, Lee returned to the fire, prepared to spend a comfortable evening with a book and a pipe. Lee had a secret fondness for the briar, but as he fancied it went very ill with his tubby little figure, he smoked it only when alone. "I am no Sherlock Holmes, alas!" he would say. He was reading *The Case of Madeleine Smith* in connection with his work. The pipe drew well, the case was well presented, but the feeling of comfort would not come. The sad, pale, tear-stained face of Mrs. Yohe rose between his eyes and the printed page. Half a dozen times he jumped up swearing, took a turn up and down the room, and sat down again with a determined effort to concentrate on the book.

The doorbell rang; the button was pushed three times, long, short, long.

This was a private signal known only to Jermyn, to Fanny and Judy and one or two of Lee's closest friends. He heard it with pleasure and jumped up; anything would be preferable to his own nagging thoughts. Trundling down the hall without a thought of danger, he opened the door.

It was not a friend. Lee saw a tallish, well-made young man, very well dressed, smiling like a book agent. He had glasses on and wore a neat, black beard like a young doctor trying to make himself look more impressive, or a Bohemian from south of Fourteenth Street. His bared teeth gleamed with extraordinary whiteness against the black beard. He had blue eyes.

"Mr. Mappin," he began ingratiatingly.

Lee, angered by his effrontery, began to say: "I'm sorry, sir, I cannot . . ."

The elevator had gone down again and the little hall was empty. The young man suddenly lunged with his shoulder against the door, thrusting it open and sending Lee staggering back. He coolly entered, closing the door behind him, keeping his extraordinarily bright eyes fixed on Lee's face and smiling in that maddening fashion. In addition to the Yale lock, there was an ordinary lock in the door and the key was sticking in it. He turned the key and, pulling it out, dropped it in his pocket. He kept saying:

"I'm so sorry, Mr. Mappin! Honestly I hate to do this!"

He seemed to be struggling to keep from laughing outright, and that made Lee feel wild with anger. Suddenly he thought of the house phone on the wall. The young man thought of it at the same instant and reached it first. He already had a pair of cutters in his hand and he snipped the wires leading to the instrument.

"I'm so sorry!" he said, biting his lip.

A cold fear struck through Lee; the fellow was so much bigger than he, and twenty years younger. He was undoubtedly armed. Lee's gun was in the drawer of the chiffonier in his dressing room at the other end of the apartment.

"I must ask you to enter the pantry ahead of me," the young man said.

Lee was forced to obey. There was a miniature telephone switchboard in the pantry. Here incoming calls were received and could be plugged to the several extensions in different rooms. The young man snipped the main wires leading to the board.

"When I go out," he said deprecatingly, "I'll phone for a trouble shooter so service can be restored tonight."

Lee felt absolutely helpless. The building was of steel and concrete construction and it would do him no good to shout for help or pound on the floor. "What do you want of me?" he demanded. "I keep no money about me."

"I don't want your money," answered the young man, smiling afresh. "Lead the way to your dressing room, please."

They proceeded through the gallery. Lee's feeling that he had been betrayed by one whom he trusted was bitterer than fear. "How did you get up here?" he asked.

The young man read his mind. "Jermyn didn't sell you out," he said. "I decoyed him over to Brooklyn with a fake telephone call. I guessed that the boys downstairs would be instructed not to let anybody up without telephoning, so I didn't ask for you; I just walked into the elevator as if I belonged in the house. 'Top floor,' I said, and the operator was bluffed."

They entered Lee's little dressing room and the young man went direct to the chiffonier and pulled out the drawer where Lee's gun lay. Certainly if Jermyn had not betrayed his master, somebody had. Lee thought of the girls and his breast was curdled with bitterness. However, the first shock had passed and his wits were working again. The drawer was filled with socks and handkerchiefs and the young man had to dig for the gun.

Lee was standing behind him at the moment and the dressing table was behind Lee. A crazy plan began to work in his brain. He felt behind him for a nail file and a tiny sewing case that lay on the table. He found the objects, and transferred them to the pocket of his dressing gown.

The young man dropped the gun in his pocket and turned around. "Shall we go into the living room and sit down comfortably?" he suggested. He had the pleasantest voice in the world, damn him! thought Lee.

Lee with an effort changed his face. "Well, I suppose I might as well make the best of it," he said.

"Sure!" cried the other. "I'm really not a bad sort of fellow. I mean you no harm. I want you to be my friend."

Lee had guessed who it was. Searching for a way of distracting the fellow's attention from himself, he said: "Will you have something to eat? My supper is still on the table."

"Thanks, I don't mind if I do," was the instant reply. "I've been so busy this afternoon I couldn't stop for supper."

"Preparing for this visit?" suggested Lee.

"Yes, sir. It took some close planning."

They proceeded to the dining room and sat down. There was plenty of food left on the table; a cold pâté, a salad, a Camembert cheese spreading on its plate. The young man's blue eyes glistened at the sight. Pulling the dishes toward him, he set to with a hearty appetite.

"You and I have similar tastes," he said.

Lee was listening intently. Faint sounds reached his ears which suggested that Tod Larkey on the floor below was having a party. One of Lee's living-room windows was open and there must have been an open window somewhere in the Larkey apartment also. It was the party which had given Lee his idea. He had only a nodding acquaintance with Larkey, but it would serve.

While the young man ate he kept a bright eye on Lee, but he could not look at him steadily because of having to attend to his food. Lee was trying to think of a way to escape from his eye for half a minute at a time. Half a minute would be enough.

Lee rose. "I'll fetch you a bottle of cold beer from the refrigerator."

"Sit down, Mr. Mappin!" said the young man quickly. "I can't risk having you pop out through the service entrance, you know. You sit here and I'll fetch the beer. Will you join me in a bottle?"

"Don't mind if I do," said Lee.

The young man went through the swing door into the pantry. Lee had gained his half minute. Whipping out his notebook, he wrote on a page: "Help! Lee Mappin," tore the page out and returned book and page to his pocket.

The young man came in with the beer.

As he sat down again he said: "I reckon you have guessed who I am."

"I have guessed it," said Lee dryly.

The young man said with his gleaming smile: "The beard is false, the hair dyed and the spectacles unnecessary." As he spoke he transferred the glasses to his pocket. Lee recognized him as the host of the Sourabaya night club.

An appealing quality came into his smile. "I took an awful risk in coming here against your will, but I was desperate. Only you can save me and my little family."

Lee hardened his heart against him. "You took no risk at all," he said coolly. "Your errand was doomed to failure before you started."

"Don't say that, Mr. Mappin."

"Did you think you could win me over at the point of a gun? I may look like a timid little fellow, but after all! . . ."

Al Yohe's face fell. "I haven't pointed a gun," he said. "As a matter of fact, I didn't bring one."

"You've got mine!"

Al pulled himself together. "Well, anyhow, as long as I'm here, you might as well hear my story."

"I can't avoid hearing it," said Lee.

While they talked, his hand was busy in his pocket. The sewing case was a little roll of leather which contained two spools of thread, a few needles and pins, a thimble. Old-fashioned people call it a bachelor's companion. Unrolling it, Lee worked one of the spools out and measured off thread as well as he could in his pocket. He glanced at the height of the ceiling; say nine feet; he would need ten feet of thread.

Al said glumly: "This is not going to be easy if you have resolved to set your face against me. . . . However, I must do the best I can." He spread Camembert on a cracker and put it in his mouth. "My interview with Mrs. Gartrey last Monday was a stormy one. She didn't mention that, I suppose."

"Were you in love with her?" asked Lee.

"No, that was the trouble."

"She was in love with you?"

"Yes, God forgive me, and how! I couldn't string her along any further. She insisted on what she called a showdown. There was . . ."

"Wait a minute," interrupted Lee. "This doesn't exactly recommend you to me. Under the circumstances, why did you continue going to her house?"

"Mr. Mappin, I'm not going to try to make myself out any better than I am. You may call me a buccaneer or worse, if you like, but I'm no murderer." He broke off to say with a boyish smile: "Lord! I wish I could call you Pop like the girls at the office. It suits you so well!" He paused, studying Lee's face, then said with a sigh: "But I guess I better not try it!"

Lee said to himself: He's just turning on his "charm."

Al resumed: "When I came to New York and was introduced to cafe society, those people, rich as Croesus, unstable as monkeys, empty as blown eggs, I made up my mind to prey on them in a perfectly legitimate way. They craved amusement, being too stupid to amuse themselves, and I was clever enough to furnish it. They were ripe for the picking! I amused them and I flattered them. My God! do you blame me? The merest fraction of Jules Gartrey's income would keep my family in luxury for years!

"As to the reputation I have acquired as a great lover, I didn't foresee that. I swear to you, Mr. Mappin, that I never made love to their women, you can believe me or not. If you were to ask an honest woman, a woman, say, like Delphine Harley, she would bear me out. As a matter of fact, those empty-headed bits of artifice didn't appeal to me. I like a more natural article. But 'making love' is the principal occupation of these monkeys, and out of sheer perversity, just because I *didn't* make love to them, the women began throwing themselves at my head. It became the fashion to fall for Al Yohe. My God, could I help it?"

Lee was sufficiently well acquainted with the gilded crust of society to recognize the truth in what Al said. But it didn't make him feel any kinder toward Al. He said: "Perhaps not. But you haven't answered my question. Why did you continue stringing Agnes Gartrey along when you saw how things were going?"

"Excuse me, Mr. Mappin. I thought the answer to that was obvious. The Gartreys are topnotchers in that set. He was one of the richest men in New York and she is called the most beautiful woman. They were necessary to me. You may think I have an easy job. Well, so has the man who dances on a slack wire. But he can't relax. I was all puffed up by publicity, but a prick would have deflated me. I had to have eyes all round my head to watch for danger. After all, I was nobody; I had to hang on to those who had something. That's why the Gartreys were essential to me. Particularly the old man. It may surprise you to learn that that hard-boiled old geezer was susceptible to flattery. Well, he was, and I knew how to feed it to him. It was he who put up the money to decorate La Sourabaya in its present sumptuous style. A cool two hundred thousand. And, by the way, I wish somebody would give me a reason why I should have killed the goose that laid the golden eggs."

"All right," said Lee dryly, "my question is answered. Let's get back to Monday afternoon."

Al Yohe rose from the table. "Thanks for a swell meal," he said. "I feel like a new man. Shall we go into the living room?"

They passed through glass doors into the larger room. Al looked around him appreciatively. "Gosh! what a swell place! It looks like the home of a gentleman and a scholar!"

Lee pushed the embers of the fire together and put on fresh wood. Al accepted a cigar and, lighting it, drew in the smoke gratefully. "This must be a private importation," he said. "Such cigars are not for sale."

He dropped on a settee at right angles to the fire, stretching his long legs before him.

Lee looked down at him grimly. Handsome, well made, gay and clever, Lee could not help but be attracted. A young man nowadays finds the world a pretty rotten sort of place, he thought; can you blame him for turning buccaneer? He shook this feeling off. Are you going to let him charm you, too? he asked himself.

Lee by this time had broken off ten feet of thread in his pocket, as nearly as he could judge it. He needed another minute alone in order to tie thread to nail file. He went to his little wall cupboard. "Have a liqueur?" he said. "I have brandy, Cointreau, and some of the veritable Chartreuse. For myself I prefer Scotch and soda."

"Me, too," said Al.

"You'll have to fetch ice cubes from the refrigerator, then."

"Sure!" Al hastened out.

Left alone, Lee measured his piece of thread against his arm. The length was about right. He tied the end to the nail file, and pinned the file through the note he had written. Hearing Al coming back, he thrust it all in his pocket.

The drinks were mixed and they sat down facing each other on the two sofas. "Go on with your story," said Lee.

"Agnes Gartrey was bent on having what she called a showdown," said Al contemptuously. "I expect you know what that means; crying, beating herself, pulling her hair out straight. Lord! if I could have photographed her then! Most men are scared out of their wits by that kind of show, but not me! It turns me hard."

"Did she want you to marry her?" asked Lee.

"No indeed, she had no intention of separating herself from Moneybags."

"Go on."

"I was afraid somebody would hear her. I knew Gartrey would be home sometime or other, though I didn't expect him so soon. I didn't want him to smell a rat. He has a mortgage on the Sourabaya. So I suggested to Agnes that we go somewhere where we could talk privately."

"Where could you go where you wouldn't be recognized?"

"To my place. It was all I could think of. She rose to that; thought she'd have me dead to rights in my place, but I didn't have any intention of taking her there. So she went into the next room, her dressing room, to get ready."

"Was the maid in there?" asked Lee.

"Yes."

"Then she must have heard all that was said."

"Sure. Probably had her ear glued to the crack of the door. However, I don't suppose that Eliza has many illusions about her mistress left. Women like Agnes feel pretty safe with their maids, because, you see, if a maid ever blew the gaff on her mistress and it became known, no other woman would hire her."

"I am learning," said Lee. "Go on."

"When Agnes went into the dressing room, she left the door partly open and we continued talking back and forth, though of course she wasn't cursing me like she did before. Then after a bit somebody pulled the door shut and I could hear no more from in there."

"You couldn't hear the two women talking?"

"Not a sound."

Lee got up. "Don't you find it a little chilly here?" he casually suggested.

"Suits me all right," said Al.

Lee went to the open window. That end of the big room was in darkness.

Leaning out of the window, he satisfied himself that it was not the window immediately underneath which was open. So much the better. It gave him a larger area of glass to tap on. Keeping hold of the end of the thread, he dropped the nail file over the sill and had the satisfaction of hearing it knock against the glass below. He pulled down the sash, pinning the end of the thread under it.

"Lovely night," he said, returning to the fire, "but turning colder. . . . Go on with your story."

"I was sitting in the boudoir, twiddling my thumbs while Agnes changed into street clothes in her dressing-room. Quite a while passed. I thought nothing of that, because getting dressed to a woman like Agnes is the most important thing in life." Al paused, staring straight ahead of him.

"God! how vividly that moment comes back! Me sitting there in the pink boudoir surrounded by Agnes' gimcracks—she collects antique porcelain figures just because they're expensive . . . and the shot out in the foyer!"

He was silent so long that Lee was forced to prompt him. "Go on!"

Al passed a hand over his face. "It gave me a horrible shock! I guess things have always come to me too easy. First time I ever had to face anything serious. . . . I thought Agnes had turned a gun against herself. I had never for a moment taken her seriously, but you can't tell about a woman. What a spot for me to be in! Made me feel sick. My one idea was to get out of the place, but I couldn't get out without passing through the foyer. I ran out there . . ."

"Which way?" put in Lee.

"By the corridor. Agnes was lying against the door into the foyer. But when I turned her over I saw she had no wound. She had fainted. I stepped over her and went into the foyer. I saw Gartrey lying on the parquet floor with a bullet hole in his head. I knew he was dead. I saw the gun and I thought he had shot himself. That made me feel a little better because it wasn't my fault if his wife. . . . Well, anyhow, my one idea was to beat it away from there. Can you blame me? I got my hat and coat out of the hall closet and started for the service entrance. Unluckily I met the butler on the way out and that put the kibosh on my chances of clearing myself. Naturally I looked wild."

"When you ran into the foyer did you see anybody?" asked Lee.

"Nobody but the dead man."

"It's your idea, I take it, that Gartrey was shot by his wife?"

"I'm not saying so," said Al. "I want you to figure it out for yourself."

"What motive had she for killing her husband?"

Al shrugged. "How can a man tell what goes through a crazy woman's mind? A spoiled beauty like Agnes believes that nothing can touch her. She would figure that with her money and her position she could get away with it. Perhaps she thought that after she had inherited Gartrey's millions I would be crazy enough to marry her. But I don't think that. If she had all that money, why should she marry again? I believe she planned to plant the crime on me, thinking she could get me off later and that she would then have me under her thumb for keeps. Or perhaps in her rage she was deliberately trying to send me to the chair. That would explain the gun."

"How did your gun get there?" asked Lee mildly.

Al shrugged. "All I know is, it was stolen from me."

"When?"

"I can't tell you that. I didn't miss it until after this happened. It's a couple of months since I have seen it."

"Where did you keep it?"

"In a chest of drawers in my bedroom."

"Did Mrs. Gartrey know it was there?"

"She did."

"Has she ever been in your apartment?"

"Sure!"

"In the bedroom?"

"Yes." Al smiled suddenly. "But not with me! She went in to powder her nose."

"Has Robert Hawkins, her ex-butler, been to your place?" asked Lee.

Al looked at him quickly. "Why do you ask that? . . . Oh, I see, you are canvassing all the possibilities. Yes, Hawkins has been there on two occasions. The old boy had an interest in photography, and I told him to come around and get a few pointers on developing. The last time was about ten days ago. I left him in the kitchen, washing prints while I went into the dark room I have improvised. He could have gone into the bedroom without my knowing it."

"And the maid, Eliza Young?"

"She has been to my place three or four times with notes from Agnes. Agnes considered telephoning unsafe because the calls at her home went through a switchboard in the pantry. Eliza might have been in my bedroom—she's a sly one!—because sometimes I was busy with my work in the kitchen when she came and had to let her wait in the living room for a while."

"Have other people visited your rooms?"

"Oh, many others. It was a kind of hangout; there was always something to drink there. They made themselves free of the place; they would roam around. I was often busy in the dark room or kitchen. . . . I'll make a list of everybody I can remember and send it to you."

"Thanks," said Lee dryly. "I have not yet promised to give my time to this matter."

Al smiled in his most ingratiating manner. "What have you got against me, Mr. Mappin?"

"Let's not go into that. Answer one question. If it is true you thought Gartrey had killed himself, it is not unnatural you should have thought only of getting out of the place; but next day, when you read the newspapers and learned that he had not killed himself, that, in fact, you were accused of the crime, why didn't you give yourself up? That's the natural impulse of an innocent man."

"Try to put yourself in my place, sir," Al said cajolingly. "Hawkins' story was enough to send me straight to the chair! And such an honest-looking old bozo; anybody would believe him. I could see that I was already convicted in the minds of the public. What kind of a defense had I? I could only clear myself by accusing Agnes. What would everybody have said then? Believing that we were lovers, they would say that I had allowed the woman to do the killing so we could come together, and was now accusing her to save my own skin. By God! I couldn't bear that. I would sooner . . ."

At this moment the bell of Lee's apartment sounded. Al jumped up all alert. "You'll have to go to the door," he said. "They know you're home."

Lee's first thought was regret that he had hung out his tick-tack so soon. He wanted to ask Al more questions. Somebody began to pound on his door and voices called for him. Al was already half-way through the dining room; Lee followed him. Through the pantry door he went; and into the kitchen. He opened the service door. With his hand on the door, smiling still, he said:

"Good-by, Pop. You're a good fellow! Sorry I couldn't win you over!"

The door slammed, and Lee stood staring at it blankly. A renewed uproar at the other door recalled him to himself. Running to it, he shouted to those on the other side. "This door is locked and the key is gone! Alastair Yohe is on his way down the service stairs!"

"Who?" they shouted.

"Alastair Yohe!"

"My God!"

"Ring for the elevator and cut him off at the bottom! Some of you run down the stairs in case the elevator is slow in coming."

"Use the house phone!" a voice shouted.

"I can't! The wires are cut."

He heard the door to the stair well being pulled open and running feet on the steps. He doubted, however, if any of Tod Larkey's guests were nimble enough to beat Al Yohe to the bottom. All would depend on how quickly the elevator came up. Lee returned to his living room and mixed himself a stiff drink.

In ten minutes or so they were back at Lee's door. They had the superintendent of the building with them, who brought a duplicate key.

Half a dozen men pushed in through the door. Tod Larkey's party, it appeared, was a stag affair. His guests were flushed and a little unsteady on their pins.

"He got away!" they all cried at once.

In spite of the self-discipline he had exerted, Lee's first feeling was one of gladness. He took care to hide it. One man cried:

"I saw him! I ran around the corner to the service entrance and he was getting in a car. The engine was running. The rear light was out and I couldn't read the license number."

All together they demanded to know what had happened.

Lee was in no humor to take this noisy bunch into his confidence. "I'm sorry," he said, "I can't tell you the story until I have reported it to the police. You'll learn it soon enough. Mr. Larkey, if you'll allow me, I'd like to call up Inspector Loasby on your phone. My wire is out."

They trooped down the single flight of stairs to the Larkey apartment.

Larkey and his guests had their ears pricked to hear Lee's report over the phone, but upon getting Loasby at his home, Lee merely said:

"Inspector, can you come down to my place right away? It's important."

"Well," said Loasby reluctantly, "I have guests. Can't you tell me what it is over the phone?"

"No," said Lee.

Loasby knew, of course, that Lee was neither a trifler nor a scaremonger, and he wasted no more words. "Okay," he said, "I'll be there in ten minutes."

Declining all offers of a drink, Lee, after thanking his "rescuers," went back upstairs.

CHAPTER SEVEN

JERMYN GOT HOME before Inspector Loasby arrived. The good fellow was flabbergasted when he learned what had happened. "I'll never leave you alone in the apartment again!" he vowed.

"Nonsense!" said Lee, "This sort of thing isn't going to happen twice!"

"My friend wasn't sick at all. It was a fake call, Mr. Mappin."

"So Al told me," said Lee dryly. Lee could not help but believe Jermyn; his honesty was transparent. It was clear, however, that somebody else had furnished Mr. Al with advance information.

Loasby was astonished and outraged when he heard the story. "The fellow is a devil! a devil!" he cried.

"Well, after all he didn't do me any harm," said Lee; "though I confess it is rather humiliating to be kept a prisoner in your own house. . . . Anyhow, I'm in this case up to my neck now, but I'm working with you, Inspector, not with Al Yohe."

"Good!" cried Loasby. "We'll soon collar him. . . . What do you suggest, Mr. Mappin?"

"You must comb the town. We know the nature of his disguise now, and he's hardly likely to get up another as good. Every young man with a beard of any color should be detained for questioning."

"Sure. Somebody is keeping him under cover. Some woman."

"Undoubtedly." Though he knew he was doing wrong and suspected that it might very well get him into trouble with the police later, Lee simply could not bring himself to tell Loasby about the little wife and her baby.

After the excitement in the apartment house, Loasby insisted that they must give the story of Al Yohe's visit to the press. "They'll get a garbled version of it anyhow from those guys downstairs, and if the newspaper boys get the idea that we're holding out on them, they'll sour on us."

"I wouldn't care if they did," said Lee, "but I suppose it's important to you."

"Sure! Sure!" said Loasby seriously. "In a free country every public official has to keep in with the press."

So the story was given out. But not the whole story. They took care to omit all reference to Agnes Gartrey and her maid.

Lee gritted his teeth when he read it next morning. It put him in a ridiculous light with the public. Wounded thus in his professional pride, he hardened his heart anew against the beguiling Al Yohe. I'm going to bring him in, he vowed to himself, if I have to do it single-handed!

Fanny and Judy received him demurely at the office. Neither of them made any reference to the story in the newspapers; they were waiting for Lee to speak about it. They fussed about him, with an added affectionateness and care to carry out his wishes. Lee would not speak about the newspaper story and that put the girls in a false position. Finally, Fanny was obliged to say:

"Pop, dear, I was horrified to read about what happened last night. I didn't like to speak of it because I thought it was a painful subject."

"Not at all!" said Lee. "I enjoyed my visitor thoroughly!"

Fanny looked at him, not quite knowing how to take this.

JUST AS HE WAS BEGINNING to think about lunch, Lee, to his astonishment, saw Robert Hawkins entering the outer office. The old man was greatly agitated. Fanny brought him into the private office. Hawkins took care to shut the door before stating his errand.

"Mr. Mappin, sir, an extraordinary thing has happened. It scares me, sir. I don't know what to make of it. I took the first train to New York to consult with you, sir."

"What is it?" asked Lee.

Hawkins produced an envelope and from it drew a credit note bearing the heading of the Girard National Bank. His hand trembled. "On Saturday morning, sir, somebody deposited five thousand dollars to my credit in the bank. My first knowledge of it was when I received this credit note in the mail this morning."

Lee, studying him, thought: If he has learned about my visit to the bank, this is exactly what a clever crook would do. He said: "You have no idea who it was?"

"No, sir! Who would give me five thousand dollars?"

"It does seem odd, doesn't it?"

"Five thousand dollars! It's a fortune! After a lifetime of work I have only succeeded in saving half that sum!"

If the old man's astonishment and consternation were faked, it was a good piece of acting. Lee made believe to take his story at face value.

"Hawkins," he said, "this is an attempt to implicate you in the Gartrey murder!"

"That is what I feared, sir! What a blackguardly trick to play on an innocent man!"

"You have been to the bank?" asked Lee casually.

"Yes, sir! I was waiting when they opened their doors this morning. I asked if there wasn't some mistake, but they said no; the amount had been paid in in cash on Saturday morning."

"Whom did you see at the bank?"

"One of the vice presidents, sir, and he sent for the teller who had received the money."

Lee would have liked to know if the bank people had told Hawkins of *his* visit on Saturday. He did not put the question, for that would have been to show his hand. "Did the teller describe the man who deposited the money?" he asked.

"A handsome, fashionable young man. That suggested nothing to me, sir."

"Well, Hawkins," said Lee affably, "you did right in coming direct to me. It was without a doubt the actual murderer who had the money conveyed to you. Five thousand dollars is a biggish sum; it ought not to be too hard to trace it. This may lead us to the man we want."

"I pray that it may, sir!"

"Meanwhile, I don't suppose you want to use the money."

"Use it!" cried the old man in horror. "I wouldn't touch it with a pair of tongs!"

"Then I suggest that you make out a check to the order of the Police Commissioner to be held by him until the mystery is cleared up."

"I'll do that, sir. I have my checkbook with me. I'll leave the check with you."

"Good! That will clear your skirts."

Hawkins produced his checkbook and, drawing up a chair to Lee's desk, proceeded to write the check. Lee watched him steadily. It was a vast sum to an old man who had worked for wages all his life. If he felt any reluctance to hand it over, he hid it well. Handing over the check, he asked with an innocent air: "What should I do now, sir?"

"Go back to Philadelphia and act as if nothing had happened. Tell nobody about your windfall. We don't want the man we're looking for to take alarm."

"Very good, Mr. Mappin."

As soon as he had gone, Lee got Loasby on the wire. "The man you assigned to watch Robert Hawkins," he said; "can you depend on him?"

Loasby chuckled. "I reckon so. He followed Hawkins to the bank this morning, rode to New York on the train with him and tailed him to your office. My man was waiting in a store across the street while Hawkins was with you, and he phoned me from there."

"Very good," said Lee. "As an extra precaution, notify the bank in Philadelphia that if Hawkins should try to draw out more than the sum he deposited himself, he is to be detained for questioning."

"Right! What's up, Mr. Mappin?"

"I'm coming down to your office after lunch. I'll explain when I see you."

At Headquarters, when Lee had described the scene with Hawkins to Loasby, the latter said: "What do you make of it?"

"There are three possibilities," said Lee. He ticked them off on his fingers: "First, Al Yohe is the murderer and is trying to throw suspicion on Hawkins. Judging from what he told me, Al is well heeled. Second, Agnes Gartrey had the money conveyed to Hawkins to bolster up her suggestion that the butler is the guilty man. There are two sub-theories here: (a) it was Agnes herself who shot Gartrey, or (b) she believes that Al Yohe did it. Third, Hawkins shot Gartrey and the five thousand is his pay, or part of it. We have got to follow up all these lines simultaneously until they are disproved or proved."

"Right. What do you want me to do?"

"You have men who are experienced in Wall Street affairs investigating Gartrey's business relations?"

"Sure."

"Well, let them dig deeper. We've got to know who Gartrey had injured, who were his enemies, who profited by his death."

"Right."

"Here's something else you can do. Suppose for the moment that old Hawkins is telling the truth. Suppose Mrs. G. sent the money to Philadelphia. There are two men who have been trying to make time with her since this happened. One of them, Alan Barry Deane, we know has been lying. Arrange it so that the bank teller can have a look at Deane and at Rulon Innes without their knowing it."

"I'll do that. What line are you going to take?"

"I'm going to cultivate the acquaintance of the beautiful widow," said Lee with a smile.

"What about Al Yohe?"

"I was hoping you might be able to give me some news about him."

Loasby shook his head gloomily. "In addition to my own men every uniformed cop on the force is looking for him. No reports."

"I'm going down to Hasbroucks from here," said Lee. "There are several questions which I have no right to ask there, but the police are entitled to the information."

"What are they?"

"Get Mr. Gartrey's private secretary. Find out from her if Gartrey got a phone call on November 3rd before he went home, and so on."

"I'll see to it," said Loasby.

Lee proceeded further downtown to the offices of Hasbrouck and Company in the great building on Wall Street which bore their name. Hasbroucks, oldest and wealthiest private bankers in New York, was a name to conjure with in financial circles. None of the present generation of Hasbroucks was in the bank; one was an artist; one raised race horses; a third was simply an ornament to Newport and Palm Beach. For upwards of ten years Jules Gartrey had been president of the concern. On the day following his death, at a special meeting of the directors, George Coler, first vice president, had been elected president in Gartrey's stead. Everybody took it as a matter of course that Coler should succeed the man who had trained him.

The executive offices were on the top floor of the skyscraper. Lee, whose first visit it was, looked around him appreciatively; he enjoyed quality wherever he found it. Here, the lofty ceilings, the walls paneled with rare woods, the thick-piled rugs caressing the feet, expressed the highest quality without any suggestion of showiness. And space, plenty of space, the greatest luxury of all. This was a thoroughly modern office.

The handsome young clerks and the beautiful secretaries moved through the rooms smiling, stopping to converse with each other cheerfully in order to show that there was no slave-driving here. Lee was particularly struck with the charming manners of the lovely receptionist at her desk. She smiled at him confidently as one nice person to another.

"You wish to see Mr. Coler? Have you an appointment, sir?"

Lee was obliged to confess that he had not.

Her face fell. "Oh, I'm so sorry! It is difficult to arrange a meeting on the spur of the moment. But I'll see what I can do. What name, sir?"

"Mr. Mappin. Amos Lee Mappin."

Her eyes widened. "Mr. Mappin! Oh, sir, I know Mr. Coler will want to see you. Please be seated for a moment." She swam away.

In no time at all she returned. "Mr. Coler will be delighted to see you, Mr. Mappin. Please come this way."

Lee was led through one magnificent room after another, where smiling employees worked at their desks or conversed happily together. "This cannot be a bank," said Lee to his beautiful conductress; "it is more like Heaven!"

She giggled politely, but it was evident she did not quite get it.

Arriving at last at the holy of holies, the corner office, she announced:

"Mr. Mappin," and disappeared. The door was ostentatiously left open.

Lee received an impression of an acre of rare Kermanshah rug, tulip wood panels, a beamed, polychrome ceiling. From behind a gigantic desk with a whole brigade of telephones on it, George Coler was rising to greet him.

Coler was in perfect keeping with the rich, conservative apartment; well-groomed, handsome, smiling and natural; indubitably one of Wall Street's aristocrats.

"Mr. Mappin! This is an unexpected pleasure!"

"Sorry, if I'm interrupting you," said Lee.

"Not at all! I am always at your service. Sit down, sir!"

"Thanks," said Lee dryly. "I am a little overwhelmed." He took in all the details of the room.

Coler laughed pleasantly. "Silly, isn't it?" he said, waving his hand about. "But, of course, a bit of swank is expected of Hasbroucks."

"I like swank," said Lee.

A shadow passed over Coler's face. "I have been promoted to the highest seat here," he said. "But how gladly I would give it up if I could have my friend back!"

"I feel for you," said Lee.

"To what do I owe the pleasure of this visit?" asked Coler.

"You have read this morning's paper, I take it," said Lee.

A frown distorted Coler's handsome face; he struck his fist on the desk.

"I have!" he cried, "and it is disgraceful that such a thing could happen! And I looked on the fellow as my friend, Mr. Mappin. I've been seeing a lot of him lately. His impudence passes all bearing!"

"Oh, you have got the wrong impression," said Lee. "Yohe's manners were most agreeable. I quite enjoyed his visit."

Coler wouldn't have it. "Disgraceful!" he repeated. "That a murderer should be able to thumb his nose at decent folk like that. What is the matter with our police?"

"Obviously, somebody is concealing Yohe," said Lee. "The police are up against it."

"If I was at the head of the force I would get something done!"

"Naturally, Yohe's visit to me was a kind of challenge," Lee went on, "and I have engaged myself to help the police in this case."

"Good!" cried Coler. "Then we'll get results. How can I help you, Mr. Mappin?"

"Mr. Coler," Lee said blandly, "the rumor persists that it is Mrs. Gartrey who is keeping him hidden."

Coler leaned toward Lee. "Mappin, there is nothing in it! I am with her part of every day—she depends on me for everything, you see, and I know what I am talking about. Mind you, I'm not saying that she wouldn't assist him; I will be very frank with you; there is an infatuation there that it grieves me to see. One can only hope that she may get over it quickly. But I know from her uncertainty, her anxiety, her desire to get some word of him, that she does not know where he is."

"I don't doubt you're right," said Lee, "but I must investigate this rumor along with everything else, just as a matter of routine."

Coler said: "Apart from assuring you that there's nothing in it, I don't see how I can help you."

"Yes, you can." Lee had come to the point he had been leading up to. "If there is any connection between Mrs. Gartrey and Yohe, she may be supplying him with money. I want to check her expenditures during the past week. Have you paid her any large sums?"

"From the estate, do you mean? Not a penny. Mr. Gartrey died intestate. She'll get the estate eventually, of course, but not until the preliminaries are settled."

"Intestate? You shock me! A man of his wealth?"

"It seems that he had lately destroyed his last will and had procrastinated in making another."

"Have you made payments to Mrs. Gartrey from other sources?"

"No. She doesn't require it. Besides having credit everywhere, she has a fortune of her own. Gartrey settled money on her when she married him."

"Does she bank here?" asked Lee.

Coler laughed. "No indeed! She wouldn't have her account in a place where her husband could overlook it. She banks with the Fulton National."

"Has she more than one account?"

"Only the one account."

"Let me see, who is President of the Fulton?"

"Canby Griffiths."

"Will you give me a note to Mr. Griffiths that will smooth my way?"

"I'd rather not," said Coler with his engaging frankness, "because it would look as if I were going behind Agnes' back. You don't need any note from me. Your name is a sufficient password anywhere in town."

When Lee arose, Coler accompanied him to the outer office. "I'm so glad you came in. We must keep in touch with each other. Our interests are the same. If money is needed for the prosecution of the case, you may call on me for any amount."

"Thanks, Mr. Coler. It won't be necessary for the present."

Coler opened a door exhibiting another handsome office only less grand than the one they had left. "My former office," he said.

It had the same collection of telephones. "Why does a banker need so many telephones?" asked Lee.

"Well, there's the inter-office phone, the connection with the regular switchboard, a connection with the banking office downstairs, a private wire to the Stock Exchange, my own personal telephone, and so on."

As they shook hands at the outer door, Coler said: "Dine with me some night, will you? So we can go into things more particularly."

"I'd be glad to," said Lee.

LEE MAPPIN'S NAME proved to be sufficient to pass him into the private office of the President of the Fulton National. Mr. Griffiths was so anxious to help Lee, and so impressed with the necessity of keeping the matter secret, that he went himself to consult the book which contained Mrs. Gartrey's checking account. The result, as far as Lee was concerned, was nil. Mr. Griffiths said:

"Mrs. Gartrey's balance as of yesterday was $113,000. She has made no withdrawals this past week. She hasn't visited the bank. All the checks that have been paid on her account were dated previous to the tragedy. I expect she has been too prostrated since to attend to any business."

"I expect so," said Lee dryly. "Anyhow, thank you very much."

ON HIS WAY UPTOWN in a taxi, Lee read the latest extra on the Al Yohe case. Every edition of the newspapers furnished an avid public with added details of Al's spectacular life; his love affairs, his wardrobe, his tastes in food and wine. Al had a passion for fresh caviar, Lee read, and it made him thoughtful. Fresh caviar had become a scarce article since the war, and scandalously expensive. It ought not to be too difficult to discover who still had a stock of the delicacy and to trace the sales during the past week. Al's present host, whoever he was, might try to procure some. It was a faint lead, but worth following up.

Lee stopped at the office of Stan Oberry, a private investigator whom he had employed with success in former cases, and put the matter in his hands. "Fresh Beluga caviar is the choicest sort," said Lee.

CHAPTER EIGHT

IT WAS NOW THAT HOUR OF THE AFTERNOON when a gentleman might properly call on a lady, and Lee drove on uptown to the Gartrey apartment. The door was opened to him by a manservant he had not seen before, a dark young fellow, handsome in the face and shapely of limb. His eyes, however, were too close together; it gave him a foxy look.

"Are you Denman?" asked Lee.

"Yes, Mr. Mappin."

"Do you mind if I ask you a few questions?"

"Certainly not, sir. Mrs. Gartrey said you might wish to question me."

Lee thought: The deuce you say! I'm sorry I didn't get hold of you before she did.

"Mrs. Gartrey said I was to give you every assistance I could," added Denman.

"Thanks," said Lee. "I understand that you were out of the house when the tragedy occurred."

"Yes, sir. Mr. Hawkins, the butler, had given me leave to take my watch to be repaired."

"Where did you take it? You understand, this is merely a formal question."

"Oh, quite, sir. It's all right with me. I have nothing to hide. I took my watch to a jeweler called Lohmeyer on West Thirty-fourth Street, and waited for it while he put in a new escapement."

"What time did you get back here?"

77

"It would be about half past four, sir."

"What did you find here?"

"Oh, sir, it was terrible. The master was still lying where he had fallen! The place was full of police, medical examiners, finger-print men, photographers, I couldn't tell you who all. And the maids hysterical and all!"

"Your mistress?"

"I didn't see her, sir. She was in her room under care of the doctor."

"What did you do?"

"Mr. Coler told me to stand at the service door and keep every-body out. Mr. Coler had taken charge of everything. Mr. Hawkins was minding the front door. Many people were trying to get into the apartment. Seems people have no shame at such a time."

"What is your theory as to what happened?" Lee asked bluntly.

Denman was startled. "Oh, sir, how should I know what hap-pened? I wasn't here. Some of the servants seem to think it was Mr. Hawkins did it, but I wouldn't go as far as to say that. I am only an underservant; I don't know anything."

Lee shrugged and let it go at that. The young man's manners were perfect, but somehow he left a bad taste in the mouth; he was too smooth, too watchful. Lee made a mental note to check his story with the watchmaker.

"Can I see Mrs. Gartrey?" he asked.

"I'll see, sir."

Lee was shown into the music room, which lay between the vast living room on one side and Agnes' boudoir on the other. In order to reach it he had to step over the spot where Jules Gartrey's dead body had lain on the parquet. Denman betrayed no consciousness of recent tragedy. The windows of the music room looked out on the familiar panorama of the park with its leafless trees, the East Drive, the reservoir beyond, the towers of Central Park West in the distance.

In a surprisingly short space of time, the door from the bou-doir was thrown open and Agnes Gartrey appeared, holding out both her hands. Lee thought: Hm! I appear to be welcome. Meanwhile Denman had disappeared.

"Mr. Mappin!" Agnes cried breathlessly; "this is like the answer to a prayer! Oh, I wanted so to see you! An hour ago I could stand it no longer and I called your office. They said you were out, didn't know when you'd return. I didn't leave my name, of course. And here you are! It is too good to be true. Come into the boudoir. There's a fire and it's cosier!"

She led the way into the adjoining room. She was wearing a kind of house gown with a lustrous black skirt that trailed on the ground and a cerise waist. Lee watched to see how she avoided walking up the front of the long skirt; there was art in the way she kicked it out of the way with every step. She made an extraordinarily graceful picture. In the boudoir the curtains were drawn together and a flattering rosy light filled the room.

"Cigarette, Mr. Mappin? Shall I ring for tea? I'm sure you'd rather have a highball, and so would I." Suddenly she dropped the fine lady air and turned to him with a face all broken up and working like a child's. Lee couldn't help but be moved, though he told himself this was just art like everything else about her.

"Oh, before I ring for the man, tell me about Al," she murmured, clasping her hands. "How does he look? Is he well? Who is taking care of him? How is he bearing up under this frightful charge?"

"He looks grand," said Lee dryly. "In the pink of condition. Bubbling over with high spirits."

"Ah, that's just his line," she said quickly. "I expect in his heart he is almost ready to despair!"

"If he is, he concealed it well."

"Where is he hidden? Who is taking care of him? Oh, I am sure you know more than you told the newspapers!"

"I don't know where he is," said Lee. "I wish I did."

"What was his purpose in coming to see you at such a risk?"

"To protest that he was innocent; to ask me to prove his innocence."

"And you will, Mr. Mappin?"

"I'm going to work on the case," said Lee, "but I cannot under-
take to prove his innocence."

"Oh, he is innocent! He is! He is!"

"I hope so," said Lee demurely. "I took quite a fancy to the fellow, confound him!"

"Did he send me any message?" Agnes asked eagerly.

"No," said Lee. "I am not in his confidence. He would hardly
send it by me."

"But he spoke of me?"

"Oh, yes, but guardedly."

She caught her breath. "Guardedly? He . . . he is not angry with
me?"

"Bless my soul, no!" said Lee; "only trying to protect your good
name."

Mrs. Gartrey paced the room. Her agitation had increased. Lee
began to perceive that it was not anxiety for Al Yohe which lay at
the bottom of it, but fear of what Al might have told him, Lee. She
said: "He told you, of course, that he was out of the apartment before the shot was fired?"

Lee lied with the utmost blandness. "Yes, he told me that."

She drew a long breath, her worst fears relieved. "You must be
dying for a drink!" she said, pressing a bell for the servant. "Sit
down, do!" She draped herself on a low chair beside the fire, and
resting elbow on knee cupped her chin in her palm, an infinitely
graceful pose. "Did he tell you that I sent him away on Monday
afternoon?"

"No. He merely said that he left. I must tell you that we were
interrupted by my well-meaning neighbor before I had finished
questioning him. That's why I came to you this afternoon; to get
you to fill in the blanks."

She swallowed this whole. "You did right," she said with restored complacence.

"You said you sent him away on Monday. Why?"

"I had an engagement."

Denman entered and was ordered to bring Scotch whisky, soda,
ice. His face was as expressionless as paper.

When he had gone out, Lee said: "You had an engagement Monday afternoon—where?"

"At Madame Helena Rubinstein's establishment. I don't know if you have heard of it, but Madame Rubinstein possesses a marvelous collection of antique doll's furniture. It is all arranged in miniature rooms down both sides of a corridor, perfect in every detail of each period, and beautifully lighted. . . ."

"Marvelous, I'm sure," said Lee, "but we're getting away from Mr. Yohe."

"Sorry. Madame Rubinstein had arranged to give a public view of her collection on Monday in aid of Polish Relief and I had to be there since I am on the Committee and . . ."

"Mr. Yohe left here at what hour?"

"About half past three. I couldn't tell you to the minute. My maid ushered him out."

"And you?"

"I went into my dressing room to change for the street. My maid joined me there."

"And then?"

Agnes bit her lip. "Wait a minute," she said. "Wait until we get rid of the servant." When she heard Denman coming she turned on her social chatter like a phonograph record, starting in the middle. ". . . perfectly fascinating, Mr. Mappin! There are Spanish rooms, French rooms, American Colonial and English rooms of different periods, each one complete even to the tiny china utensils in the bedrooms. Madame has been collecting the furnishings for years. They say that Robert Edmond Jones painted the little interiors for her."

"How interesting!" said Lee.

The servant entered bearing a tray which he placed on a little table beside his mistress.

"You needn't wait," she said.

When he had closed the door behind him, Lee said inquiringly: "Well?"

She held up a delicate hand. "Let me mix the highballs first. I always begin to tremble when I approach that moment in my mind."

When she handed Lee his drink, he held it up. "To happier days!"

"Ah, you're so kind and understanding!" she murmured grate-fully. After she had taken a swallow of her highball—and a big swal-low, Lee noted, she picked up her story at the precise point where she had dropped it. "I was dressing in there when I heard the shot." She put a hand over her eyes.

"You ran out?" prompted Lee.

"Not immediately. I was paralyzed with terror. Nothing brutal has ever been allowed to approach me, you know. I am spoiled. I am no better than a hothouse plant. I couldn't move. And Eliza was just as bad. We clung to each other. I picked up the house phone then—the switchboard is in the servants' hall, but I could get no answer, no answer! 'Eliza,' I said, 'we have *got* to go and see!' It was the hardest thing I ever had to do in my life!"

"You ran out together?"

"Yes . . ." She quickly corrected herself. "Not together. I ran across this room and through the music room to the foyer. Eliza went by the corridor."

"Why did you separate?"

"Don't ask me! Neither of us knew what we were doing!"

"How long a time passed after the shot before you got out in the foyer?"

"I couldn't answer that either. It seemed like ages."

"Well, say two or three minutes. And what did you find?"

She covered her face. "My husband lying on the floor . . . bullet hole . . . gun . . . Hawkins kneeling beside him . . ."

"Was anybody else there?"

"The maids. Maybe they came afterwards. I don't remember."

"And then?"

"I think I cried out: 'Pick him up! Pick him up!' It seemed so dreadful to see him lying there on the floor, an old man. And Hawkins said: 'He is dead, Madam.'"

"What did Hawkins look like when he said it?"

"Look like? He looked like a butler. A butler's expression never changes. If the house was blown to pieces he would say, without changing his tone: 'Do you require anything more, Madam?'"

Lee ironed out a smile; Agnes did not mean to be funny. "Were you completely dressed when you ran out in the foyer?" he asked.

"No . . . yes . . . no . . . Why do you ask me that?"

"Well, in Hawkins' story, he said . . ."

"That I was fully dressed. I see. And it would have been impossible, of course, for me to make a complete change in five minutes. You had better disregard Hawkins' story entirely . . ."

"But the other servants also . . ."

"I had my suit skirt on when the shot was fired. Before I ran out I put on the jacket of my suit, so I had the appearance of being completely dressed."

"The jacket was buttoned, I assume."

"How can I be expected to remember such a detail as that?"

"What did you have on beneath the jacket, Mrs. Gartrey?"

. She hardened. "Why do you ask me that question?"

"A man like Hawkins might easily have been mistaken, but it seems strange that the maids should have testified that you were fully dressed. Including your own maid, Eliza."

Agnes changed color under her make-up. She was breathing quickly. "Are you intimating that I have not been telling the truth?" she demanded.

Lee looked shocked. "My dear Mrs. Gartrey! I never dreamed of such a thing!"

She was not satisfied. Her lips had drawn back in an ugly fashion. "When Al, Mr. Yohe, told you that he was innocent, did he express any opinion as to who had shot my husband?"

Lee shook his head. "The poor fellow was all at sea. That is why he insists on remaining in hiding."

"Did he . . . did he by any chance suggest that I might have had a hand in it?"

Lee deliberately paused a moment before answering. "He did not."

"Oh, God, what perfidy!" she breathed.

"My dear lady!" Lee assured her, "you are disturbed without cause. Al Yohe never said a word that would lead me to suppose such a thing. On the contrary, his thought was all of you. . . . I am merely trying to get a clear picture of what happened. . . . If you did not start to dress until after he left, how *could* you have been fully dressed a moment or two after the shot was fired?"

"I was not completely dressed," she said sullenly. "For an obvious reason my servants were not telling the truth. They wished to protect my good name."

Lee struck his forehead. "Of course! How stupid of me not to have perceived that at once!"

She drank off the rest of her highball. Slowly she recovered her self-possession. "You must have patience with me," she said with a return of her caressing manner. "My nerves are gone! Sometimes I scarcely know what I am saying!"

"Naturally," said Lee soothingly. "I am so sorry that I have to trouble you at such a time."

"Such a charge could never touch me!" she said with proud confidence.

Lee was reminded of something Al Yohe had said the night before.

"And if it should be brought, it would fall," Agnes continued, "because at the moment the shot was fired my maid and I were together."

Lee inwardly resolved to talk to Eliza Young without the knowledge of her mistress.

He rose and opened the door into the corridor. "I am trying to fix the layout of this building in my mind," he explained deprecatingly. "On the other side of the corridor wall must be the public hall and passenger elevator."

"That's right," she said carelessly. "Will you have another drink?"

"No more, thank you." Lee returned to his chair leaving the door open. "What did you and Mr. Yohe talk about while he was here?"

Again suspicion made her eyes narrow. "Didn't you ask him that question?" she countered.

"I did ask him," said Lee with an innocent air, "and his answer was evasive. That made me think that perhaps it had some bearing on what happened later."

"You're wrong," she said. "Our talk was completely unimportant—so unimportant that it has passed out of my mind. . . . I suppose we talked about the Polish Relief Ball in which we are both interested. We discussed mutual friends—just such talk, in fact, as you would expect between old friends."

Lee thought: That is a little too good to be true, my lady.

While he sat with her he heard from the other side of the corridor wall a slight rumble and, after a pause, a click. Insignificant sounds, but unmistakable to apartment dwellers. It was the elevator door opening and closing again. It was important to Lee to know that these sounds could be heard from where he sat. Either Al Yohe or Agnes Gartrey could have had warning that Gartrey was about to return. Lee heard the distant sound of the doorbell.

"Bother!" said Agnes with an intimate smile. "I hope we're not going to be interrupted."

"Well, I've told you all I know," said Lee. "Have you anything more to tell me?"

"Oh, I'm so stupid, Mr. Mappin. I don't know what are the important things. You must question me."

"Can't think of any more questions now. But we'll meet again."

"We must."

The manservant entered. "Mr. Coler, Madam." Lee felt a little uneasy. It might be difficult to explain this visit.

Agnes said: "I'll see him directly. Did you show him into the living room?"

"Yes, Madam."

"Did you close the door?"

"I . . . I think so, Madam."

"That means you didn't," she said sharply. "Close it on your way out. How many times must I tell you to close doors, all doors!"

"Yes, Madam." He went out.

"It's just as well not to advertise the fact that you and I are friends," Agnes said to Lee. Agnes was keeping certain things from Coler, then. Lee was relieved and also a little puzzled.

"Quite!" he said. He got to his feet. "There's just one thing that bothers me. I'm not sure how Al is fixed for money. If I should find out that . . ."

She didn't wait for him to finish. "Oh, you must come to me for anything that may be needed!" she said eagerly. "Shall I give it to you now?"

"I wouldn't know how to reach him," said Lee. "But if he communicates with me again . . ."

"If he does, you must find out how he is fixed for money. Make him tell you. And call on me for any amount. You needn't tell him it comes from me."

"It would be dangerous for you to draw a check to me," suggested Lee.

"I don't need to! I always keep a store of cash by me, quite a large sum. Always have done so. Checkbooks are apt to be dangerous."

"Quite," said Lee.

They laughed together agreeably—but not for the same reason.

"If you hear from him again, beg him to communicate with me," she said longingly.

It had the sound of a genuine plea.

He went out thinking over all she had said. It did not hang together at all. She was acting alternately as if she adored Al Yohe and as if she hated him poisonously. Lee thought: Hell knoweth no fury like a woman scorned!

CHAPTER NINE

ON TUESDAY MORNING, as Lee got out of a taxicab in front of the little building on Madison Avenue which contained his offices, he was accosted by a breathless woman:

"Mr. Mappin . . . if you please . . . I recognized you from your picture in the newspaper . . . may I speak to you?"

Lee sized her up. While extremely agitated, her aspect was not at all dangerous; a stout woman of fifty-odd, with a plain, pale face; well dressed in a sober style; no make-up, no effort to appear younger than she was. She never had been beautiful, but she looked honest, well meaning, sensitive in her distress. Obviously, it had required a great effort for her to nerve herself up to speak to a strange man.

"What can I do for you?" asked Lee.

"I have some information about the Gartrey case."

"Won't you come into my office?"

"I intended to call at your office," she stammered, "but . . . but my courage failed me. There will be other people there . . . clerks, perhaps newspaper reporters. If I could see you alone!"

"Well, there's a hotel on the next corner," said Lee. "Let us go in there and order a cup of coffee."

She thanked him gratefully.

They sat down in the coffee room of the hotel with a little table between them. Lee made conversation to put the nervous woman at her ease. Her faded eyes had a good, kind expression; he believed in her honesty.

"My name is Bertha Cressy, Mrs. Cressy," she said. "I have been a widow for over twenty years. I was a friend of the late Mr. Gartrey's." She hesitated painfully.

"How long have you known Mr. Gartrey?" asked Lee to help her out.

"Mr. Mappin," she said distressfully, "will you give me your word that you will keep what I am about to tell you to yourself? I could not bear to have it printed in the newspapers. I have a horror of publicity. If the newspaper reporters found me out, I . . . I don't know what I'd do!"

"I certainly will not relay your story to the newspapers," said Lee kindly, "but how can I give you the assurance that you require? If you have evidence to give in this case it must be brought into court."

"I have no evidence to give," she said. "I don't know who killed Jules Gartrey. I only want to see justice done to my dead friend. The newspapers are making him out a perfect monster! He was kind to me. It seems so unfair!"

"The newspapers do that sort of thing in order to heighten interest in the case," said Lee. "It sometimes makes me indignant, too. Unless there is something in your story that requires to be told in court, I promise you I will keep what you tell me to myself."

She thanked him profusely. "I have known Mr. Gartrey from the time of his first marriage, but not intimately," she said. "That is thirty years ago. I was a girlhood friend of his first wife, Mona Hawley. We were schoolmates and we continued to be friends until she died eleven years ago. Long before that, the death of my husband had left me in very straitened circumstances and Mona helped me out, in fact she supported me. Her husband knew nothing about it, and when she died it ceased. I didn't see Mr. Gartrey for some time after that. A year after Mona's death he married for the second time. Do you know about that?"

"Only that it turned out badly," said Lee. "There was an ugly scandal of some sort."

"Yes. I wouldn't pretend that Jules was an easy man to get along with, but he was far from being the cold and selfish being that the newspapers make out. Sometimes while my friend was alive it made me angry to see the way he treated her. But Mona never complained. You see, she had fallen in love with him as a young man, before he became rich. She always saw him in that light. His second wife was a young actress—not that I have anything against actresses, but this one was a bad-hearted woman. She married him for his money and repented of her bargain. She was a flaunting, conspicuous creature, always getting in the newspapers, and she made Jules, who hated that sort of thing, very unhappy.

"It was at this time that he looked me up. I was working as a saleswoman in a department store; poor pay and very hard work for a woman of my age. You can imagine my surprise when the rich man came to my shabby little furnished room. He had found some of my old letters to Mona, he said, and after reading them was convinced that Mona and I were the only good women he had ever known. He said it was not fitting that a friend of his dead wife's should be living in such poverty, and he arranged to have an annuity paid me that enabled me to give up my job and live in modest comfort ever since. What an act of kindness! To lift the awful dread of insecurity from my breast forever! I could never sufficiently express my gratitude.

"In my new home he came to see me regularly. It relieved his breast to talk to me about Mona and to confide in me how the other woman wounded him in his pride. There soon began to be talk of other men in her life. I don't need to go into detail about that; it is long past. Matters went from bad to worse with his marriage; he finally paid the woman an immense sum of money and she went to Reno and got a divorce. So far, that was all right, but when she returned to New York, out of pure malevolence she made a statement to the newspapers that almost wrecked my poor friend."

"What was that?" asked Lee.

Mrs. Cressy blushed slightly. "Don't ask me to repeat it in detail. A coarse and shameless woman! She had his money and she had her divorce and she didn't care what she said. I only mention this to enable you to understand what happened later. What she said reflected on Mr. Gartrey's manhood; she intimated that . . .

that he had never been a real husband to her. He was a proud man. There was nothing he could do but suffer in silence. Only I knew what he suffered. The wound that that woman dealt to his pride never healed.

"Six years ago he married for the third time. I was not consulted in advance or I might have warned him—but I don't suppose it would have made any difference if I had. His new wife was a young girl living on the island of Barbados. He met her while he was cruising in the West Indies on his yacht. Her father was a clergyman; she had never been away from the little colony; she was innocent, simple, unsophisticated, and as beautiful as an angel. He thought she would make him an ideal wife; he thought when he introduced her to the great world it would be like fairyland to her and he the Prince Charming.

"Of course, it didn't turn out like that. He made the initial mistake of settling a million dollars on her at the time of their marriage, so that from the beginning she had an independent income of forty thousand dollars a year. She was corrupted by luxury; her beauty made her famous and her whole character altered. It was the story of his second marriage over again, but this time he suffered worse and for a longer time.

"Gradually he learned that she was unfaithful to him, though he had no legal proof of it. And she knew that he knew; she didn't care because she believed that he would put up with anything rather than face a second scandal. When they were alone together she was completely cynical; she twitted him with his advancing age. She made his life a hell on earth but he was a proud man and he never let the world guess it. As before, I was his confidante. I don't think anybody else ever knew except possibly Mr. George Coler, who was his closest male friend.

"Finally, like the other one, Agnes Gartrey offered to go to Reno to divorce him, but she demanded such an enormous settlement that he refused. He could not bear, he said, after having given her one fortune to reward her unfaithfulness with another. He made up his mind that if there had to be a second scandal this one should not be at his expense. He was preparing to divorce her on statutory grounds here in New York State. Then he would not have to give her a penny. His suspicions settled on Alastair Yohe, the society photographer, and a precious young scoundrel!"

"Have you ever seen him?" put in Lee.

"No! And I have no wish to! . . . In order to further the affair, Mr. Gartrey made friends with Yohe and even lent him a large sum of money to refurnish his night club. Mr. Gartrey engaged private detectives to watch the couple, but nothing came of that. He then arranged with one of his own menservants to inform him by telephone when Yohe came to the house. I assume that it was such a message which took him home so early on the afternoon he was killed."

"There can be no doubt of that," said Lee.

"That is my story," said Mrs. Cressy. "About a month ago, when Mr. Gartrey was in my apartment, he tore up the will he had made in the woman's favor and burned the pieces. At that time he wanted to make a will leaving me a great sum of money, but I protested against it. He put off making another will and now, I suppose, she will inherit his fortune anyhow."

"Certainly the greater part of it," said Lee. "Unless she should be convicted of his murder."

Mrs. Cressy's eyes widened. "Do you think . . . do you think? . . ." she stammered.

"Ah, that I can't say," said Lee. "All the evidence so far appears to point to the young man."

"I've told you the story for your own information," said Mrs. Cressy. "I am not a revengeful woman, but I should like to see her punished. Even if it was the young man who fired the shot, morally she is just as guilty as he."

"So it would seem," said Lee. "I am exceedingly obliged to you, Mrs. Cressy. You have thrown much light on a dark subject. I shall respect your confidence."

CHAPTER TEN

LATER IN THE MORNING, Lee and Inspector Loasby were in conference at Headquarters. Loasby said:

"Yesterday I asked Jules Gartrey's personal secretary to come and see me, and she stopped in after office hours. A beautiful girl, and very intelligent; name of Coulson. She said that Mr. Gartrey had received a message over his personal telephone on the afternoon of the third—she was in his office at the time, and it threw him into considerable agitation. This was at three o'clock. He sent for Mr. Coler, but word came back that Mr. Coler was not in his office. Mr. Gartrey then went home without a word to anybody and was never seen again at his office. It looks as if he had been lured to his death, Mr. Mappin."

"Possibly," said Lee.

The Inspector had another piece of information to impart. "I asked Mr. Alan Barry Deane to come down this morning on the pretext that I wanted to question him further in respect to the visit that he said Al Yohe had made to his apartment on the afternoon of the murder. I had the receiving teller of the Girard National Bank in the building, and I arranged that he was to come into my office while I was talking to Deane and lay some papers on my desk. After Deane had gone, the bank teller positively identified him as the man who had deposited five thousand dollars to the credit of Robert Hawkins. What do you think about that?"

"It does not surprise me," said Lee. "We are dealing with amateur plotters here."

"I don't see that it gets us much farther forward," said Loasby. "There is no charge that I could bring against Deane."

"Let it go for the moment," said Lee. "Deane is of no importance as compared with the woman who sent him to Philadelphia. The fame of a beautiful woman is apt to obscure the fact that she is a fool. This foolish woman is almost certain to bring disaster on herself and everybody connected with her before we are through."

Loasby was very glum; criticism in the press had risen to such a point that the Mayor had talked to the Commissioner of Police about it. Loasby feared for his job. Lee's conscience was troubling him sorely, for he possessed a clue that would very much have simplified Loasby's search for the elusive Al Yohe. Having suppressed it in the beginning, Lee could not very well bring it forward now— at least not openly. He determined to feed the information to Loasby by degrees.

Loasby was saying: "The Stieff Building where Al had an apartment is on Fifth Avenue near the Plaza. Stieff's store is at street level. It's a small building but the rents are very high because of the choice address. Al's flat consists of kitchen, dinette, living room, bedroom and bath. He has set up a portable dark room in the dinette. The building furnishes maid service to the tenants and the maid told me that Al never slept there more than two nights a week and sometimes not at all for a week running. He never kept any food in the place except maybe a box of biscuits or the like, but there was a whole closet full of liquor. We broke into it. Nothing there but liquor, the most expensive brands. We sealed it up again.

"The elevator and the hall boys told me that Al worked at his photography in the place. He had many visitors day and night. Sometimes they made so much noise at night the other tenants complained. After all his visitors had gone, though it might be three or four in the morning, Al would change into his day clothes and go out whistling. Wouldn't return until late the next day. Was never there week ends, yet he didn't take a bag when he started out."

"What does this picture suggest to you?" asked Lee.

"Why, that he had another hangout, and a woman waiting for him. It is she who is hiding him now."

"Obviously."

"If I only had a description of that woman!"

"Let us look over the photographs that were found in his place," suggested Lee.

Loasby sent for the photographs and they were presently put on his desk. The prints were contained in hundreds of manila envelopes filed alphabetically in two drawers. Al had generally used a tiny Leica which could be carried in his pocket; also there were many enlargements of the original negatives. Each envelope was endorsed with the name of its subject and there was a date on the back of each picture. Lee thumbed them over rapidly. Many of the greatest names in New York were included. He was surprised to find a picture of himself for he did not know that he had ever been the object of Al Yohe's attentions. It had been taken in La Sourabaya and made him look like a cross between an underdone apple dumpling and a baldheaded owl. He showed it to Loasby with a laugh.

"Let me destroy that," said Loasby scandalized.

"Not at all," said Lee putting it back in its envelope. "It adds to the gaiety of nations."

"Am I in there?" demanded the handsome Inspector apprehensively.

"No," said Lee, "I have been through the Ls."

At the back of the second drawer he found a bulky envelope without endorsement. He emptied the contents on the desk and went over the scores of little prints one by one. These, as he had hoped, proved to be the pictures Al had taken for his own amusement; views of New York, street scenes, odd characters—and the little wife!

"There's the girl," said Lee, tossing it over.

"How can you be so sure?" said Loasby.

"She's the only girl in the lot who is not named."

Loasby studied her through his magnifying glass. "She's pretty," he said, "but so simple-looking. You wouldn't think Al Yohe would fall for that after the queens he was accustomed to."

"How little you know of human nature!" said Lee grinning. "Here's another of her . . . and another."

"A sweet little thing," said Loasby.

Finally Lee found a prize; a picture of Charlotte pushing a baby carriage. The baby unfortunately was asleep and did not show. "Look at this one!" he cried. "Al Yohe is married to the girl and they have a baby!"

"Your mind jumps to conclusions like a grasshopper!" grumbled Loasby.

However, he had a great respect for Lee's mind, and was prepared to believe what he was told.

"Here's a picture of the baby," said Lee, tossing over another print. "The spitting image of Al."

Loasby studied it. "Damned if I can see it."

"Examine the eyes. It's the way the upper lid is folded that gives Al such a beguiling look, and the little fellow has it, too."

"How do you know it's a boy?"

"Oh, if you've had any experience of babies you can always tell." Lee's conscience felt easier now because Loasby was in possession of as much knowledge as he had himself; it was up to him to use it.

Among the pictures Lee found one of Al himself that had been enlarged. The young man was shown seated sideways on a wide windowsill silhouetted against the light. The house across the street showed faintly in the background. Al's hair was gracefully tousled, his shirt open at the throat. "Al at his ease in his own place," Lee said, exhibiting it. "Let us see what this tells us."

"There are millions of windows in New York," grumbled Loasby.

"Not exactly like this window."

"It may not even be in New York."

"But it is New York. I'll prove that to you directly. Al would never choose a suburban hide-out. The transit facilities are not good enough at three or four o'clock in the morning."

"It might be Brooklyn."

"No. For Al to be continually taxiing over to Brooklyn in the small hours would leave too broad a trail. Why should he waste all that time when there are good places in Manhattan?" Lee went over the pictures again and found two that represented the interior of the same room without the inclusion of figures. The first showed a bit of the same window; the second a side wall of the room with a marble mantel. It was an old-fashioned room but luxuriously furnished. There was a "steeple" clock on the mantel. Lee spread the three pictures before him. "Now, we've got something to go on!" he said.

Loasby grinned incredulously. "Do you actually think you can locate that room from a study of the interior?"

"Let's see. For forty years it has been my principal diversion to mosey around this town. I know it pretty well. . . . Notice the width of the window seat; ten or twelve inches; this house was built in the days when walls were walls, in the late 1870's, say, or the early 1880's. The style of the interior woodwork and the mantel bears out the date. It is not a one-family house but a flat; one of the walk-up flats which began to be built at that period. It has a brownstone front . . ."

"The front doesn't show in the photographs."

"All the houses built for respectable people at that time had brownstone fronts. This is obviously not a tenement house. Tenement houses may be much older, of course."

"How do you know it's a flat, anyhow?"

"In a dwelling house they would never put in so elaborate a mantel on the top floor."

"Wait a minute! What do you mean, top floor?"

Lee explained patiently. "I know it by the house across the street. Even at that distance the ground floor does not come into the picture. Al's flat must be on the fourth or fifth story."

"Why not higher?"

"The walk-up flats of that period were not built any higher. Elevator flats began to come in about 1888." Lee made a new study of the photographs. "It would be natural for Al to rent a walk-up flat," he continued, half to himself, "even if the little wife had to carry the baby up and down stairs. If there were hall boys or elevator boys the risk of their recognizing him would be too great. . . .

An old house but well kept up; notice the parquet floor, Loasby. Al has to pay a good rent for it because it is still in a smart neighborhood."

"Are there any old houses in smart neighborhoods?"

"Surely. An old house will often be left standing next door to a swanky apartment house to protect its light on that side."

Loasby came around the desk to study the pictures over Lee's shoulder.

"This house is on one of the wider streets," he said, "judging by the distance of the house across the street."

"Right," said Lee, smiling.

"It might be West Fifty-seventh Street. That's one of the widest streets and it has both old and new houses. Also Seventh-ninth, Eighty-sixth and Ninety-sixth are all wide."

"They weren't built upon as early as 1880."

"Then let's go over and take a look through Fifty-seventh."

Lee shook his head. "This is a street running north and south."

"How do you know that?"

"Thanks to Al's methodical habits. All these photographs of the room are dated the same day, May 23rd. I am assuming that they were taken about the same hour. Notice the clock on the mantel; quarter to one. Now note that as Al sits sideways on the window sill the sun is just coming around into his face. That's why he placed himself in that position. Opposite his face the window frame is in shadow. At one o'clock in the afternoon that must be a window on the east side of a street running north and south."

"My God!" murmured Loasby. After a moment he went on: "That complicates the search because all the north and south avenues are wider than the cross streets."

"Right, but not as wide as this one. Take a good look at the picture, Loasby. Notice the distance of the house across the way. There are only two north and south streets as wide as this indicates; upper Broadway on the West side and Park Avenue on the East."

"That's right," said Loasby excitedly. "But there's also the Grand Concourse in the Bronx."

"A new street. It has no houses as old as this one. . . . Upper Broadway is out, too."

"Why?

"In the 1880's it was called the Boulevard and was lined with country houses. It never had any buildings like this one."

"Then it's on Park Avenue!" said Loasby excitedly.

Lee smiled.

Loasby's face fell. "No, it won't do, Mr. Mappin." He rapped the photograph. "You said yourself this was built for a middle-class house. There were never any middle-class houses on Park Avenue."

Lee took a pinch of snuff. "You forget, Loasby. Park Avenue was not considered a desirable street in 1880. The top of the railway tunnel was open and the locomotives filled the air with smoke and sulphurous fumes. It was not until the railway was electrified that Park Avenue began to grow exclusive."

"It's three miles long," said Loasby glumly.

"Surely; but any house built as long ago as 1880 will stick out like a sore finger."

Loasby got up. "Well, let's put it to the test." He did not sound hopeful.

"We mustn't use a car with police plates," said Lee. "I suggest you order a convertible town car. With the top up we can see without being seen as we drive through the streets."

"Right."

A few minutes later they were on their way. Loasby was in civilian clothes. Deprived of his usual motorcycle escort with blaring sirens, the chauffeur had to take his chance with the traffic and the Inspector became very impatient at the slowness of their progress. It was a long way uptown.

"By God! what a lot of imbecile drivers there are in the streets!" he cried.

Lee smiled.

At Thirty-third Street Lee suggested that their chauffeur use the motor tunnel. "We don't need to bother with this part of Park Avenue. Murray Hill has always been fashionable; there were never any middle-class flat houses. Let's begin on the other side of Grand Central."

Issuing from the tunnel at Fortieth Street, they crossed the viaduct, encircled Grand Central Station, and dove under the arches of the New York Central Building beyond. Issuing at Forty-sixth Street, the magnificent vista of Park Avenue stretched away to the north before them.

For the first few blocks the street was built solid on both sides with palatial apartment houses, hotels, and an occasional grand church. Above Fifty-ninth Street, relics of the past began to appear between the modern buildings and the chauffeur was instructed to slow up and keep as close as possible to the curb.

Here and there Lee was able to point out an old building that answered in a general way to what they were looking for, but not exactly. Loasby began to get excited.

"There are things in New York you never see until they're pointed out to you," he said sententiously.

They drove on slowly for a mile and a half further. Suddenly Lee said with complete confidence, "There it is!"

He was pointing to a pair of old-fashioned flat houses with brownstone fronts in the middle of the block between Eighty-seventh and Eighty-eighth Streets. Obviously they had been left standing to save the light of two huge modern apartment houses, one on each corner. The old houses had neighborhood stores at the street level. Though out of date, they were well kept up. It could be seen by the curtains at the windows that well-to-do people lived in them.

"How are you so sure it's one of these?" demanded Loasby.

"Look at the apartment house across the street. That's the building in the background of the photograph."

Their chauffeur found a parking space at the curb. Loasby was all keyed up now. "I might take a look at the names in the vestibule," he suggested.

"Won't do you any good," said Lee calmly. "You certainly won't find the name of Yohe there." He looked up and down the street. "Judging from the number of babies I see, this is the fashionable hour for their parade. If Mrs. Yohe has the baby out for an airing, she'll be bringing him home presently to be fed."

They waited; Lee watching the sidewalk throng with a half smile; Loasby chewing a cigar and fidgeting.

In the end, up at the corner Lee saw Charlotte coming. She was pushing a folding gocart with the baby in it. He waited a moment, savoring his triumph, then said very casually:

"Here she comes, Inspector."

Loasby's full blue eyes seemed to start from his head. "My God, it's miraculous!"

Lee was helping himself to a pinch of snuff. "Elementary, my dear Watson," he murmured.

"What's that?"

"Nothing. I was only talking to myself."

Charlotte, with the deft, assured movements of the young mother, lifted little Alastair from the gocart and planted him on the house step. She folded the cart, and picking up the baby, seated him within her arm, took the handle of the cart in her free hand, and disappeared within the house.

"What a sweet little mother!" murmured Loasby. "Seems a kind of a shame!"

The words echoed in Lee's breast and all his feeling of triumph faded.

Loasby was for clambering out of the car to follow Charlotte, but Lee detained him with a hand on his arm. "Better wait a minute. It is possible that Al may be following her, watching to see if the coast is clear."

They waited. Al did not appear. "He's inside the house," said Loasby excitedly. "He wouldn't dare show himself in the street by day. By God, we have him!"

"What are you going to do?" asked Lee.

"I'll telephone for assistance and wait here until my men come."

Lee sat in the car while Loasby disappeared in a cigar store close at hand. In five minutes he returned, saying: "I made a few discreet inquiries in the store. She calls herself Mrs. Matthews and she lives on the top floor. There's only one apartment on a floor. Her husband is not known in the store, but she buys cigars for him."

Lee was profoundly depressed. "Well, I'll be leaving you," he said. "There's nothing more that I can do."

Loasby was glad to see him go. Naturally he didn't want to share the glory of this capture.

Lee, not caring to show himself at the office under the circumstances, went home. He tried to do some work on his big book, but found himself unable to shape a coherent sentence. The expressionless Jermyn, who took in a good deal more than he seemed to, tried to distract his master with a galantine and a half bottle of Pouilly that he had in from the Colony, but Lee had small appetite. With an unusual burst of confidence he said:

"It's that damned Gartrey case, Jermyn! It's got under my skin."

Jermyn said: "I quite understand, sir. For myself, I cannot believe that Al Yohe is guilty."

"What reason have you for saying that?" Lee asked sharply.

"Oh, I wouldn't go to set up my opinion against yours, sir. But I'm all for the little mother and the baby."

"So am I," said Lee. "That's what makes the situation so hellish!"

After lunch there was a telephone call. Jermyn presently came to Lee, saying doubtfully: "It's a gentleman, sir. I do not know the voice. Won't give his name, but says it's very important. Do you care to take it?"

Lee eagerly picked up the instrument. He heard a fresh young voice, strained with anxiety. "Mr. Mappin? Do you know who this is?"

"Yes, I know you," said Lee grimly.

"I'm in a jam, sir. I had to go out to attend to a piece of business this morning. Before coming back to the house I always call up Charlotte from a block or two away to make sure the coast is clear. I called her up and she didn't answer, though I was sure she was there because it was the baby's lunch time. After a few minutes I called again and somebody took down the receiver but said nothing. It makes me think the police must have stumbled on our hide-out careful as I have been. They must be cleverer than I gave them credit for."

Lee was conscious of a feeling of relief. After all, the police had not yet taken Al. He said nothing about his own knowledge of the situation.

"What can I do?" he asked noncommittally.

"If the police are there, poor little Charlotte must be nearly out of her mind with fright and anxiety. She has nobody to turn to. Tell her from me that . . ."

"Wait a minute!" Lee grimly interrupted. "If you give me a message for Charlotte I must turn it over to the police."

There was a silence while Al presumably mastered his disappointment and anger. He uttered no reproaches. "Well, that's that!" he said. "But please tell Charlotte this for me—and I don't care if the police overhear it; tell her that I have a safe hide-out and I'm all right. Tell her to keep up a good heart and carry on until I can find a safe way to communicate with her."

"Yes, I can tell her that," said Lee.

A pleading note came into Al's voice. "And will you be Charlotte's friend, Mr. Mappin? That won't commit you to anything. God knows she's not to blame for what has happened."

"I will be her friend so far as I am able," said Lee gravely. "I wish to be your friend, too. You can't keep this up, Yohe. You *must* face the situation."

"Not yet!" he said with the incorrigible break of laughter in his voice. "Thanks for everything, Mr. Mappin." He hung up.

Soon afterwards there was a call from Loasby. In a grumbling voice like a schoolboy's, he said: "He gave us the slip, Mr. Mappin."

"I know it," said Lee dryly.

"Hey?" cried Loasby startled. "How did you know it?"

"He just called me up."

"The hell you say! What for?"

"To ask me to tell Charlotte that he was all right and not to worry."

"Damned cheek!" growled Loasby. "By God, what pleasure it will give me to attend the death chamber when he burns!"

Lee said nothing.

"I went to the apartment myself," Loasby resumed. "He was not in it. Charlotte was frightened but I couldn't get a thing out of her. You know the type. You could kill her by inches and she wouldn't speak."

"I know," said Lee.

"I left a man there to wait for his return. The house is watched front, rear and from the roof. My man has reported that the telephone rang twice, but Charlotte refused to answer it. He heard Al's voice on the wire. So I take it he's warned now, and won't be back."

"Too bad!" Loasby couldn't see him grin.

"However," said Loasby, "at that we have separated him from his hide-out; he is certain to be picked up within twenty-four hours."

Lee's grin widened. "Surely!" he said.

"I want to talk things over with you," said Loasby.

"Why not stop at my place on your way uptown?" suggested Lee. "I had better not be seen around Headquarters too much or the newspaper boys will have a rag baby."

"Right. I have to go to a banquet at the Ambassador. Expect me about ten o'clock."

"Very well. And look, Inspector; I recommend that you don't let out a word about the flat on Park Avenue."

"Not a word! Not a word!" said Loasby fervently; and Lee knew that he could depend upon it, since the story showed up the handsome Inspector in a ludicrous light.

After these conversations, Lee felt a little better. He paced up and down his living room smiling at his own discomfiture. Duty points one way and inclination another, he thought. I have got to break this case or it will break me!

CHAPTER ELEVEN

LEE CALLED UP THE GARTREY APARTMENT. A manservant answered. "I would like to speak to Miss Eliza Young," said Lee.

"What name, please?"

"Never mind my name. It's a personal matter."

The voice hesitated. "The servants do not use the phone for personal calls, sir. Mrs. Gartrey's orders."

"It is rather important," said Lee.

"Hold the wire a moment, please. I will find out." After a considerable wait Lee heard Agnes Gartrey's cold, crisp voice on the wire. "What is it?" Smiling to himself, he quietly hung up. She was always on guard!

At eight o'clock he called again. He figured that at this hour Mrs. Gartrey would certainly be at dinner, and the manservant presumably waiting on the table. Though he had obeyed orders, the man had probably told Eliza of the call for her and she would be on the *qui vive* for another. A female voice answered on the wire.

"I would like to speak to Miss Eliza Young, please."

"This is she."

Lee smiled at his success. "This is Amos Lee Mappin speaking,"

"Oh, yes," she answered eagerly.

"Can you speak freely, Eliza?"

She lowered her voice to a whisper. Evidently her lips were close to the transmitter. "I'm speaking at the switchboard, sir. So you can say what you like. But the other servants are in and out of the pantry, here."

"I understand. I think you and I ought to have a talk, Eliza, *privately*. There has been too much publicity."

"Indeed you're right, sir."

"Would you be willing to come to my home to discuss the case?"

"Yes, sir, I would be glad to."

"When will you have time off?"

"I could make it about nine o'clock tonight, sir, if convenient to you."

"Very good. I'll be looking for you." He gave her the address.

WHEN JERMYN BROUGHT HER in to him, Lee was sitting by the fire with a whisky and soda before him. Eliza was a comely woman with a tall, matronly figure and white hair. Her clothes, while of good material, were soberly made without any concessions to the style of the moment. She was of a type unusual in America and seen on the street it would have been hard to place her. Thirty years' service had rendered her face smooth and expressionless. She wore a pince-nez that she was continually adjusting and readjusting.

"Sit down, Miss Eliza," said Lee in friendly fashion. "You see I am having a little refreshment. Will you join me?"

Eliza bridled a little. "I take that kind of you, Mr. Mappin. I don't mind if I do, seeing it's after working hours." Her voice was unexpectedly small and flat, conveying the impression that her soul was too small for its ample frame. She sat stiffly on the edge of the sofa facing Lee. Lee looked at Jermyn over her head, and Jermyn, comprehending, mixed her a stiff highball at a table behind her. Lee perceived that the offer of a drink had stiffened her guard. He thought: That's all right, my lady; it wouldn't be the first time that good liquor had loosened a woman's tongue in spite of her. He started a general conversation.

"I take it you are English, Miss Eliza."

"Yes, Mr. Mappin."

"How long have you been in this country?"

"Twenty years."

"Really! Then you are quite one of us by this time. What brought you to America in the first place?"

"I came with an American family, Mr. Mappin, who had been living in England. And the wages was so much higher in this country that I stayed."

They chatted on about life in America and in England. Eliza, who set a good value on herself, was not at all put about by Lee's condescension.

At first, she took dainty little sips of her drink, but as it warmed her, the sips became larger and in the end it was finished as soon as Lee's.

Getting up, Lee took both glasses to the little table behind her.

"No more for me, thank you, Mr. Mappin," she said primly.

Nevertheless he mixed her a good one. When he put it before her, her expression suggested that she did not intend to touch it. However, she did.

"Miss Eliza," said Lee, "do you believe that Al Yohe killed Mr. Gartrey?"

"No, Mr. Mappin!" she said positively. "On the contrary, I know that he could not have done it!" She emphasized it so vigorously that the pince-nez slipped down her nose and had to be shoved back. "I let him out of the apartment myself a good five minutes before the shot was fired."

Lee held up his glass and looked through it. "Perhaps he came back," he said casually. "Did he have a key?"

Eliza was shocked. "No, Mr. Mappin! That would have been impossible! . . . Matters had not gone as far as that," she added.

This was not what Lee had expected. *Matters had not gone as far as that!* He took a swallow and turned it over in his mind.

"If Mr. Yohe would only come back!" sighed Eliza.

Lee said: "He says he won't until he sees a chance of clearing himself."

"My evidence would clear him, Mr. Mappin!"

"But, don't you see, Miss Eliza, your evidence is canceled out by that of Hawkins."

"It is supported by Mr. Alan Barry Deane," said Eliza sharply, "and he's a gentleman of position."

"I'm afraid Deane wouldn't make a very good witness."

"Hawkins is a liar!" said Eliza viciously. "If he would only fall dead it would simplify matters."

Lee wondered if Eliza was echoing her mistress. Agnes Gartrey had men to do her bidding and unlimited money. Hawkins must be warned.

"Even if Hawkins should testify," Eliza went on, "there would be a conflict of evidence and they wouldn't dare convict Mr. Yohe."

Lee thought: Somebody has been coaching her in the legal aspects of the case. He said: "We can't be sure of clearing Mr. Yohe until we find the real murderer. What is your opinion, Miss. Eliza?"

She stiffened. "Find the liar in the case and you'll have the murderer, Mr. Mappin."

"Obviously," said Lee.

He took her over the whole ground of Monday afternoon. Eliza told precisely the same story as her mistress and Lee felt that he was getting nowhere. Every question he put reminded Eliza that she must be on her guard. He was working to get her to the point where she would talk on without prompting, but it was a slow business. He thought he had her when she said in answer to one of his questions:

"Every time he came Mr. Yohe would have a highball."

"He was a frequent visitor, then," put in Lee casually.

"Why, Mrs. Gartrey told you he was," said Eliza.

Lee, taken aback, applied himself to his drink. This innocent-sounding answer opened up a vista. Agnes Gartrey had foreseen that Lee would question her maid and had drilled her in all the answers. That explained why Eliza not only told the same story but told it in Agnes' very words.

Lee took another line.

"While the door was standing open between the boudoir and the dressing room, what did Mr. Yohe and your mistress talk about? You could hear that part?"

A look of fright came into Eliza's eyes; apparently this was outside her lesson. She recovered herself quickly. "You must be mistaken, Mr. Mappin. Madam did not go into the dressing room until after Mr. Yohe left the apartment."

Lee let it pass. "Did you have warning of Mr. Gartrey's return?" he asked.

Eliza stared. "I don't understand you, Mr. Mappin."

"The other day when I was sitting in the boudoir," said Lee mildly, "I could hear the sound of the elevator door opening and closing on the other side of the wall."

"We could hear nothing," said Eliza sullenly, "because the door from the dressing room into the corridor was closed."

Notwithstanding her prim airs, Eliza loved whisky and apparently had not often tasted any so good as Lee's. A tinge of pink crept into her pale cheeks and her tongue became nimbler. When Lee placed a third highball on the stand beside her, she affected not to notice what he was doing. In the end it was a simple remark of Lee's about Jules Gartrey that loosened the curb on her tongue. After that Lee had only to sit back and listen.

"A hard man, Mr. Mappin; a hard man! Inhuman! Nobody could get along with him because he was so suspicious. He believed that everybody was trying to wrong him. He looked on all servants as thieves. It is no wonder that his two previous wives left him in spite of all his riches."

"Only one wife left him," Lee pointed out mildly.

"Well, the other died," said Eliza.

"My mistress was an angel the way she tried to placate him and to hide his bad temper from others. . . ."

Lee smiled inwardly at the thought of Agnes in the role of angel.

"Always so polite and good-tempered with him, deferring to all his whims. He was never satisfied. And, of course, no servant could please him. Though the servants worshiped the mistress, they were always leaving because they could not stand him. I have been there the longest and I hope to stay with the Madam until I retire from service. She says she wants me to. Of course, as Madam's own maid he had very little to do with me. I kept out of his way as well as I could, but even that put him in a temper. He said that I failed to show him proper respect and that Madam should discharge me. She refused. It was the only time I ever knew her to oppose him. . . ."

Lee, listening to this farrago, wondered how the belief had gained credence that the truth always came out when whisky loosened the tongue.

"Oh, Mr. Mappin, nobody would ever believe what my madam had to put up with from that man! You could tell the moment you entered the apartment whether he was home or not. All day we would be so happy and peaceful, and when he came home in the afternoon a blight would fall on the house. He would always ring the bell and then open the door with his latchkey. When we heard that sound our hearts would sink. That day I didn't hear the bell but only the sound of the latch and then, right away . . . a shot in the foyer! I will never forget that moment! I was tidying up Madam's dressing table . . ."

So Agnes had finished dressing, then! Lee's face gave no sign.

Eliza, unaware of the slip she had made, plunged on. "I was tidying up Madam's dressing table, and I stopped dead in my tracks. My first thought was of her and I ran out into the corridor . . ."

"So she had left you," put in Lee mildly.

Eliza realizing then where her tongue had led her, was transfixed with terror. "No, no, no," she stammered. "She was right there in the dressing room with me."

"Then what did you mean by saying your first thought was of her?"

"I mean . . . I mean, I thought there was an assassin, a madman loose in the house and I wanted to save her from him."

Lee affected to believe her. "So you ran out into the foyer with the idea of grappling with him?"

"Yes, sir. That was what was in my mind. But I didn't get far because she called me back to her and we clung to each other like two sisters! And my madam said: 'Eliza, we've got to go out there . . .'"

From that point Eliza recited her lesson to the end without any slips.

Lee preserved a bland face. "Drink up," he said amiably. "It is so distressing to recall these things."

Eliza shook her head. She was still trembling at the narrowness of her escape. She could not be persuaded to touch the glass again.

"When you and Mrs. Gartrey finally got out into the foyer, what did you see?" he asked.

"Hawkins was kneeling beside the body, Mr. Mappin."

"Did he appear to be agitated?"

"Not to say agitated, Mr. Mappin. He was cool enough. But there was a horrible look in his face. There was murder in it."

Lee got no more out of her. He had no desire as yet to corner the woman.

First satisfy himself as to the truth of what had happened was his plan, then go after the evidence. In the meantime, Eliza and, more particularly, Agnes Gartrey, must not be put on their guard.

When Eliza finally rose to go, she drank off the rest of the highball, feeling that she was then safe. Lee rang for Jermyn to show her out.

"It was very good of you to come to me tonight, Miss Eliza. I trust you will accept this trifle for your trouble."

Eliza was not at all abashed. "I thank you kindly, Mr. Mappin," she said, slipping the folded bill in her glove.

Lee rubbed his hands when she had gone. He felt that he was making a bit of progress. Agnes had been fully dressed when the shot was fired. This bore out Al Yohe's story. And, what was more, the two women were *not* together at the moment when Jules Gartrey met his end.

CHAPTER TWELVE

INSPECTOR LOASBY came into Lee's apartment with a heavy, downcast air, and dropped on a sofa. Lee made haste to mix him a highball.

"Fetch another bottle of Scotch, Jermyn," he said cheerfully.

Loasby said with a groan, "I have three hundred men on the case, Mr. Mappin, besides the help of the uniformed force. Since one o'clock the town has been combed from the Battery to Kingsbridge and we have not turned up a single clue as to that —'s whereabouts. Some other woman is hiding him now, I suppose. He seems to hypnotize them!"

"Women love to aid a fugitive," said Lee. "It's something we have to reckon with."

"If it should ever get out how close I was to Al today and how he slipped through my fingers, it would break me, Mr. Mappin," mourned Loasby. "You must help me!"

"But you said there were no clues."

"Can't you dope out something?"

"I'm not a magician, Inspector. He's a clever fellow. He will probably do the last thing we would expect him to do."

"You might be able to get something out of Charlotte."

"Excuse me. I'm not going to try to induce a wife to betray her husband. . . . Look, Inspector, to drop Al Yohe for a minute or two, I'm a little anxious about old Hawkins in Philadelphia." Lee hastily sketched the scene with Eliza Young earlier in the evening. "It is on the cards that they might try to get the old fellow in order to

save Yohe. Are you in touch with the man who is watching Hawkins?"

"Sure, I've got two men spotting him; Besson and O'Mara. I
can communicate with them any time."

"I suggest you call them up now."

Loasby called a number in Philadelphia. In a moment or two,
he got the small hotel in the suburb of Frankford that served his
two men as headquarters. Besson was asleep upstairs, he was told,
and O'Mara was out on the job. He held the wire while they sent
up to waken Besson. When he got his man, Loasby said:

"Besson, I've had a tip that the people who are trying to clear
Al Yohe may try to rub out old Hawkins to keep him from testify-
ing. In addition to watching Hawkins, therefore, your job and
O'Mara's is to protect the old man from possible danger. He should
be on his guard against strangers."

After listening to Besson's answer, Loasby repeated it to Lee.
"Besson says that will be easy because he has scraped acquaintance
with the old man, who now looks on him as his friend."

Lee said: "Why don't you suggest that Besson or O'Mara or both
of them should take a room at Mrs. Quimby's if there's a vacancy."

Loasby did so. "I want you to get in touch with O'Mara now,"
he added. "Find out what the situation is tonight and report back
to me." He gave Besson the number of Lee's telephone.

Lee made up the fire and they resumed their discussion of Al
Yohe's possible whereabouts.

"At the moment I can't suggest anything but routine measures,"
said Lee.

"You must go deeper into the question of who were Al's closest
associates. When he was left out in the air today, he would have to
go direct to somebody he could trust."

"I have it in hand," grumbled Loasby. "Trouble is more than
half the people in cafe society claim to be Al's intimate friends."

After twenty minutes had passed, the telephone rang. This was
detective officer O'Mara who, as soon as Besson relieved him, had
sought out the nearest telephone to report. Loasby held the receiver away from his ear so that Lee could hear what he said.

"About six o'clock this evening, old Hawkins came out of the house and proceeded to a little restaurant on Frankford Avenue. He met a young fellow at the door. Hawkins seemed surprised when the young fellow spoke. They went in and had dinner together. When they came out they were real friendly."

"Describe the young man," said Loasby.

"About twenty-five years old, Chief. Five foot eleven in height, weight 170, slender and well built. Wore a gray suit, a tan topcoat and a gray fedora. His clothes looked new but cheap material. Black hair, fresh color, blue eyes. Wore glasses with thick lenses that gave him a funny squint."

"Sounds as if it might be our Al with his hair dyed," murmured Lee dryly.

"Was it Al Yohe?" Loasby sharply demanded.

"Why, no, Chief," came the startled answer.

"Have you ever seen Al Yohe?"

"No, but I studied his photographs plenty. This couldn't a been him, Chief." Nevertheless, the voice did not sound altogether positive.

"Go on," said Loasby.

"After dinner they come back and went in Mrs. Quimby's together and the light went on in old Hawkins' room, third floor, front hall. The young man stayed a couple of hours. At nine o'clock the light went out in Hawkins' room and a minute later the young man come out of the house and turned in the direction of Frankford Avenue. I followed him long enough to see him go up the steps of the Elevated and then I returned to my post."

Lee's face had turned as grim as stone. "*The light went out before the young man left the house!*" he murmured. "Instruct O'Mara to return to Mrs. Quimby's immediately and investigate." Loasby gave the order and hung up.

Thoroughly alarmed now, there was nothing to do but wait for a further report. Loasby poured himself a stiff drink; Lee paced the long room with his hands behind him. Both men became aware simultaneously of the loud ticking of the ormolu clock on the mantel. A tug whistled in the river below like the blast of doom, and they both started. Utter silence followed.

In the end they heard Jermyn's voice in the distant pantry as he answered the call. Loasby snatched up the instrument without waiting for the bell.

"Hello? Hello?"

He held the receiver away from his ear and Lee heard O'Mara's lugubrious voice saying: "You didn't warn us soon enough, Chief. A terrible thing has happened. Old Hawkins is dead. Poison in his whisky. Bottle and glass are standing on his bureau, also the rest of the poison. No label on the bottle. There's been an attempt to make it look like suicide. A scrawling pencil note on the bureau as if he was already dying when he wrote it. It says:

> I can't stand it any longer. I have drunk poison. It was me who killed Jules. . . .

"He started to write Gartrey but didn't get any further than G-a. The paper was under his forehead as if he had fallen forward on it while writing. The pencil was placed as if it had just fallen from his hand. But the killer slipped badly when he put out the light because the old fellow couldn't have been writing in the dark, of course. He has been dead a couple of hours."

"Is the lodging house aroused?" asked Loasby.

"Oh, my God, yes, and people gathering in the street already."

"Is Besson with you?"

"I have sent for him, Chief."

"I'll come right down. I'll get a plane. Notify the Philadelphia police. Don't let them disturb anything until I have had a look at it."

"Okay, Chief."

Loasby hung up. The two men looked at each other. "My God, I am cursed with fools!" Loasby cried bitterly. "At nine o'clock both those men should have been on the job. Then one of them could have followed the killer!"

Lee, lost in a grim study, was not interested in what might have been.

"A stupid crime!" cried Loasby, thumping the table. "Nobody will profit by it."

"As it has turned out, yes," said Lee. "Under other circumstances it might not have had such a stupid look. I don't see how Hawkins could have taken up so readily with a man he didn't know. We must look into that. Notice that the killer avoided going to Mrs. Quimby's to ask for Hawkins. When the two of them returned to Mrs. Quimby's, Hawkins opened the door with his key and the chances are that nobody in the house saw the killer, either coming or going. Note that he was clever enough to break off the suicide note before he came to the signature. If he had not put out the light, and if O'Mara had not happened to be watching from across the street, it would have been accepted as a suicide."

"This is some more of the work of that brute, Al Yohe!" cried Loasby.

Lee shook his head. "Impossible!"

"Why couldn't it have been?"

"You forget that Al Yohe admitted to me he was in the Gartrey apartment at the moment Jules Gartrey was shot. In fact, his story bore out that of Hawkins in every particular. What good would it do him to put the old man out of the way?"

Loasby stared at Lee with widening eyes. "Then . . . then, it must have been done at the order of that love-crazed woman! The most prominent woman in New York. My God, Mr. Mappin, this will blow off the roof of the town!"

Lee shrugged. "She's just a woman like any other!"

"We could never in the world convict her!"

Lee's lips were pressed out in a thin line. "I promise you I will, if she's guilty!"

"Will you come down to Philly with me?"

"No. There's nothing for me there. I'll go over the findings with you when you return."

Loasby hastened away.

Lee continued to pace the living room. "Poor old man!" he murmured. "His only crime was that he told the truth!"

CHAPTER THIRTEEN

THE PHILADELPHIA MURDER OCCURRED just at the moment when the Gartrey case was beginning to lose some of its first impetus in the press for lack of fresh fuel. On the following morning it blazed anew across the headlines of America in four-inch type. There was a kind of ghoulish joy in the reporting of the news. To the newspapers it was like a gift from heaven.

The printed description of the killer reminded everybody of Al Yohe, and the public (led by the press) instantly made up its mind that Al had added this second murder to his first. The police were roundly abused for allowing so dangerous a man to remain at large. A threatening undertone was heard in the angry mutterings of the street crowds. The electric chair was too good for such an inhuman wretch. Citizens who ought to have known better, expressed themselves in the newspapers to the effect that anybody who might come face to face with Al Yohe would be performing a public service by shooting him down.

Lee, reading all this, thought: "If Al were to call me up today, I would not dare advise him to give himself up."

He made up his mind to go and see Charlotte as soon as he had breakfasted. Lee's heart was very tender for the little wife. The poor thing had been through such frightful trials during the past few days that these hideous stories might well finish her.

It was about ten when he alighted in front of the flat on Park Avenue. He was very thankful that no hint of Charlotte's existence had as yet got into the newspapers. There was no crowd on the sidewalk. Upstairs the door of the apartment was opened to him by a plain-clothes man with an eager expression. The man's face fell when he saw who it was, and Lee smiled.

"Did you think your bird had come home to roost?"

"Well, I was hoping it might be something in the shape of a clue," the man grumbled.

"I want to talk to Mrs. Yohe."

"She's up on the roof with the kid. Go right up."

The last flight of stairs brought Lee out on the roof. It was a beautiful morning and warm for the season. His eyes took in the false floor protecting the roof proper; the posts and the lines strung from side to side for the tenants' washing. On either hand, an immense modern apartment house rose to the sky; a murmur of traffic came up from the street.

Charlotte was seated on the coping of the low wall that separated the roofs of the two smaller houses. The baby slept in his gocart before her. The girl did not immediately perceive Lee. She was knitting some sort of little garment of blue wool, and to Lee's astonishment her face was calm. Yet she had read the newspapers, for one of them lay at her feet. On the other side of the roof sat another plain-clothes man, bored and yawning. Lee thought: Wants to make sure she gets no message by carrier pigeon. All of Inspector Loasby's men knew Lee by sight, and this officer made no attempt to interfere between him and Charlotte.

Charlotte arose at Lee's approach, smiling delightfully, and flushing pink with pleasure. "Mr. Mappin! What a nice surprise! How good of you to come and see me!"

Lee was more than a little taken aback. She looked adorable. "Well . . . I just wanted to make sure you were all right."

"I'm all right," she said with a lift of her chin. "I have to keep cheerful on Lester's account. The little fellow feels it when I give way . . . I don't like to go down in the street," she continued, "because the neighbors know that this house is being watched by the police, though they don't know why. I don't want anybody to connect it with Lester and me. Lester gets good air up here, and I can order anything I need for the house by telephone. Of course, it's a bore to have the police around all the time, but they're not bad fellows. They make it as easy as they can for me."

"Hum!" said Lee, caressing his chin. He sat down beside her. "Will it wake the young fellow if we talk?"

She shook her head. "No fear! He will sleep until his hour is up, though the heavens fall!"

"Hum!" said Lee again. "I see you've read the newspaper."

She poked it with her foot. "Yes. Such stuff!"

"I came to tell you," said Lee, "that I know, and the police know, that Al had nothing to do with what happened in Philadelphia last night."

She turned pink again. "It was kind of you to think of me, but as far as I'm concerned the assurance wasn't necessary." She smiled suddenly and bit her lip as at some humorous recollection.

Lee wondered what was going through her mind. "Even so," he said, "these ugly stories about Al must have distressed you."

"Oh, I don't pay any attention to what I read in the papers, Mr. Mappin. I knew that Al couldn't have been in Philadelphia at six o'clock last night."

"How?"

She laughed outright. "Because he was with me in New York until after four!"

Lee stared. "Excuse me," he said, "but I'll be damned! . . . *Where* could you have seen him yesterday? . . . No, don't tell me," he quickly amended, "for after all, I'm working with the police."

"I don't mind telling you," she said, "because we won't meet again in the same place. It was in Central Park."

"What about your watchdogs?"

She laughed. "There was only one of them. I gave him the slip."

"How were you able to make a date to meet Al?"

"There was no date. It was this way. We were out of money and Al had gone out to get some."

"Where was he going to get it?"

Charlotte's lips closed tight. "I mustn't tell you that."

"Well, go on."

"There is a certain unfrequented spot in the park that Al and I call ours. I kept thinking that he might come there to look for me, so I asked my watchdogs, as you call them, if I could take Lester for his usual walk up and down the avenue, and they said yes. One of them carried Lester downstairs for me. Well, when we set off I took care never to look behind me, but I knew perfectly well that the man was following me. At Eighty-sixth and Park there is a big store that has two entrances, one on the avenue side, one on the street. At the avenue side I lifted Lester up and went in, leaving the gocart at the door. Outside the other entrance there's a taxicab stand, so I just got in a taxi and told the driver to take me in Central Park. He had to drive back to Park Avenue before he could turn and I saw my policeman watching the gocart and knew I was safe from being followed. So I went to our certain place in Central Park, and sure enough, Al came along. . . ."

"Good God!" ejaculated Lee. "Disguised?"

"A little bit. But I knew him at once." Her laugh sounded. "Oh, it was clever! Nobody but Al would ever have thought of anything so simple!"

"Was he alone?" asked Lee grimly.

She hesitated. "I don't think I'd better answer that."

Lee thought: Then he was not alone!

"He sat down beside me," Charlotte continued, "and we talked. He was mighty thankful to see me. He gave me money and also the key to our safe deposit box. He told me how to cut some coupons if I needed more money. Lester was so glad to see his daddy, too. Al wasn't so much disguised but the baby knew him. He adores his father. I wouldn't let Al stay but a few minutes. We weren't far from Eighty-sixth Street and there was just a chance that one of the watchdogs might stumble on the spot. I drove back to the side entrance of the store in another taxi and when I came out of the Park Avenue entrance, there the man was, still watching the gocart. I made out not to see him. The whole thing didn't take more than half an hour, so I walked the baby up and down the street for a while before taking him in."

"You're a clever woman, my dear," said Lee soberly. "I am sorry to see you playing a losing game."

Charlotte merely looked obstinate.

"Al can keep up this merry game of hide-and-seek for a while, but it can only have one end."

"Aren't you working for him?" she said.

"I am working to discover the truth."

"Well, if he didn't have anything to do with this Philadelphia murder, doesn't that prove that he didn't . . ."

"Robert Hawkins was probably killed by some friend of Al's who supposed that Hawkin's death would help Al."

"You mean that woman," Charlotte said coolly. "You are right, of course. And it was she who killed Jules Gartrey. I am surprised that you can't see that."

"Why should she?" asked Lee mildly.

"Because it was hateful to have to live with him. He hampered her liberty. . . . And by his death she becomes one of the richest women in the country and free!"

"If she hired a man to put Hawkins out of the way, she was putting herself in the murderer's power for life."

Charlotte shook her head. "No. Because the murderer wouldn't dare say anything. And, anyway, she's a beautiful woman; she's able to reduce men to a slavish obedience."

"I'm not saying you're not right," said Lee.

There was a silence. The endless murmur of traffic in Park Avenue came up to them, ceased abruptly as the lights changed; commenced again. Lee watched a skywriter, a black speck against the blue, darting, turning, spinning out his gigantic white script. Charlotte's needles twinkled and clicked. Her lips were tight. She said at last:

"Do you know what I think? I think the story of Lester and me ought to be published in the papers."

"Good God, no!" cried Lee involuntarily.

"If that woman learned that Al had a wife and baby, it would put her in such a fury of rage that the truth might come out."

"But, my dear child, think what it would mean! Life would become impossible for you and the baby!"

Charlotte's chin went up again. "I could stand it. As for Lester, he's too young to know what's going on, thank God!" She bent over the gocart.

"He still thinks the world is full of kindness and love."

"Have you discussed this with Al?" asked Lee.

"No, indeed. He would never consent to such a thing. He wants to spare me. But if I was sure it was the right thing to do, I would act without consulting him."

Lee laid a hand on hers. "No, my dear, no! Your position is difficult enough as it is!"

LEE CONTINUED ON TO HIS OFFICE. There he found Fanny Parran and Judy Bowles holding court for a dozen newspaper reporters. Ordinarily, the sight would have pleased him, for he was proud of the attractiveness of his office assistants and he liked to see them enjoying themselves. Lee insisted that he was an amateur and, as such, he said, no speeding-up process was necessary in his office. Consequently, Fanny and Judy adored their jobs. But this morning the gay wise-cracking back and forth made Lee sore. He thought ruefully: This damned case is spoiling my sunny nature!

Tom Cottar of the *Herald Tribune* acted as spokesman for the others: "Mr. Mappin, what do you think of this Philadelphia murder?"

"What a foolish question!" said Lee sharply. "A brutal, cold-blooded crime! What would you expect me to think of it?"

"Do you believe that Al Yohe had a hand in it?"

"I never express an opinion as to a man's guilt until after he is tried."

"Nobody but Al Yohe had any interest in Hawkins' death."

"The officer who saw the killer asserts that it was not Al Yohe."

"Maybe the cop was just trying to save his face."

"Maybe. But there is also another possibility."

"We are aware of it," said Tom Cottar dryly, "but we're not allowed to say anything about that."

Lee shrugged.

He got rid of them at last. They went away and each cooked up his own story of the interview in which Lee had not admitted anything.

Fanny was as sweet as peaches toward her employer this morning. She was a little uneasy, Lee saw, and keen to find out what he was up to. She said casually: "I called you at eleven, Pop, but Jermyn said you'd been gone for an hour."

Lee kept an impassive face. "What did you want?"

"Inspector Loasby phoned to say he had returned to New York and would like to see you at his office. Or, if that was not convenient, he'd come up here."

"I'll go down to Headquarters," said Lee.

Loasby gave Lee the gist of his findings in Philadelphia. Robert Hawkins had been poisoned with cyanide. Cyanide, of course, would betray itself by its taste, but Hawkins, like all men who took their whisky straight, had swallowed it at a gulp and tasted it too late. No fingerprints had been found except Hawkins' own. Mrs. Quimby reported that Hawkins had received a letter on the morning of his murder. She had taken notice of it because he received so few letters. A plain, white envelope without any printing on it, posted in New York. Addressed in an ordinary kind of hand, like a clerk's. The maid had handed it to Hawkins, and after reading it the old man had remarked: "From a young man I used to know."

He had then sent word down to Mrs. Quimby that he would have his dinner out that evening. Neither letter nor envelope had been found in his room, the killer evidently having taken care to remove them. Nobody in Mrs. Quimby's house had had a sight of Hawkins' visitor the previous night.

"There is nothing in Philadelphia to furnish a clue to his identity," said Loasby. "I am working at this end to discover Hawkins' former associates. He was registered at the Tuckerman agency before going to work for the Gartreys. I'm also having the sales of cyanide traced."

Lee stroked his chin. "There's one odd feature of the situation. If the killer made a date with Hawkins to meet him at the restaurant, why should Hawkins have been 'surprised' to find him at the door?"

"I asked O'Mara about that," said Loasby, "and he stuck to it that Hawkins did not appear to know the young man when he greeted him."

"This is the way I would explain it," said Lee. "Somebody was looking for a man to liquidate old Hawkins. It is hardly possible that a man could be found who knew Hawkins and was willing to take on the job of rubbing him out, just like that. It is likely that they signed the name of one of Hawkins' acquaintances to the letter and gave the job to a professional killer. This one explained to Hawkins why he had come instead of the friend he expected, made friends with the unsuspicious old man during the meal, and afterwards suggested going to Hawkins' room for a drink."

"That's the way I figure it," said Loasby.

While Lee was at Headquarters, Fanny called up to say that Mr. George Coler of Hasbrouck and Company was trying to get in touch with him.

"I'm not far from his office," said Lee. "Tell him I'll be there directly."

Once more Lee was led through the magnificent suite of lofty rooms to George Coler's private office. The beauteous receptionist swam before him as gracefully as a swan. Today, however, the astute banker was far from showing his usual *savoir-faire*; his high-colored face was mottled in hue and etched with harassed lines; one eyelid twitched nervously; he was unable to keep still. Today he took care to close the door of his office after Lee had entered.

"So good of you to come down, Mr. Mappin. I'm really in no shape to do business today, but I have a dozen important meetings." He attempted to carry it off with a laugh. "I suppose the market would break if I went home."

"What's the matter?" asked Lee mildly.

"It's that damnable murder in Philadelphia last night!"

Lee wondered why the murder of a poor old butler should upset the great and powerful banker to this extent. While Coler railed on against the crime, he quietly waited to find out.

"Horrible! . . . Absolutely cold-blooded! . . . The man must be insane! . . . What's the matter with the police? Is Al Yohe to be allowed to go on killing at his own sweet will?"

"This one wasn't Al Yohe's work," said Lee.

Coler whirled on him. "How do you know that?" he demanded.

"Well, there is certain evidence in the hands of the police that proves it couldn't have been Yohe."

Coler's agitation increased. "Good God, Mappin! Do you mean that the police have information that hasn't been given out?"

"Why, of course. They can't reveal their whole hand."

Coler approached him with his face working. "What sort of information?"

Lee held up his hands. "I couldn't tell you that, Mr. Coler."

"You can tell me! I'm not a newspaperman. I'm accustomed to keeping things to myself. I have a right to know this!"

Lee continued to shake his head. Coler paced the room, biting his lip.

Lee thought: Coler believes that it was Agnes who had old Hawkins rubbed out and that it will be brought home to her. He's in love with Agnes.

Coler succeeded in controlling his agitation. "Mappin, whom do the police suspect?" he asked frankly. "You are safe with me."

"They don't 'suspect' anybody yet. There is no positive evidence."

Coler came close to Lee and let a hand drop on his shoulder. His air of candor was very winning. "Mappin, you are no policeman," he said. "You don't belong in that galley. You belong with us. I want you on my side."

Lee affected to look blank. "I'm afraid I don't understand you."

"I will be perfectly plain with you. I want you to work for me, Mappin—may I call you Lee? This is your profession and you are at the head of it. In a matter as important as this you can ask me any fee you like. But it's not a question of pay. I know you don't care particularly for money. This affects your own self-interest, Lee."

"I don't quite get you," said Lee.

"You and I belong to the so-called better class. We've got to stick together. We are the rulers and we've got to maintain our position. Numerically we are few and the muckers, the roughnecks, the mob, they are many. We've got to keep them down, by any means. How glad they would be to get back at us, led by the sensational press. We mustn't give them such an opening, Lee!"

Lee continued to look blank.

"Suppose a woman of our class, an infatuated woman, lost her head and . . . and became implicated in a nasty crime. Think what an opportunity it would give to all the rabble rousers in the country to stir up the masses, to preach hate against the upper class. Especially in a time of excitement like this. It would be a terrible blow to our prestige, Lee!"

"I think you exaggerate the importance of the situation," said Lee dryly. "The newspapers, yes, but they don't cut very deep; they have to be finding new sensations all the time. I can't see it becoming a national issue. And, anyhow, I never could feel that I belonged to any particular class, either upper or lower. I suppose it's a defect in my make-up."

As Coler began a fresh tirade against the unruly masses, Lee stopped him with a gesture. "I see your point, Mr. Coler, but I cannot change my course now. I have handed over certain evidence to the police and in return Inspector Loasby has taken me into his confidence. So you see . . ."

Coler heard only one phrase of this. "What evidence have you turned over to the police?" he demanded excitedly.

Lee held up his hands.

The interview did not last much longer. It was something new for the powerful banker, accustomed to obedience and subservience from all, to meet with firm opposition and he did not take it well. There was the hint of a threat in his final shot at Lee.

"You are making a serious mistake, Mappin! We are powerful; we know how to defend ourselves; we stand by our own!"

Lee got out.

CHAPTER FOURTEEN

ON WEDNESDAY NIGHT Miss Delphine Harley was opening at Gilbert Miller's Theatre in *Trumpet-vine,* a new comedy by Philip Barry. Since the star, the manager and the playwright all enjoyed the highest popularity, it promised to be a triple-barreled social event, the most important of the pre-Christmas season. Miss Harley had sent Lee a couple of seats. When the night came he was in anything but the right mood for the furor of a fashionable first night, but it was Judy's turn to be taken and he could not bear to disappoint her; he dressed for it with a sigh. Judy had been looking forward to this for days ahead. Lee had presented her with a new dress that he had picked out himself, a soft, royal-purple satin with a billowing skirt. Choosing costumes for his girls was one of his most delicate pleasures.

Police were holding back the dense crowd in front of the theater. It was music in Judy's ears to hear the exclamations of the people as she crossed the sidewalk—and Lee did not find it exactly unpleasant. "Ahh! ain't she beautiful! . . . That's the prettiest one we seen. . . . Who are they? . . . The little fellow is Amos Lee Mappin, the writer. I seen his pitcher in the paper."

The rear of the theater was jammed with people from the cheaper seats who had come down to see the arrival of the notables. From the stairway, which provided the best point of vantage, came shrill cries: "Look! there's Kitty Carlisle! . . . Oh, there's Vera Zorina! . . . Madge! Madge! there's Jimmy Stewart! . . . You're crazy! It's just a hall room boy thinks he looks like Jimmy. If it was Jimmy in person, he'd be mobbed!"

It was a long, slow business to get through to the aisle. "What a childish people we are!" grumbled Lee. "Will we ever grow up?"

Judy squeezed his arm. "I love it, Pop! I really feel like somebody when I am out with you!"

After the usual delay, the performance started. From the start it was evident that Gilbert Miller had another hit on his hands. The usually difficult first-night audience was lifted out of itself. Miss Harley's first act entrance was greeted with applause that stopped the show. She was playing the part of a county girl from Maryland who, when transplanted to New York, revealed all the devious cleverness of another Eve. The audience loved her. She gave a most brilliant performance, yet Lee, who knew her pretty well, had a feeling that something was amiss. Her art was perfect, but the natural, spontaneous humor that constituted her special charm, seemed a little strained, and when the curtain went down he said as much to Judy.

"Oh, I thought she was lovely!" said Judy enthusiastically.

It occurred to Lee that the girl's voice sounded a little self-conscious.

After the second act, while the theater rang with applause and the curtain was raised again and again to allow the smiling Miss Harley to acknowledge it, Lee wrote on the back of his card: "Congratulations! You were immense!" and sent it to the star's dressing room by an usher. He and Judy remained in their seats to avoid the awful crush at the back of the theater. Before the curtain rose again the usher brought Lee a note within a sealed envelope. It read:

> Dear Lee:
> I must see you tonight. Don't come to my dressing
> room, there'll be a mob there. I'll shake them as soon
> as I can and come to your place. So don't go to bed!
>   Yours, D.

Lee handed the note to Judy. "There *is* something wrong!" Judy looked so queer while she read it that he was impelled to ask: "Do you know what it is?"

Judy was startled. "Good heavens, Pop! How should *I* know what's the matter? I scarcely know Miss Harley. I haven't seen her for ages. Whatever put such an idea into your head? I'm sure I'm not in Miss Harley's confidence . . ."

"Methinks she doth protest too much," murmured Lee, and Judy fell silent.

Anyhow, Judy lost a supper by it, for Lee felt that he ought to hasten home. He stopped at his favorite delicatessen on the way to buy smoked turkey and other delicacies, for Jermyn had not been instructed to stay up and he wasn't sure what there might be in the refrigerator. Jermyn was in bed, and while Lee waited for Delphine he bustled around setting the table, beating up eggs ready to scramble when she came in, and so on. Lee loved to fuss around kitchen and pantry, and was fond of complaining that he never got a chance.

Delphine did not keep him waiting too long. Looking through the open door into the dining room, she flung her arms around Lee. "Darling! How did you guess that I would be starved to death!"

"Well, you've done a good night's work," said Lee.

She accompanied him out into the kitchen while he cooked the eggs. "I love kitchens! Scrambled eggs and smoked turkey! My favorite combination. I hope you put water in the eggs instead of milk. Milk makes them tough."

Lee could see that she was nervous. He let her take her own time in coming to the point. She asked him questions without waiting for the answers.

"What did you think of the show tonight? Everybody said it went all right, but I know I was terrible. I couldn't keep my mind on the play. I was just an automaton. What a time I had getting away afterwards! I know I've made a hundred enemies. There was a supper party at Pierre's. I never should have got away if Gilbert hadn't helped me. He saw that I was all in . . ." And so on. And so on.

They carried the food into the dining room and sat down. Delphine refused a cocktail and Lee poured her a glass of Montrachet.

"Let me eat a mouthful before I tell you what I came for," she pleaded. "Honestly, I'm famished."

"Take your time," said Lee. "We have all night."

She ate, but did not on that account stop talking. "This play has been the very devil to lick into shape! Casting trouble; one part after another. They wanted me to open cold in it, but I absolutely refused. So we were booked for Monday and Tuesday nights in Syracuse. That meant two performances and two whole days of rehearsing. I got back to New York at four this afternoon and had to drive direct to the theater to run through my scenes with Claude Danforth. A good actor, but he will not *listen* during a scene. It's maddening! This turkey is delicious. So I didn't get home until after six, just time enough for a bite and back to the theater again. . . ." She suddenly laid down her fork and looked at Lee imploringly. "Good heavens, Lee! I don't know what you will say to me! I am frightened out of my wits!"

"How can you be afraid of me?" said Lee. "I am so little!"

"You're little," she said, "but, Oh, my! . . . Lee, I found that I had a guest in my apartment. . . . Whom do you think it was? . . . It was . . . It was Al Yohe."

"Good God!" said Lee. He was not, however, greatly surprised. He had felt it coming.

Delphine nodded her head violently. "Yes, Al Yohe. Did you ever hear of such a colossal nerve? Making himself perfectly at home. Waited on hand and foot by my two adoring maids."

"Is he still there?" asked Lee grimly.

"I don't think so. You can call up if you like. I told him I was going to tell you."

"Then he won't be there now," said Lee, resuming his meal.

"Of course, I ought to have called you up before the performance," Delphine went on, "but I just couldn't bring myself to do it! The poor lad had flung himself on my mercy with complete confidence that I wouldn't betray him. And those terrible stories in the papers today and all! And if I *had* given him up, I would certainly have lost both my maids. Just at the beginning of the season, too, it would have been beastly awkward. As soon as I settle down in this part I want to do a little entertaining. . . ."

"So you had dinner with him."

She nodded with a guilty smile. "And I never was better entertained, Lee. He's so beguiling! I tried to be stern with him, but he made me laugh!"

"How long had he been there?"

"Since yesterday at half past one."

"Was he disguised?"

"His hair was dyed black and he wore a cunning little mustache. That was all except a grocer's apron and a basket of vegetables."

"Vegetables!"

"Yes, he came to the service door yesterday with his basket. He sat down in the kitchen, and within half an hour, I gathered, had my cook and my housemaid completely charmed. He told them who he was. They knew he was a friend of mine and they put him in my spare bedroom and went out to do his shopping for him. Later in the afternoon—this is the most incredible part, Lee—he told them his wife was short of money and he wanted to get in touch with her and give her some. His *wife*, Lee! Did you know he had a wife? A wife *and* a baby! *Al Yohe!*"

"I knew it," said Lee. "Go on."

"It didn't make any difference with those two infatuated females. . . . Well, it didn't make any difference with me, either! Al is *such* a lamb! But I'm truly sorry for the woman who married him! He put on a pair of black glasses Cook had bought for him, and took a stick, and Cook led him through the streets as if he were blind. Cook is so respectable, you know, she in herself would be the best of disguises. Everybody looked at them so sympathetically, she said."

"What's your cook's name?"

"Rose. Mrs. Rose Craigin. She's sixty if she's a day, but still romantic!"

"Al Yohe is a devil!" said Lee.

"That's what I said. But so beguiling, Lee! The way his eyelids fold at the corners. . . . They met his wife in the park. Such a sweet girl, Cook said. And the baby, of course. He gave her money and Cook led him back to my place. Nobody suspected them. Nobody would ever suspect them."

"He spent the night in your apartment?"

"Yes. And all day today. Incidentally, Lee, he couldn't have gone to Philadelphia yesterday, because both girls swear that the three of them played five hundred all evening with a dummy in my dining room. But wouldn't it be terrible if they had to testify to that. I'd be disgraced!"

"Perhaps it won't be necessary," said Lee dryly. "I am already satisfied that he wasn't in Philadelphia."

"Well, if he didn't kill the man in Philadelphia, perhaps he didn't kill the man in New York, either. Lee, I simply cannot believe that Al Yohe is a murderer!"

Lee snorted indignantly. "Just because his eyelids fold so sweetly at the corners! Really, Delphine, you are as bad as your maids! I thought you had more sense!"

"Well, I'm only a woman," she retorted with spirit, "and perhaps weak where a handsome young man is concerned. But I have not altogether taken leave of my senses at that. I've been around; I've known a lot of men and I would be willing to bet my last dollar that this man has not got a murder on his conscience!"

"I hope to God you may be right," said Lee. "Drink your wine."

As soon as she left him, Lee dutifully conveyed Delphine Harley's story to Inspector Loasby by telephone. The Inspector was bitter.

"You are always telling me just too late where Al Yohe could be found!"

"I lost no time in passing it along," said Lee.

"By God!" exploded Loasby. "I'm going to prosecute those two maids for concealing a criminal! I'll make an example of them!"

"You'll have to arrest Miss Harley, too," Lee pointed out. "Do you want to take that responsibility?"

Loasby subsided in sullen profanity.

"Don't waste your time in such side issues now," Lee urged. "After we clean up this case it will be time enough to decide who's to be punished."

Loasby immediately sent men to Miss Harley's apartment, but, of course, the bird had flown hours before. The frightened maids asserted that he had left immediately after Miss Harley went to the theater. At that time he had no disguise except his dyed hair and his little mustache. Once more the city had swallowed Al Yohe.

CHAPTER FIFTEEN

ALL DAY WEDNESDAY AND WEDNESDAY NIGHT Loasby was engaged in rounding up the underworld characters of Manhattan. Every young man suspected by the police of being a potential killer was brought into Headquarters and questioned. At noon on Thursday, the Inspector called up Lee in high satisfaction.

"At last we've had a break, Mr. Mappin. We have got the man who killed Robert Hawkins."

"Good!" said Lee. "You are certain?"

"Absolutely. O'Mara has positively identified him as the man who ate dinner with Hawkins in Frankford and afterwards accompanied Hawkins to his room."

"What about the waitress who served their dinner?"

"I've sent to Philadelphia for her."

Later Lee drove down to Headquarters to have a look at the prisoner. Loasby said:

"His right name appears to be Dominick Stacey, but he has gone under many aliases. They call him the Jocker, or Jocker Stacey. He has a long police record. Has been suspected of a gangster killing but has never been up on a homicide charge. A thoroughly bad egg."

"He's been questioned, I take it."

"Questioned?" said Loasby grimly. "And how! Going on four hours now. By the best men I've got. He hasn't weakened. Claims that he spent Tuesday afternoon and night with his girl. She's been brought in; swears that Jocker was with her in her room the whole time; that she cooked supper for him. The alibi is worthless because

they can't name anybody who saw them between the hours of four
and midnight on Thursday."

"You have searched his place and hers for the price of the murder?"

"Sure. No results."

"I suppose he's been told that he would get off easier if he told
who hired him."

"Sure. And laughed in our faces."

While Lee was in Loasby's office, the waitress from Philadelphia was brought in by a detective. As soon as he saw her, Lee felt
dubious of the result. A pale, anemic little woman, excitement and
terror had reduced her almost to a gibbering state. The heavy,
fatherly air that Loasby adopted toward her only frightened her
the more. She could scarcely articulate.

On an upper floor at Headquarters, the usual scene was staged
in the theater where the line-up took place every morning. The
woman from Philadelphia was seated in the dark auditorium along
with Lee, Loasby and several detective officers. A strong light was
thrown on the stage and six men, all of about the same age and
same general appearance were led upon it to stand in line. Five of
them were presumably police officers. Each in turn was required
to stand this way and that, to walk, to assume a pair of thick-lensed
glasses, to answer a few questions. They were then all taken off
the stage and sent back upon it, one at a time.

While the fourth man was standing in the strong light Loasby
nudged Lee to let him know that this was the prisoner. Lee was
saddened by the sight of him, he was such a fine physical specimen;
tall, muscular and hard. A four hours' grilling from the police had not
so much as ruffled his nerves. He was smiling a little. Under other
circumstances, Lee thought, he might have been a hero.

To Inspector Loasby's delight, the woman picked the right man.
But when the performance was repeated, she chose another man,
and when they went through it again, still a different one. Loasby
swore under his breath and she broke into a hysterical weeping.
The performance was called off and Lee saw the prisoner being led
away with a contemptuous smile. They all trooped downstairs.

"Well, at any rate," grumbled Loasby, "we're no worse off than we were before. O'Mara's identification is positive."

"After the woman's nerves quiet down, try her again," suggested Lee.

As LEE AND HIS GIRLS were preparing to close the office for the day, there was another phone call from Headquarters. Loasby's voice sounded agitated.

"Mr. Mappin, Charlotte has given us the slip."

"Hey?" said Lee.

"Shortly before four she expressed a wish to take the baby out for an airing. She had been before and they let her go. She was followed, of course. She went into a store at the corner of Eighty-sixth, leaving the gocart in the street. This store had a second entrance on the side street and my man stood on the corner where he could watch both doors. She was in the store quite a while. Then he saw her run across the sidewalk carrying the baby and get in a taxi. It was the only taxi on the stand. My man commandeered a car to follow, but the driver was rattled, he says. Anyhow, the taxi made a getaway in the traffic."

"Maybe she'll be back," suggested Lee.

"I doubt it. The taxi returned to his stand in a couple of minutes. Said he'd driven her just a little way into the park. He took my man to the place, but of course there was no sign of Charlotte. I'm convinced she's gone to join Al. We have the gocart."

Lee sympathized with the harassed Inspector.

"Well, this may prove to be Al's undoing," said Loasby with forced optimism. "It is possible for a single man by disguising himself to keep out of our hands, but a wife and a baby will treble his risks. You can't disguise a baby. I'm confident we'll have all three of them within twenty-four hours."

Lee smiled into the transmitter. "I trust so," he said.

"I called you up," Loasby continued, "to warn you that I could no longer keep the wife and baby out of the picture. I must send out a general alarm for them now."

"I'm sorry for that," said Lee, "but, of course, I see the necessity. When are you going to give the story out?"

"Immediately."

After he had said good night to the girls, Lee had himself driven up to the Gartrey apartment. He wanted to be present when Agnes Gartrey heard the news. He was shown into her boudoir. She was alone. Her greeting was invidious. Very likely George Coler had warned her against Lee; perhaps she was wondering if it was really worthwhile any longer to keep up the pretense that they were friends. Lee was not at all put out by her insolent indifference. It was more comfortable to be on an honest footing.

As always, he enjoyed Agnes as disinterestedly as he enjoyed a fine work of art. He didn't want her for his collection. The last few days had left their mark on her; make-up could no longer hide the little hollows in her smooth cheeks, the slightly sunken eyes. Lee, regarding her as a connoisseur, considered that these evidences of human passion really made her look handsomer than before. When everything was going well, her face was too smooth, too perfect. In order to explain his presence, he said:

"I thought you'd like to hear some of the latest developments in the case that concerns us both so deeply."

"That was good of you," she murmured. "I know nothing but what I read in the papers. I have to act a lie with everybody who comes here. It is only with you that I can be myself!"

So she had decided that it would be worthwhile to flatter him a little further!

Lee heard a slight sound as of someone approaching in the corridor. It aroused his suspicion because he did not hear it go away. For the moment he said nothing.

Watching Agnes closely without appearing to, he started to tell her in detail of what had happened in Philadelphia. Moving about the room in her silken draperies, indifferently arranging her bibelots, she was listening with the keenest attention. But the story did not appear to come close to her at any point. This woman was armed against surprise; she had only one weakness—Al Yohe. Lee

thought with professional admiration: Agnes Gartrey has the mak-
ings of a great criminal!

"Such a stupid crime!" he said.

Agnes shrugged. "Aren't all crimes stupid?"

Lee finished his story by saying: "The police believe that they
have the murderer. He goes by the name of Jocker Stacey."

Agnes lit a cigarette. "Has he confessed?" she drawled.

"No. He offers a phony alibi."

That was all. She was turning the dials on the radio. It was overdone. More natural if she had shown some elation at the death of
one she looked on as her enemy, and a little curiosity in respect to
his killer.

Again Lee heard the merest breath of a sound in the corridor.
"Do you know," he said softly, "I think somebody is listening at
that door?"

Agnes strode silently to the door and threw it open. The servant Denman was standing there. "The latest newspaper, Madam,"
he said coolly. "You asked me to bring it to you at once."

She took the newspaper, staring at him hard. The man's face
was smooth and obsequious. He bowed and retired. Agnes watched
him until he had disappeared into the foyer. Closing the door, she
tossed the newspaper on a chair. Out of the tail of his eye, Lee saw
that the story of Charlotte had not yet broken. Agnes said:

"I don't know if he's a spy or not. I suppose I'd better discharge
him just to be on the safe side."

"Don't," said Lee. "If he is a spy, let us do a little spying on him
and we may learn something to our advantage."

"Perhaps you are right," she said, returning to the radio.

The small incident made Lee thoughtful. He knew that Denman
was a spy. But now that his original employer was dead, whom was
he spying for?

Agnes said: "Do you mind if I turn on the news broadcast? I
have noticed that when the police have anything to give out it usually comes at this hour."

"Go ahead." Lee braced himself.

They listened to war news, to a stock-market report, to a well-known movie star's endorsement of a brand of beer.

"What a lot of tripe you have to endure before you get what you want," drawled Agnes.

From the radio the pleasant male voice continued:

> "Inspector Loasby, head of the New York City detective force, issued an important statement concerning the Al Yohe case at Headquarters this afternoon. Inspector Loasby said, quote:
>
> "'The police have known for some days past that Al Yohe is married and has a baby, Alastair, Junior, about nine months old. . . . '"

Lee was looking blandly at Agnes. Her face showed no change of expression, but under her make-up her color subtly changed, making her face suddenly look like a badly painted waxwork. Lee turned his head away. The voice continued:

> "'For more than a year past Mrs. Yohe has been occupying a walk-up apartment at number — Park Avenue under the name of Mrs. Matthews, and Al has spent as much time there as he could spare from his duties as host and publicity agent of La Sourabaya night club. He is described as a very affectionate husband and father. This information was withheld from the public while the house was kept under police surveillance in the expectation that Al might steal home to see his little family, but he has not done so. On the contrary, this afternoon Mrs. Yohe took the baby and succeeded in evading the police guard at the house, and it is assumed that she has gone to join her husband. She was last seen at 4 P.M. on an unfrequented walk in Central Park in the neighborhood of the East Drive near Ninetieth

Street. She was then carrying the baby. A general alarm for them has been issued.'"

Agnes Gartrey rose suddenly—and dropped limply back on her chair. Her eyes were devoid of all sense. She had forgotten Lee.

"'Mrs. Yohe's first name is Charlotte. She is twenty-three years old, five feet four inches in height, weight 118 pounds; has a graceful, well-formed figure. Her skin is very white and she has a faint natural color in her cheeks; blue eyes, light brown hair. Has a sweet and gentle expression except when roused to defend her husband. When last seen she was wearing a black cloth skirt and black pumps; a finger-length coat of beaver fur cut very full; a small hat of beaver with a touch of red velvet. All her clothes are of expensive materials.

"'The baby is nine months old, weight eighteen pounds, blue eyes, fine, soft hair just beginning to come in. A sturdy child. Is at the age where he likes to pull himself to his feet. Will soon be walking. Wore an oyster-white beret, pleated coat and leggings, all of a soft material resembling velours. As his mother left his gocart behind, she will have to carry him until such time as she can procure another. A small, pretty, expensively dressed girl carrying a child that is really too heavy for her, ought to be a conspicuous object wherever seen. The nearest policeman should be notified.'"

The speaker passed to another subject and Agnes switched off the radio.

Unable to bear Lee's bland, steady gaze, she turned away from him. After a moment she murmured hoarsely:

"You have known this from the first?"

Lee said: "I have known it for a few days past."

"Why didn't you warn me?"

"I was forbidden by the police."

"Surely *I* had a right to know!"

"They gave me no latitude."

After a silence she said in an uncertain voice: "You had better leave me."

Lee sat still. He could imagine the hell of bitterness that filled the woman, supposing that she had had a man murdered for nothing—possibly two men, but he was unable to feel much pity for her. He kept his mouth shut, knowing that a passionate woman cannot endure a silence.

Her voice scaled up hysterically. "Did you just come here to gloat over me?"

"No," said Lee.

"You lie! You're enjoying this!"

"Far from it," said Lee soberly.

She whirled around. Her beautiful face seemed to have disintegrated. She looked awful. Her voice rose almost to a scream. "Then what did you come nosing here for? What are you after? What are you after?"

"The truth," said Lee.

She laughed in an ugly fashion. "The truth: A fat lot you care for the truth! You came here to see me suffer! You're just an idler, a sadist! It gives you pleasure to humiliate people and watch them suffer!"

Lee took a pinch of snuff.

Her voice rose higher. "Well, I'll tell you the truth! Nothing can be hidden now! I'll pay him off, at any rate. I don't care if it destroys me, too. The truth is I have ruined myself for a liar and a murderer! It was Al Yohe who shot my husband! He hadn't left the house when Jules came home. He was sitting here in this room while I dressed. I lied and I forced my maid to lie in order to save him! Al was sitting here; the door into the corridor was open; he could hear the elevator door slide back; he ran out into the foyer and shot Jules. He had threatened to do it!"

"Why?" asked Lee mildly.

The little question pulled her up short. "Why? Why?" she repeated, staring wildly.

"He couldn't have planned to marry you if he had a wife to whom he was devoted."

She sneered. "How do you know he was 'devoted' to her?"

"He arranged to have her join him today, though it would double the risk for both of them. Apparently he can't do without her."

A spasm of pain passed over Agnes' face. With a frantic gesture, she tore part of the lace at the bosom of her negligee and let it hang. Even in her abandon, there was something theatrical in her aspect. "Oh, God!" she cried, "and this is the man I lied to save!"

"You haven't answered my question," Lee reminded her.

"I don't have to answer your questions!"

Lee faced her down. "What reason could Al have had for shooting your husband?"

With an effort she obtained control over herself. "I'll tell you . . . I'll tell you. Al owed Jules two hundred thousand dollars for the decorations in La Sourabaya, and he couldn't pay it! Two hundred thousand dollars! That's what he killed him for!"

"He'll have to pay his estate," suggested Lee.

"He'll gain time."

"Did you see Al shoot Gartrey?" asked Lee.

"I almost did. I almost did. When I heard the shot I ran into this room. Al was gone. I ran into the music room. Through the opening I could see Jules lying on the floor in the foyer and Al standing over him with the gun in his hand, staring down with an expression of fiendish rage. The gun was smoking! Al didn't see me. He dropped the gun, snatched his coat and hat out of the closet and ran back into the service corridor. And I . . . I went to my poor husband."

She put a hand to her eyes in a heartbroken gesture. Lee was not impressed. "Where was Eliza?" he asked dryly.

"She joined me in the foyer."

"Let us have Eliza in here," said Lee.

Agnes dropped the sorrow-stricken pretense. "I'll do nothing of the sort!" she said furiously.

Lee was standing near the fireplace. He put out his hand and pushed the bell button. Agnes ran to intercept him but was too late. She was panting like a runner, almost speechless with rage.

"How dare you . . . how dare you presume to give orders in my house!"

"This is hardly the time for good manners," said Lee. "I want to see the woman before you have time to rehearse her in a new story."

Denman entered. His black eyes were as bright and soulless as shoe buttons. Agnes, walking quickly away to a window, kept her back turned to them.

"Is Miss Eliza about?" asked Lee mildly.

"Why . . . why, I believe so, sir."

"Please ask her to step here for a moment."

Agnes, without turning around, spoke from the window. "Do no such thing! I forbid it!"

The man looked sharply from one to the other. Lee, when it suited him, had a powerful eye. He said quietly: "You heard me. Fetch Miss Eliza here."

The man went out like an automaton, closing the door after him.

As it turned out, Eliza was in the adjoining room, the dressing room. Lee heard a rush of feet in the corridor. Hastening to the door, he flung it open, but was only in time to see Eliza disappearing through the door into the foyer. She slammed it after her.

The manservant was standing openmouthed in the corridor. His expression of innocent confusion was overdone. "I . . . I told her, sir," he stammered, "but she ran away."

Lee could not very well chase the lady's maid through the apartment. He turned back into the boudoir, closing the door and helping himself to another pinch of snuff as an aid in recovering his poise.

"Now you get out!" snarled Agnes.

Lee's eyebrows ran up. "Shouldn't we have a little further talk?" he mildly suggested.

"Get out! Get out!" she screamed. "I want no further talk with you! Oh, how I hate you, nasty, sneering little man! Making believe to be my friend! Pretending that you knew nothing and all the time leading me on! I see now what your game is. That was just a cock-and-bull story you told the police about Al Yohe forcing his way into your place. You know where he is! Al is your favorite, isn't he, and you are bent on getting him off at *my* expense! Not if I know it! Not if I know it! I'll tell all now. I don't care who is hurt by it. Eliza and I together will convict him! I'll see him burn!"

"You had better sleep on it first," said Lee.

"Get out!" she screamed. "I know what I've got to do! You're a liar and a cheat! You're a traitor to your own class. . . ."

Lee thought: She has seen George Coler.

Agnes flung at him what was to her the final insult: "Communist!"

Lee couldn't help himself; he laughed. "Good afternoon," he said bowing.

On his way out he had a sense that somebody was keeping out of sight in the music room, but he did not investigate.

CHAPTER SIXTEEN

WHEN LEE LET HIMSELF into his own apartment, Jermyn was in the gallery. He said: "Mrs. Gartrey just called you up, sir."

Lee smiled grimly. "Already?"

"Wanted you to call her up the moment you came in, sir. Said it was vitally important."

Lee went to a telephone. Agnes had changed her tune. "Oh, Mr. Mappin, what must you be thinking of me!" she wailed. "I lost control of myself. Will you believe me when I say I didn't mean a word of what I said! It was due to the shock of what I learned over the radio."

"I quite understand," said Lee soothingly.

"And can you ever forgive me?"

"Certainly!" said Lee. "I am not at all a sensitive person. You are freely forgiven."

"Oh, how good of you!"

She went on protesting her remorse, while Lee waited, smiling, for the real object of her call. Finally it came.

"I hardly dare ask it after what has happened, but will you please, *please*, come back to me right away? We must, as you said, talk things over. You are the only one who is in my confidence, the only one who can help me to do what is right."

Lee's smile became broader. "Surely, I'll come right back."

"Don't take action of any sort until you have seen me!"

"Certainly not, Mrs. Gartrey."

"Oh, *thank* you!"

In the magnificent entrance hall of the Gartrey apartment house, Lee found George Coler pacing up and down, biting his lip. His face still had a mottled look. He slipped his hand under Lee's arm as if they had been intimate friends and led him away out of hearing of the hall attendants.

"Mappin, I am so thankful I was able to intercept you," he said. "Don't go up to Mrs. Gartrey now."

"But why not?" said Lee. "She sent for me."

"I know, I know, I have just left her. She is beside herself."

"I understand that. I was here earlier."

"She told me you were . . . Mappin, this story given out by the police today has administered a frightful shock to her. She is half out of her mind. Doesn't know what she is doing."

Lee wondered what the man's game was. Perhaps he was actually telling the truth. It's the last thing one suspects of a prominent man nowadays.

"It will be a good thing in the end," Coler continued. "It will cure her of this insane infatuation for Al Yohe. I had hoped to see her get over it gradually. I knew I could trust her good sense in the long run. But to get it like this has completely bowled her over. . . . Just give her a little time to find herself, Mappin. It is cruel to press a woman in her condition."

"I'm not going to press her," said Lee. "Just what is it that you are afraid of?"

"She appears to be determined to tell her story to the newspapers, to the police, to publish it to the world! It would ruin her whole life. In mercy, Mappin. . . . "

"I'm not going to allow her to do anything like that," said Lee, "not if I can prevent it."

Coler stared. "You mean that?"

"Surely. I am no believer in the sensationalism of the press. It not only feeds the public's worst appetites, but sometimes obstructs justice as well."

"And the police?" asked Coler anxiously.

"I have no intention of passing on her story to the police at this juncture."

Coler picked up Lee's hand and pumped it up and down. "Thank God!" he exclaimed. "I knew you were a good fellow, Mappin! We had some hasty words in my office that I am sorry for; I knew you were sound at heart!"

"Well, thanks!" said Lee.

"I couldn't do a thing with Agnes!"

"It may not be as bad as you think. I have often noticed that a woman is most obstinate when she is at the point of giving in."

Coler laughed heartily. "That's good!" he said. "I must remember it. You don't mind if I bring it out as my own, do you? We can't all be as witty as you are."

"Not at all," said Lee.

"Call me up after you have talked to her," said Coler with a glint of ugly eagerness in his eyes.

"I can't promise to do that," said Lee coolly. "Not if she talks to me in confidence, you know."

Coler gave him a hard look and strode on out of the building.

Upstairs Lee was once more shown into the pink boudoir by young Denman.

The servant's face was as smooth and waxen as ever. Agnes received Lee with an air of deprecating wistfulness. She had changed the torn negligee for a sober black and white robe, and her face had been made up anew.

When the servant left the room, she reassumed her heartbroken air and made play with a lace handkerchief.

Lee cut short her self-reproaches. "Please," he said, "I have forgotten what happened here earlier. I made all allowances for the shock you received. Let's begin over."

"You are so good," she murmured, touching the handkerchief to her eyes. "Have you telephoned what I told you to the police?"

"No!" said Lee.

"To the newspapers?"

"Certainly not!"

Agnes lowered her head to hide the look of satisfaction in her face. "I am suffering cruelly," she murmured in a piteous voice. "No man could ever understand what I am going through! . . . Long practice has made Al Yohe expert in deceiving women. I didn't realize that. His air of frankness and honesty was perfect! Day after day he came here to pour out his pretended passion for me. I laughed at him, then I listened, then I weakened. I led such a loveless life, you see. And all the time he had murder in his heart! He was just using me as a means of reaching my husband! Could a woman suffer a more awful humiliation!"

Lee thought: Your story does not hang together very well, my lady.

"I am only a woman," she continued, "with all a woman's faults and weaknesses. The only way I can heal the frightful wound he has given me is by helping the law to punish him. I want to see him suffer. Do you blame me for that?"

"Not in the least," said Lee briskly.

"He no doubt still believes that he can do anything he likes with me and I don't want him to be warned that I have turned against him. The only dangerous witness against him, as he thinks, has been removed by death and he may give himself up now, thinking that he can brazen out his crime with my help. I want my pitiful story to remain a secret until after Al Yohe is lodged in jail. I will then tell the whole truth as a warning to other women."

"That is exactly what I would advise," said Lee.

"Then I can depend on you to say nothing?"

"Absolutely!" Lee, delicately probing like a surgeon, asked casually: "Why didn't you say this to George Coler just now and put him out of his anxiety?"

Agnes looked at him sharply. "What about George Coler?"

"I met him downstairs. He was half sick with anxiety because you had told him you were going to publish the whole story. He begged me to reason with you."

She shrugged pettishly. "George irritates me so that I say things to him I don't mean. I suppose he's the best friend I've got, but he's in love with me."

"So I gathered," said Lee.

"It's horrible to me to be reminded of that now. I'm done with men forever! I hate love!"

Lee thought: I wonder!

"However," she went on, "I promise you I will make it up to him. George is really a good fellow."

"Quite," said Lee. "Can we depend on Eliza to keep her mouth shut?"

"Absolutely. . . . You wanted to talk to Eliza, didn't you? I'll call her."

She went to the door of the dressing room and opened it. "Eliza, come in, please. Mr. Mappin wants to talk to you."

Lee thought: Not much use now since they've had their heads together.

Eliza entered self-consciously. Her large, pale face wore an expression of lugubriousness fashioned after that of her mistress. She, too, had a handkerchief. She was perspiring and the pince-nez kept slipping down.

"Sit down," said Lee. "I don't like to see you standing when you're in such distress."

"Oh, sir!" moaned the lady's maid, seating herself on the extreme edge of a chair.

"Tell me precisely what happened on that tragic Monday afternoon."

Eliza wiped her eyes. "Sir, I said what wasn't true when I told you that I had let Mr. Yohe out of the apartment before the shot was fired. He was still here. He was sitting in this room while I dressed Mrs. Gartrey. At first, the door was open and they talked back and forth, but before I disrobed her I closed the door."

Lee thought: So far, this is true. He asked with a casual air: "Was the door from the dressing room into the corridor open?"

The question took Eliza off her guard. "Yes . . . no . . . I don't remember, sir."

"It was closed," put in Agnes sharply. "All the doors are closed while I am dressing."

"Naturally," said Lee. "Please go on, Miss Eliza."

"I had almost finished dressing Mrs. Gartrey when we heard the shot. Mrs. Gartrey jumped up and ran in here."

"What did you do?"

"Me? I was paralyzed with fright, sir. For a moment or two I couldn't move. Then I thought of my mistress. My mistress came first with me. I ran in here after her. The room was empty. I ran on into the music room and she was there. I was in time to see Mr. Yohe disappearing through the rear door in the foyer. He didn't see us. After a little, Mr. Hawkins, the butler, came into the foyer and kneeled down beside Mr. Gartrey's body."

Lee looked questioningly at Agnes.

"I must make a correction in my statement there," she said quickly.

"Eliza is right. Eliza and I remained clinging to each other in the music room until after Hawkins came out into the foyer."

"I see," said Lee. He turned to the maid. "In your former statement you said you ran through the corridor into the foyer."

Eliza hung her head. "I was not telling the truth, sir."

"But what reason did you have for saying that?"

"No particular reason, sir."

"Hawkins stated that you came out of the corridor door."

"Hawkins was a liar," said Agnes sharply. "What difference does it make, anyhow?"

"You are right," said Lee soothingly. "It makes no difference. But this is important. Miss Eliza stated to me that you had left the dressing room before the shot was fired; that she was alone in there when she heard the shot."

Agnes looked daggers at the maid. Eliza was terrified. Her nose glasses fell off. "No, sir! No, sir! You have that wrong, sir. We was together!"

"I made a note of it at the time."

"No, sir! I never said such a thing, sir. I couldn't have said it, it's not true! We was together!"

"Think what you are saying, Eliza," put in Agnes acidly. "Mr. Mappin mustn't get the impression that we have anything to hide."

The maid adjusted her glasses with shaking fingers. "No, Madam, I know that. You and me was together. Please believe me, sir."

Agnes said harshly: "Sooner or later you will have to go on the witness stand, Eliza. Will you be able to swear to what you say?"

"I will swear it before any judge in the land!" cried Eliza. "We was together in the dressing room when we heard the shot. And you said: 'What's that?'"

"That's all, Miss Eliza," said Lee. "And thank you very much."

Eliza went back into the dressing room holding her handkerchief to her face.

"So you see," said Agnes, "there cannot be the slightest doubt that Al Yohe is guilty."

"I have no doubt," said Lee.

"Will you have a drink?"

"No, thank you. I mustn't wait for that."

Lee walked home. The act of walking supplies a gentle stimulus to the brain, and he saw things in a clearer light. He had spoken truly when he told Agnes he had no doubt. He believed that he at last knew what had happened. When a liar repudiates his lie and tells another, he gives away more than he is aware of. His successive lies point the way to the truth.

But Lee had not a scintilla of evidence to take into court. I must have evidence! he said to himself.

CHAPTER SEVENTEEN

MEANWHILE INSPECTOR LOASBY was working hard on the Robert Hawkins' murder and on the following afternoon, Friday, he telephoned gleefully to Lee that he had built up a complete case against Jocker Stacey. Lee went down to Headquarters to hear his report.

"The Philadelphia waitress has recovered her nerve," Loasby said to Lee. "Today she picked out Stacey from among six men three times running without any hesitation. That in itself is enough to send him to the chair. But I have also been confronting him with different trainmen and conductors of the Pennsylvania Railroad as they came into New York on their runs, and he has been positively identified by two men as having been on the 2:30 train from New York on Tuesday afternoon. Another trainman swears that he was aboard the 9:38 from West Philadelphia to New York Tuesday night. It's lucky for us that the Jocker is a striking looking fellow. A clerk at the Information Desk in the West Philadelphia Station has identified him as the man who asked how to get to Frankford Tuesday afternoon. It all fits together, you see."

"Does he know you have secured this evidence against him?"

"Sure! I told him that he might as well come clean now, but he only laughs. He has engaged Harry Brummel for his attorney."

"Hm!" said Lee. "Stacey must have been handsomely paid for this murder."

"You said it, Mr. Mappin. Brummel comes high. The most conspicuous criminal lawyer in New York, and the most unscrupulous. A sinister figure, if you ask me; I hope I may live to see him disbarred. He has the reputation of never having lost a homicide case. The crooks of this city look on him as a superman. But I don't see how even Brummel can get this killer off."

"The District Attorney had better watch his jury," said Lee dryly. "There are millions available to beat this case."

Loasby was presently called on the telephone by the celebrated Harry Brummel. The Inspector first looked pleased as he listened to his communication, and afterwards suspicious. He said to him on the wire:

"All right, I'll have him brought here, Mr. Brummel. You may be present while he makes his statement, but I must warn you not to prompt him nor communicate with him in any way, or I'll have to call the proceedings off."

When he hung up, Loasby gave an order for Dominick Stacey to be brought from the Tombs to his office. Loasby said to Lee with a scowl: "Brummel says that after consulting with his client and learning the extent of the evidence against him, he has advised him to come clean, and Stacey has agreed. . . . I don't much like the look of it, Mr. Mappin. Brummel is too slick. I suspect there's a trick in it."

"I am perfectly sure there is a trick in it," said Lee coolly. "Some of the most powerful interests in New York are out to get this man off."

"How can they hope to get him off?" said Loasby, spreading out his hands, "a cold-blooded, premeditated murder and six witnesses ready to swear that Stacey is the man!"

"They're working for a verdict of manslaughter," said Lee dryly. "Stacey would be glad to take a sentence of ten years, wouldn't he, with a third off for good behavior, and a million, say, waiting for him when he came out?"

Loasby whistled softly.

The effulgent Mr. Harry Brummel was presently brought in, a man in his forties who didn't look his age, very sure of himself, very beautifully dressed—too beautifully dressed for Lee's taste. Lee disliked him intensely, but concealed it pretty well; Loasby less successfully.

Brummel, slick and obsequious as he was, nevertheless managed to convey that he didn't give a damn what anybody thought of him. He had a thick skin. His client was brought in between two officers. Jocker Stacey, tall, hard and insolent, looked pleased with himself, too.

"I understand you are ready to make a statement," said Loasby.

"That's right," said the prisoner with an impudent grin. "My lawyer tells me I'll get off easier if I come clean."

"Sure; Judge, Prosecutor, jury, will be more lenient with you if you assist in bringing the principal criminal to justice. But you understand, nobody is making any bargain with you in advance for clemency."

"I get you, Inspector."

"You can sit down if your statement is going to run to any length. I must warn you that whatever you say here can be introduced as evidence at your trial."

"I know it."

The prisoner sat down and Loasby's secretary was brought in to take his statement. Jocker asked for a cigarette and it was given him. He said:

"Last Tuesday, November 11th, I took the 2:30 train on the Pennsylvania to West Philadelphia. I asked in the station how to get to Frankford and was told to take the Elevated. In Frankford I mooched around to get the lay of the land and afterwards went into the Red Lion cafe to wait until six o'clock. I met old Hawkins outside a restaurant. I had never seen him before but he was described to me. I was told to explain to him that the friend he expected had gotten a position that day and had asked me to take his place as he wanted to blow Hawkins to a good feed. . . ."

"What was this friend's name?" put in Loasby.

"I couldn't tell you, Inspector; Jack something. I only heard the name once and it has slipped my mind. It was a fellow Hawkins had worked with some place previously."

"All right. Proceed."

"Hawkins was suspicious of me at first but I talked him around. We ate dinner and afterwards we went around to Hawkins' room to drink. I had a pint flask of rye and the poison in a little bottle. I read in the papers it was cyanide; I didn't know what it was before. I was just told to give him a few drops in his whisky. We had a few drinks together first and the old man got a little mellow. It was simple to distract his attention for a moment and put the drops in his glass. He swallowed the shot and just give me a look; he couldn't speak; he went out like a light switched off. I fixed the suicide note the way I had been told and left the balance of the whisky and the poison on the bureau and got out. Took the 9:38 from West Philly back to New York. Oh, yes, I forgot to say I was told to look for the letter the old man got that day. So I searched his pockets and I took it."

"What name was signed to that letter?"

"I never read it, Inspector. Tore it up and threw the pieces away in a toilet in the railway station."

"Why did you put the light out in Hawkins' room?" asked Loasby.

The young man betrayed no emotion beyond a slight annoyance. "You can search me, Inspector. Certainly was a dumb play."

"You were pretty excited, I take it."

This touched the killer's pride. "No, sir!" he said quickly. "That old guy was nothing to me."

"If he was nothing to you, why did you kill him?"

"It was a job. I got paid for it."

"Who paid you?"

All the men in the room were hanging on his answer. Jocker, gratified to find himself the center of so much attention, paused and grinned from one to another. "Al Yohe," he said coolly.

Muttered imprecations escaped from some of the men. Lee, however, was differently affected. So this is the plot! he thought. My course is clear from now on. I'm on Al Yohe's side.

Loasby said: "Describe the circumstances under which Yohe got in touch with you."

"It was the Monday night previous, Inspector. I was playing pool with some fellows in Slater's parlor on Grand Street. There was this guy sitting among a lot of other guys in chairs along the wall. He was disguised and I didn't recognize him; nobody in the place did. After the game was over he come up to me and said: 'You're a good player, Jocker; will you drink with me?' Well, I could see by his clothes that he was a guy from uptown and I thought there might be something in it. So we had a drink there in the back room of Slater's. 'How did you know my name?' I asked him, and he said: 'I heard the men talking about you. Guess you don't know what a famous guy you are around here, Jocker.' Trying to butter me up, see? So I let him buy me all the drinks he wanted and we talked, he all the time hinting there was something pretty good in it for me, something big.

"So before he come to the point he said: 'We better go to some place where you're not known, Jocker,' and we went out of Slater's and he said: 'How about the Biltmore bar? There's such a crowd there nobody would remember us after.' And I said okay, and we drove uptown to the Biltmore and took a table in the bar and the guy continued to buy, and we got real friendly. So finally it come out: was I willing to take on a job down in Philly? 'What kind of a job?' I ask, and he said, 'Liquidating an old guy who's got one foot in the grave already.' I give him the big laugh and made out I took him for a stool pigeon trying to get something on me. So he said: 'I'm in no position to sing to the police. Look me over good,' he said, and took off his glasses. So then I seen it was Al Yohe and I said, just to kid him, I said: 'What's to prevent me turning you over to the cops? It would square me for life with the cops. I could get away with anything after.' And he said: 'You won't do that.' And I said: 'Why won't I?' And he said: 'Look under the table.' And I looked and I seen he had a gun out and pointed at my guts. And I said: 'Put away your barker, kid, I ain't doing business with the police.'

"So I been reading about Al Yohe's case in the papers and I knew what he wanted to rub out the old guy for. He mentioned a grand and I said nothing doing. When I got him up to three grand, half in advance, I seen he wouldn't go no higher, so I said okay, and we shook hands on it. We talked over the details and Al said he would write to the old guy that night. So we made a date to meet in the same place at twelve noon on Tuesday. Al was there waiting for me at noon and it was then he give me my last instructions and the whisky, the bottle of poison, the suicide note and pencil, and the fifteen hundred dollars. Promised to pay the balance in a week. I wasn't worrying about that because he knew that if he didn't come across I could tip off the police by mail or phone."

"Did you make another date to meet Al Yohe?" asked Loasby.

"No, Inspector. Al knew where he could find me any time."

"What did you do with the fifteen hundred?"

"Gave it to my girl to keep for me. After I talked to Mr. Brummel today I sent word to her to bring it down to Headquarters and hand it to you, Inspector. Mr. Brummel said if I was going to come clean it had to be clean."

Some of the officers in the room put their hands before their mouths. None dared to grin openly in the powerful lawyer's face. Lee said:

"May I put a question, Inspector?"

"Certainly, Mr. Mappin."

"Jocker," said Lee, "if you're giving up all the money you have, how are you going to pay Mr. Brummel?"

The prisoner's hard face betrayed not a flicker of expression. "Mr. Brummel, he said he would take his chance of being paid. He wouldn't take the case, he said, unless I gave up the dirty money."

"Knowing," said Lee dryly, "that there would be plenty more where that came from."

Brummel jumped up with a great parade of indignation. "Mr. Inspector, I object to such foul insinuations in the presence of the police!"

Loasby said: "This is not a courtroom, Mr. Brummel. Mr. Mappin's remarks are off the record."

Having registered a formal protest, Brummel was immediately all smiles and obsequiousness again. He came around to where Lee was sitting and laid a hand on his shoulder. "No hard feelings, I hope, Mr. Mappin. I certainly would not like you to get a down on me. I look on you as the cleverest brain in New York today."

His hypocrisy made Lee feel a little sick at his stomach. He offered his snuffbox to Brummel, who hastily drew back. "Clever," said Lee blandly, helping himself to a pinch, "but hardly as clever as all that."

When the prisoner was taken away and his gaudy lawyer had departed, Lee and Loasby faced each other across the latter's desk. The Inspector said solemnly:

"This begins to look like a devilish plot, Mr. Mappin."

"It has the smell of it," agreed Lee.

"Their stories all fit together so neatly, and there is no evidence on the other side. How the devil are we going to expose it?"

"I don't know—yet," said Lee, "but I mean to give my whole time to it. I'm for Al Yohe now." He felt a curious lightness in saying it. The conflict between his mind and his feelings was over.

"I feel a little like that myself," said Loasby, "but it looks bad."

Lee said: "The name that was signed to the decoy letter would furnish a valuable clue. Jocker was certainly lying when he said he didn't know it. I don't approve of so-called third degree methods but any *legitimate* pressure that you could bring on Jocker to get that name out of him. . . ."

"I have it in mind," said Loasby, "but how can we accomplish anything as long as Al Yohe is a fugitive?"

"You are right. However, if I knew where Al was at this moment, I wouldn't tell you."

"Why not?"

"If Al was arrested, the case would be taken out of our hands and perhaps rushed to a fatal conclusion before we could act effectively."

"You don't know where Al is, by any chance, do you?" demanded Loasby suspiciously.

"I do not," said Lee smiling, "but I warn you, if I find him I'll keep it to myself."

Loasby frowned, not quite knowing how to take this. "Well, if I can't find him, I don't guess you can."

"Probably not," said Lee. "I suppose we can't keep the story of Jocker Stacey's confession out of the newspapers for the moment?"

Loasby shook his head. "Impossible! If we didn't give it out, Brummel would. It's part of his game to get his side of the case before the public before it can be questioned."

CHAPTER EIGHTEEN

DURING THE PAST TEN DAYS Stan Oberry, at Lee Mappin's order, had been quietly investigating the sales of fresh Beluga caviar. None had been imported since the war. Only one firm in the city, Chandler and Company, had a dwindling stock of the delicacy in cold storage. The price had soared and sales were few, but each sale was found to have a destination above suspicion.

Late Saturday afternoon, while Lee was in his apartment, Stan called to make a report. "Half an hour ago," he said, "just before Chandler's closed for the day, they received an order for a pound of that Russian stuff I thought you'd like to hear about. The order was from La Sourabaya. . . ."

"Ah!" said Lee, "Al Yohe's joint! Decidedly interesting!"

"The order was brought by François, an old waiter from the night club, who paid cash for the stuff, which seemed a little strange because La Sourabaya's credit is plenty good at Chandler's. The waiter insisted on having it packed in dry ice because, he said, it was for a customer in the country."

"Better and better," said Lee. "Go on."

"My man followed François when he left Chandler's. He took the package to La Sourabaya, right enough, and carried it in with him. I thought you'd like to know that it was a fancy, pasteboard box about a foot square, green in color, with Chandler's label on the top and a broad red stripe around the middle of the box."

"Excellent!" said Lee. "I'll get dressed and go to La Sourabaya for my dinner."

THE NIGHT CLUB OPENED at six o'clock for the dinner trade and Lee in evening clothes was on hand soon after. A new Captain received him in the foyer. Lee said:

"I am told you have an excellent waiter here called François. I'd like to have him if he is available."

"Most certainly, sir."

Lee was almost the first to sit down in the immense, dimly lighted hall, decorated to represent a night scene in the East Indies. La Sourabaya at the dinner hour had a very different atmosphere from La Sourabaya after midnight. There was no music or floor show; the emphasis was all upon good food and wines. By taking care of the finer details, Al Yohe had succeeded in attracting a small, but very choice clientele for dinner.

Among other things he had dug up three or four old waiters of the rare sort that is fast disappearing from the earth. François was one of them.

He came to the table bowing. With his pleasant, wrinkled face, curled lock of hair and side whiskers, he looked like a painting by Daumier.

"Good evening, François," said Lee.

"*Bon soir, M'sieu.* You know me, then?"

"I never saw you before, but you have been recommended to me and I asked for you especially."

"You are very kind, M'sieu."

"I am early," said Lee. "Let us take our time over dinner."

The old man was innocently pleased. "Yes, sir! Yes, sir! So one should dine! But *Les Americains* are always in a hurry!"

Lee picked up the menu. "To begin with, I would like a morsel of fresh caviar."

François' old face made a picture of distress. "I am sorry, sir, there is none. You see it has been removed from the card. We have not had any since . . . since Mr. Yohe went away."

"You are sure you could not find me a portion in the pantry?"

"Not for love nor money, sir. It is still to be had in New York, but when a customer desires it, we must be notified in advance."

Lee with a shrug appeared to let it go. Studying the menu, and consulting with François, he ordered his dinner. François entered into the choice with enthusiasm.

During the course of the meal he hovered around the table solicitously. At the moment he had no one else to wait on.

"François," said Lee, "don't you find it rather trying for a man of your years to work in so popular a restaurant? Such crowds come here every night."

"I do not serve the late-comers, sir. Younger men are required for that. I am only for dinner. My hours are from five-thirty until nine-thirty."

Lee thought: So much the better!

Later François was emboldened to ask: "If it is not presuming, *M'sieu*, what gentleman was it that recommended me to you?"

Lee said: "It was no other than Mr. Yohe himself."

The old man was curiously moved. Unable to speak, he looked at Lee with moist eyes and trembling lips.

Lee said: "You were attached to Mr. Yohe, I take it?"

"Yes, sir! Yes, sir!" François said softly. "I owe much to Mr. Yohe. The whole staff was attached to him. It is not the same since he is gone. He was a fair-minded man; he would listen to you. Always you had to laugh with him. The lowest bus boy in this place felt that Mr. Yohe was his friend."

"I, too, am his friend," said Lee. "I am convinced that a terrible mistake has been made."

The old man's eyes glistened. He would have liked to shake Lee's hand but recollected himself in time. "You are the first gentleman I have heard to say that, *M'sieu!* All were his friends before; all are against him now."

"What did you mean by saying that you owed much to him?" asked Lee.

"Mr. Yohe engaged me to work here, sir. I was having a very difficult time because everybody else said I was too old. But Mr. Yohe said he wanted men who had grown old in service. He was pleased with my work here. He said that I attracted the kind of dinner custom he wanted. Already there is a change since he is gone. I fear. . . . That is why I was grateful to you, sir, for asking to be served by me."

Lee said: "Do not fear for the future, François. There is always a place for one as good as you."

"Thank you, *M'sieu!*"

Lee found a Romanée Conti on the wine list that pleased him and he ordered a second half bottle with cheese. This spun out the meal until after eight o'clock. Upon leaving, he gave François a tip that almost reduced him to tears again. Lee felt oddly drawn to the gentle old man whose passion was for service. If there were more like François, the world would be a pleasanter place, he thought.

Lee took a taxi at the door and had himself driven around the park to kill time. Back in Fifty-second Street shortly before nine-thirty, he had his man draw up at the curb across the road from La Sourabaya. He sat back in the cab smoking a cigar and watching the service entrance.

At nine-forty, François came out with, to Lee's great satisfaction, the green pasteboard box with a red stripe under his arm. The old man hailed a taxi with a self-important air and drove off to the east. Lee said to his own driver:

"Double fare if you keep that cab in sight."

They were led east to Park Avenue and north to Seventy-fourth Street. The first cab turned the corner and stopped before the service entrance of an expensive apartment house. Lee smiled to himself. It was the house where Delphine Harley lived. Lee had his driver wait across the street. François paid off his cab and went in, carrying his box. In a few minutes he came out again empty-handed and walked away toward Lexington Avenue. As soon as he was out of sight, Lee paid his own driver and went in the service entrance. Slipping half a dollar to the attendant at the elevator, he said:

"An old man just came here to deliver a box. Do you mind telling me whom it was for?"

The young man was only moderately surprised by the question. A New York elevator attendant has to be ready for anything. "He took it up to Miss Harley's apartment, sir."

"Thank you very much," said Lee.

Outside he hailed another cab and had himself driven to the stage door of Gilbert Miller's Theatre. He knew that the second act of *Trumpet-vine* ended at a few minutes past ten, and it was almost that. The doorkeeper said politely:

"Miss Harley never sees anybody during this entr'acte, sir. She has to make a complete change."

"A very old friend," said Lee. "I'll send in my card. If she can't see me, I'll wait until the final curtain."

Delphine knew that Lee would not call at this awkward moment unless there was something in the wind, and she did not keep him waiting. He found her in the hands of her maids; she had a towel around her neck, her bright hair was caught up in a knot on top of her head, her face was covered with cold cream.

"I have to change my make-up," she explained, "because I'm supposed to be chastened in the last act."

"Don't let me interrupt you," said Lee. "I only wanted to make sure that I could carry you off after the show before anybody else got you."

"How exciting! But why, Lee?"

Lee glanced at the maids. "It's a long story and I don't want to interfere with your dressing."

"But I'm booked to have supper with the Wintringhams at the St. Regis."

"You can be a few minutes late, can't you? I'll deliver you to the St. Regis before midnight."

"Surely, I can be a little late."

"Good! I'll be waiting in a cab at the stage door."

Three-quarters of an hour later, Delphine, issuing from the stage door, started talking before she was well inside the waiting cab. "What on earth is up, Lee? I am consumed with curiosity. Where are you taking me?"

"To your place," said Lee, giving the address to the driver.

"To my place? What for?"

"Have you any fresh caviar, Beluga by preference?"

"Caviar? No!"

"Have you ordered any?"

"Certainly not. It's worth about a million dollars a pound, isn't it?"

"Not quite that."

"Well, anyway, it's too much for a working girl. What put caviar into your head?"

"I think we'll find a consignment in your pantry, my dear."

"Nonsense! Stop talking in riddles."

"I followed it as far as your house. In a fancy green box with a red stripe around it. I believe it's on its way to Al Yohe."

"Oh!" said Delphine. She fell silent.

Lee was aware that she had hardened. He put a hand on hers. "I ought to tell you, my dear, that I have had a change of heart in respect to Al Yohe. As I see the plot developing against him, I can no longer believe that he is guilty. And I promise you that if I do find him, I shan't hand him over to the police. But it is necessary for me to consult with him before I can defend him to advantage."

Delphine relaxed. She moved closer to him. "Well, that's a relief. I knew you had a good heart, Lee. As for me, I never could believe that Al was guilty. Honestly, I don't know where he is, but I suspect that Mrs. Craigin, my cook, knows. You'll have to handle her with gloves, though."

"I was hoping I wouldn't have to handle her," said Lee. "Won't she be asleep at this hour?"

"She ought to be, because I said I wouldn't be home until late. The other maid, too."

"I suppose the police have been after Mrs. Craigin."

"Good gracious, yes! They questioned me, too, but I satisfied them I knew nothing. They've been here again and again to question Cook. She stood them off. Said she hadn't seen nor heard from him since he walked out of the door, and stuck to it. I was proud of her. I think the police have given her up as a bad job now."

As they entered the apartment, Delphine whispered, "We ought to talk in normal voices. If one of them is awake we don't want to sound like conspirators."

Lee raised his voice. "Yes, I am hungry, darling. What is there?"

"Let's go and see," said Delphine.

In the pantry and in the little kitchen adjoining, there was no green box visible. Delphine called Lee's attention to a faint rumbling sound not far off. "Cook's asleep, all right," she said giggling. She threw open the refrigerator door. No box.

"There's ham," said Lee in a normal voice. "A ham sandwich and beer would just touch the spot."

"Fetch it into the dining room," said Delphine. In a lowered voice she went on: "I'll take a look in her room. If she wakes, I can make some excuse."

In a moment or two she was back in the dining room. "You're a wizard," she said. "The green box is on a chair in her room hidden under a jacket. She didn't wake."

"Where's the other maid?" asked Lee.

"She lies down on the lounge in my dressing room until I come home."

"Tomorrow is Cook's Sunday off, I take it."

"You have guessed it, wizard!"

"Do you know where she goes?"

"She has a sister in service in the country near Greenwich, Connecticut. I don't know the sister's name or whom she works for, but Cook asked me today if Martin, my chauffeur, could take her to Grand Central tomorrow morning in time for the 10:11 train for Greenwich."

"That is sufficient," said Lee.

After eating his sandwich and drinking his beer, he took Delphine to the St. Regis and went on home. Before going to bed, he called up a garage that he patronized and arranged to have a town car with a reliable driver waiting at the door of his house at 9:15 on Sunday.

It was a clear, cool day with bright sunshine. Lee sat back in the corner of his car, smoking, gazing at the scenery, revolving the problems of the Al Yohe case. After he got out of the city the glimpses of tree-bordered Pelham Bay that he obtained and the ineffable blue of the Sound were lovely.

He had some difficulty in fitting George Coler into his puzzle. He could not believe that Coler had had a hand in the Philadelphia

murder. However you looked at it, it was too hare-brained a scheme
to appeal to a man of experience. And, anyhow, George, being in
love with Agnes Gartrey, was not likely to lend himself to the job
of removing the only dangerous witness against Agnes' favored
lover. But supposing that Agnes had embarked on this without the
knowledge of George, George's anxiety after the event was perfectly
understandable. He could see what a dangerous situation Agnes
was in. It was undoubtedly George who had engaged Harry
Brummel to get her out of it.

The plot to hang the murder of Hawkins on Al Yohe bore the
Brummel earmark. It was likely to be successful, too, considering
the state of popular opinion, unless Al could produce a watertight
alibi for the hours that Jocker Stacey claimed Al had spent with
him. And who could testify for Al but Charlotte? The testimony of
a wife, and especially of an adoring wife like Charlotte, would not
have much weight with a jury.

Nevertheless, Lee resolved that if he was able to cast a doubt
on Jocker Stacey's "confession" he would advise Al to stand trial
for the murder of Jules Gartrey. After all, Eliza Young was not a
strong character, and a first-rate lawyer, an honest lawyer, ought
to be able to break down her lies—and perhaps Agnes', too. Lee
thought: I have never yet helped to send a woman to the chair—
but why not, if she's guilty?

He was in Greenwich in ample time for the train and his
chauffeur parked the car with its nose to the station platform where
Lee, hidden in the back, could see all that went on. He had
newspaper photographs from which to identify Mrs. Craigin, but
they proved to be unnecessary for when the train came in, she got
off carrying the green box with its red stripe.

Stout, good-natured, capable, Irish, Lee approved of her looks.
She was met by a rather shabby but respectable man who had the
appearance of a servant on board wages. He led her to a station
wagon parked among the other cars. Lee said to his chauffeur:

"Follow the station wagon when it backs out."

But when the station wagon backed into the clear, he could read
the legend painted on its door: *Mount Pisgah*, and he changed his

order. "Let it go," he said. "On the empty country roads they would soon get on to the fact that they were being followed."

The station wagon turned away out of sight and Lee had himself put down before a little cigar and news store opposite the station. To the man behind the counter, he said:

"Do you know a place around here called Mount Pisgah?"

"Sure thing, Mister, the Estabrook estate; five miles north. One of the biggest places in the county, but it's been closed up for four-five years. The Estabrooks, they got places all over; Palm Beach, Pinehurst, Bar Harbor, besides an apartment in New York. They haven't been up here in a dog's age."

"Are there any servants on the place?"

"Sure, Matt Rennert and his wife, caretakers. Live in a cottage just inside the gates. There are also the farm employees."

"How do I get there?"

"Five miles out on the road to White Plains. Left-hand side. You can't miss it. Hell of a big brick wall all around. There's no other wall like it. Big iron gates with stone globes on top. Brick cottage just inside. What's your interest in the place, Mister?"

"I heard it was for sale."

"Gad! I wish they would sell. It would be nice for all of us to see the place occupied again. Have you a permit to view it?"

"No," said Lee.

"Then there's no manner of use you driving out there. Matt Rennert won't admit nobody without they have a permit."

"Well, I'll take a chance on it," said Lee.

He drove on out of the village. In the rolling countryside the Mount Pisgah estate was immediately recognizable by its wall. Seeing the entrance ahead, the chauffeur slowed down. The tall iron gates were chained together and padlocked. Lee could see the tracks of the station wagon where it had come out and gone in again. Smoke was issuing from the chimney of the brick cottage inside the gates, but there was nobody to be seen. The main house was not visible. They proceeded.

The wall extended for about a quarter of a mile further along the highway, then ran back at right angles. The enclosure was laid out like an English park with thick screens of trees inside the wall. Lee stopped his car.

"Somehow or other, I've got to get over that wall," he said. "I haven't exactly the right figure for it."

"I'll give you a boost, sir," said his chauffeur. "I'll go with you."

"No, you must stay with the car."

"How will you get out again, then?"

"Oh, if I can get in, I'll trust to luck to get out again. Perhaps there are other gates."

Leaving the car, they walked along by the brick wall, only to discover that it completely encircled the park. At the back, there was a pair of high wooden gates leading out to the farm fields. These looked a little easier to scale, but Lee would not try it, fearing there might be somebody on the other side. Instead, he had the chauffeur boost him to the top of the wall in a place where the woods inside looked thickest.

Perched on top of the wall like Humpty-dumpty, Lee spoke down to the man:

"Go back to the car and keep driving around the roads in a circle that will bring you past the front gates every half hour or so."

He dropped to the ground inside the wall. It was not much of a drop, but it shook him up a good deal. A tangle of undergrowth and briars faced him; Lee was no woodsman, and after struggling through it for a few yards he had to stop to wipe his face and recover his breath. He discovered that his cheek was bleeding from a thorn scratch and that the front of his overcoat was liberally decorated with clinging weed seeds. This is no position for a philosopher, he thought, picking off the seeds halfheartedly. As soon as he started ahead he collected a fresh crop.

He finally came out on a bridle path winding away right and left through the trees. Turning to the right at random, he plodded on in the twilight of the arching trees until he discovered that he was coming up behind the cottage. Hastily retreating, he took another path that forked to the right, and presently the trees began to open up ahead. He could see a bit of the main driveway with a wide lawn beyond. As he cautiously stole toward the open, he heard the sound of a car coming and slipped behind a big tree. The station wagon passed in the driveway, heading back toward the cottage. Matt Rennert and Mrs. Craigin were on the front seat. The woman no longer had the green box in her lap.

After giving the car time to reach the cottage, Lee stole to the edge of the trees to get his bearings. Evidently the millionaire owners had been economizing on this place; only enough work was done on it to keep nature in check. There were some sheep pastured on the sweeping lawn. Off to the right the trees closed in and the cottage by the gates was invisible. On the left rose a great, square mansion in the Georgian style, its mellow brick walls half-hidden under ivy. The front door and the lower windows were boarded up; all the upper windows closely shuttered. It gave the house a blind and deserted look.

Lee plodded in that direction, keeping within cover of the trees as far as possible. Tracks in the drive indicated that the station wagon had come from around the north side of the house and Lee followed them. On this side, too, all the openings were boarded up. There was a service door; Lee tried it only to find it locked. He was not unduly discouraged, however, for he distinguished threads of smoke rising from two of the rear chimneys.

Passing around to the south side of the big house, he climbed over a rough barrier erected to keep the sheep out. The gardens were laid out on this side; a wide, formal garden, now much neglected, and beyond it a private garden enclosed within thick, tall, cedar trees. Making his way through an opening between the cedars, he saw a baby carriage tucked into a sheltered corner and smiled. Glancing under the hood of the carriage, he discovered Master Alastair Yohe sleeping peacefully. The babe stirred—it was his dinnertime—and Lee hastened to take cover behind a spiraea bush. Alastair presently lifted up his voice in a lusty cry of hunger, and Lee waited, smiling and picking the seeds off his overcoat.

CHAPTER NINETEEN

THERE WAS A RUSH OF FEET and Charlotte came running through the hedge opening with an adorable expression of anxiety. She looked as fresh and vivid as a bride. Lifting the child, she pressed him to her breast, kissing him, murmuring: "Did he think he was forgotten, poor lamb!" Lester, taking it as a matter of course, stopped crying. Lee thought: He's too young to appreciate his good fortune. Charlotte carried him out through the opening and Lee followed, taking cover from bush to bush.

From around the corner of the tall hedge, he saw her mount the steps of a side porch and disappear behind a door. Lee followed. Since all the surrounding windows were boarded up, he had no fear of being seen from indoors. Softly trying the door, he found it unlocked. He went in, closing the door behind him noiselessly. He was in a dark passage; light was issuing through an open door ahead of him and he heard the sound of voices in there. He presented himself in the doorway.

He saw a smallish room and bare, a housekeeper's room or perhaps a servants' hall. There was a hearth with a cheerful fire burning and a table set for a meal, lighted with candles. Charlotte sat with her back to him, removing the baby's outer wraps; beyond the table, Al in his shirt was sunk in an easy chair with his slippered heels cocked on another, reading the Sunday paper. Charming scene of domesticity!

Lee said: "Well, children?"

There was a silence. Charlotte, clutching the baby to her breast, turned a face of terror; Al, dropping the paper, stared open-mouthed. The baby wailed, and Lee began to feel self-conscious.

"It's no ghost," he said; "it's really me."

Al recovered himself. Springing up, he came around the table and clapped both hands on Lee's shoulders, "Mr. Mappin! What a swell surprise! You're just in time for lunch. It's a celebration! We've got champagne and fresh caviar!"

"Really!" said Lee.

Charlotte was looking past Lee toward the open door. "Are you . . . are you alone?" she stammered.

"Quite alone," said Lee. "Nobody has discovered your hide-out but me, and I'm not going to tell."

"The police? . . ."

"I warned Inspector Loasby that if I found you I would keep it to myself. If he didn't believe I meant it, that's his lookout."

"How did you get in?" demanded Al.

"Over the wall and through the briars," said Lee, exhibiting his seedy overcoat.

"What made you think you would find us inside?"

Lee described how he had followed the trail of the green box.

Al struck a fist into his hand. "I ought to have known that my gluttony would betray me!"

The worst of Charlotte's fears had subsided, but there was still a doubt in her eye. "Why did you want to find us," she asked, "if . . . if . . ."

Lee finished the question for her. "If I didn't mean to give you away? Well, I'll tell you. I wanted to consult Al about the best means of conducting his defense. I'm on his side now."

Al let out a whoop of joy and hugged Lee to his broad chest. "Didn't I tell you we were going to get a break?" he shouted at Charlotte. "I felt it coming this morning." He relieved his spirits by kicking the Sunday newspaper around the room.

Charlotte came to Lee, bringing the baby. Tears stood in her eyes. "I am so happy," she whispered. "I don't know how to thank you. Lester wants to thank you, too. Kiss him."

The solemn baby looked at Lee with dark suspicion and Lee said: "I'd rather kiss his mother."

Charlotte lifted her fresh and bloomy lips. "You're such a dear!" she whispered.

Charlotte put Lester in his high chair and fed him while Al toasted bread before the fire. He wasn't very good at it; he talked too much. Al was in the highest spirits and talk spouted from him like water from a fountain. Lee was oddly moved by the scene; this is something I shall not soon forget, he thought; the bare, candle-lighted room and the little family; young husband, handsome and confident, girl wife, adorable and adoring, and their lusty babe.

Al was full of great plans for the future. He said: "As soon as the cloud is lifted from my fair name, I'm going to invest my little capital in a small hotel. Not in New York, no, by God! I'm through with New York and its phony society. I thought of Washington, D. C.; a hotelkeeper's paradise, where the transient population grows like a mushroom bed. I've learned something about feeding people; I will introduce really good food in Washington . . ." et cetera, et cetera.

Presently they sat down to the table. The cork blew out of the champagne bottle with a report like a pistol shot, and glasses were filled. Al made outrageous jokes and Charlotte's silvery laughter was heard continually. Lee thought it one of the sweetest sounds in the world. Even young Lester became infected with the general hilarity; he made rude male noises, bounced on his fundament, and beat a spoon on his tray. Al elected himself and Charlotte members of the Popsicle; i.e., those privileged to address Lee as Pop. Lee could enter into their gaiety, but he was too old to lose himself completely in the moment like the other two. All the time in the bottom of his mind lay the anxious thought: How can I save them?

When they had finished eating, they all took a hand in clearing the table. Lester was carried out in the kitchen to keep company with his mother; Al and Lee sat down by the fire to discuss their business. Lee said:

"I see you get the newspapers. You read Jocker Stacey's so-called confession yesterday."

Al nodded. "Made out of whole cloth, Pop. I never laid eyes on Jocker Stacey nor passed a word with him in my life."

"So I supposed," said Lee, "or I shouldn't be here."

"His story was damn plausible!" said Al, scowling.

"Sure, it was plausible, because the scenes he described really took place. All he did was to substitute your name for the name of the person who actually hired him."

"How can we break his story down?"

"That's what I came to ask you about. He claimed that you spent last Monday evening with him, that is, a week after the murder, in Slater's poolroom on Grand Street."

"Suppose they bring forward habitues of Slater's who will swear they saw me there talking to Jocker?" Al asked with a sidelong look.

"They undoubtedly will," said Lee undisturbed. "It won't make any difference to me. I know Slater's and the gang that hangs out there. Where were you that Monday night?"

"At home with Charlotte and the kid. I never stirred out of the flat."

"That's good so far as it goes," said Lee. "Unfortunately, the testimony of a wife does not have much weight with a jury. A good wife is expected to lie for her husband. Jocker said he met you again on the following day at twelve noon in the Biltmore. Where were you at that hour? I know you weren't home, for at twelve on Tuesday I was watching the flat on Park Avenue."

Al considered. Suddenly he began to grin, checked it by biting his lip, and glanced queerly at Lee. "I've got a perfect alibi for Tuesday at noon, Pop, but . . ."

"But what?"

"I don't know how you're going to take it."

"What has it got to do with me?"

"Pop," said Al appealingly, "blame me for it if anybody has to be blamed. I could never forgive myself if the other party got into trouble with you on my account."

"What other party?" said Lee irritably. "What are you talking about?"

"Fanny Parran," said Al.

"Well, I'm damned!" said Lee. Al was gazing in his face with a ridiculous expression of anxiety. Lee started to laugh and the young man's face cleared like the sun breaking through clouds. "That's a good one on me," said Lee. "A week ago it would have made me sore, but now I don't mind. I shall have to eat crow, though, when I face Fanny, and that won't be so nice. What was the occasion of your meeting Fanny?"

"Jules Gartrey's death caught Charlotte and me short of cash," said Al. "Charlotte had been to see Fanny before Tuesday. Fanny said she knew a broker, and I conveyed five one-thousand-dollar bonds to her to be sold. The meeting was to enable her to hand over the cash for them."

"Where was the meeting?" asked Lee.

"At Hanley's café, a small place on Lexington Avenue, opposite one of the entrances to the Eighty-sixth Street subway station; the time 12:15. We met, had a drink together, she gave me the money and we talked for fifteen minutes."

Lee said: "It was on Tuesday that Jocker Stacey said you handed him fifteen hundred dollars."

"Don't worry about that," said Al. "I gave Charlotte five hundred and I have most of the rest on me. What I have spent I can account for."

"Go on with your story," said Lee.

"Fanny left me at 12:30 and I called up the flat to see if the coast was clear; no answer. I waited ten minutes, called up again and was then satisfied that the police were in the place. So I called you up, remember? 12:45 Tuesday?"

"Right, I can testify to that," said Lee.

"I then walked over to Second Avenue," Al continued. "I was sore on account of our hide-out being discovered. Made me feel naked, walking around the streets with a general alarm out for me; I imagined everybody was staring at me. In a secondhand store on Second Avenue, I bought a flat wicker basket and a grocer's apron; I went into the cellar of an unoccupied house and hid my hat and overcoat. I put on the apron and dirtied it, and roughed up my hair. Out in the street I felt easier then. Nobody looks at a grocer's boy. I bought some vegetables from a pushcart and carried them in my basket. I walked down to the service entrance of Miss Harley's apartment on Seventy-fourth Street. She was away but I persuaded the cook, Rose Craigin, to take me in."

"I have heard about that part," said Lee dryly. "What time did you arrive there?"

"One-thirty," said Al. "And remained there until about three-thirty. Cook and I then walked over to the east side of the park where we ran into Charlotte and gave her the money. That's how I spent Tuesday. You and Fanny Parran, the waiter at Hanley's café, and the secondhand dealer all ought to be able to bear me out. I may not be able to find the pushcart man again, but Mrs. Craigin will testify for me and the other maid at Miss Harley's."

"Excellent!" said Lee. "I can also testify that two days before Hawkins' murder you told me a story that corroborated his at every point. You therefore had no motive for putting him out of the way. . . . When this comes out it will show me up in a bad light," Lee went on ruefully, "assisting a fugitive from justice and all that."

"I'm sorry," said Al.

"Well, I expect I can live it down. You need have no further fear of Jocker Staccy's story. We can face him down in court. . . . Now about the other charge. Since the story of Charlotte and the baby has been published, my lady Agnes is in a fine rage against you."

"I never gave Agnes a thought," said Al, "but of course she would be."

"She is determined to send you to the chair for the murder of her husband. The question is, can she?" Lee went on to tell Al of Agnes' latest story of Jules Gartrey's death.

"Like Jocker Stacey's story," said Al, "it's part true and part false. When Agnes says she saw me standing over Gartrey's body with the smoking revolver in my hand, that is a pure fabrication. Why, Agnes got out in the foyer *before I did*."

"Hey?" said the surprised Lee, "you didn't tell me that before."

"Well, I didn't want to be put in the position of charging Agnes with the murder. Look what a light that would show me up in!"

"But if it's a question of you or her?"

"I am not certain that she killed him."

"Tell me what happened and let me judge."

Al said: "There I was sitting in the boudoir while Agnes changed her clothes. There are three doors in that room; all of them were closed. Agnes and her maid were supposed to be in the dressing room adjoining. Since the door from boudoir into corridor was closed, I had no warning of Gartrey's coming; I couldn't hear the elevator door; evidently Agnes did. I heard a rush of feet through the corridor, then the shot."

Lee smiled. "That's pretty strong evidence."

Al shook his head glumly. "No. At first I thought so, but the shot followed too quick. *Agnes did not have time to get out into the foyer.*"

"Hm!" said Lee. "In that case there is further work to be done on the case. . . . Think back. *After* the shot did you hear the sound of a door opening or closing?"

"I couldn't tell you, Pop. I was too excited then. I thought Agnes had shot herself. I hesitated. I didn't know what to do. I ran out into the corridor and there she lay in a heap on the floor. Her body was partly resting against the door into the foyer. I felt utterly sick. But when I turned her over, I saw that she had no wound on her and that there was no gun there. She had only fainted. I then opened the door and saw Gartrey lying dead in the foyer. . . ."

"Wait a minute," said Lee. "Could Agnes have shot Gartrey and then have got back into the corridor?"

"It is possible. But I am not sure of it. There was scarcely enough time."

"Go on."

"When I saw Gartrey, my one thought was to get out of the place. I stepped over Agnes and beat it. You know the rest."

Lee, stroking his chin, thought it over. "This killing is still unexplained," he said slowly, "but, anyhow, I believe we can get you off."

"How?"

"It couldn't have been you who ran out and shot Jules Gartrey because your hands were bare. And there were no fingerprints on the gun."

"Sure!" cried Al joyfully. "My gloves were in the pocket of my topcoat and my topcoat was hanging in the closet!" He sprang up. "Charlotte! Charlotte!"

She came running in, her pretty face all screwed up with anxiety. "Oh, what's the matter?"

"Darling!" cried Al, spreading his arms wide. "Pop has found a way to clear me! I knew he would! I knew he would!"

They embraced as if it was the first time they had come together. It lasted so long that the bystander became embarrassed. Afterward, Lee had to be embraced. Al popped another bottle of champagne.

Lester was brought in and they all lined up in chairs before the cheery fire.

"What's the next move?" asked Al. "I promised, you know, to give myself up to the police as soon as I had you on my side."

"I believe it will be safe for you to give yourself up now," said Lee, "but wait for a couple of days; I want to do a little work on the case: I want to prepare the way for you. I'll come and get you when I'm ready."

"Okay," said Al, "but don't leave us in suspense in this dark hole. I am longing to see the sun again! You can write me and enclose it in an outside envelope addressed to Matt Rennert, Greenwich. The Rennerts call me Johnny Jones. It's just a fiction because they know who I am."

"I'll write to you," said Lee. "At what hour is mail delivered here?"

"Twice a day by R.F.D. at the gate; nine in the morning and four in the afternoon."

"How can I get out of here unseen?" Lee asked. "I don't think it would be prudent to let Mrs. Craigin and the Rennerts know that you have had a visitor today."

"I'll unbar the farm gate for you," said Al. "There are no laborers about on Sunday. You can reach the highway through the fields."

"Don't go yet, Pop," Charlotte softly pleaded. "It is so good for Al to have somebody to talk to beside a woman and a baby."

"Have I complained?" said Al.

"No, darling. But I can see how cooped up you feel."

"I'm in no hurry to go," said Lee. "I am enjoying myself."

IN DUE COURSE Lee regained the highway unseen and walked along. Hearing the approach of a car, he looked over his shoulder and was somewhat disturbed to see the car behind him stop at that moment. It backed around in the road and returned the way it had come. This had a queer look. The car was a black sedan; it was too far away for Lee to read the license number or to distinguish the features of the man who was driving it.

A minute or two later his own car came along and picked him up. "There was a suspicious-looking car. . . ." Lee began.

"Sure; did it pass you?" asked his chauffeur.

"No. Came up behind and when it saw me, turned and went back. That's what made me suspicious."

"Been hanging around all afternoon," said the chauffeur. "I was going to tell you. Passed me just now doing about seventy. Driver holding his head down so I couldn't get a good look at him. Never did get a good look at him. Car had an Illinois license plate. Looked like a fake plate to me."

"May be nothing in it," said Lee, "but anyhow, go back to Greenwich and let me out at that little stationery store."

Lee was recognized in the store. "What did you think of Mount Pisgah?" asked the man behind the counter.

"I couldn't get into the place," said Lee, "I'll have to get a permit and come again."

Lee bought a couple of sheets of paper and two envelopes. He wrote:

Dear Johnny:
My chauffeur tells me there has been a black sedan
hanging about Mount Pisgah all afternoon. I can't

quite figure it out. It may be an enterprising newspaper reporter or a New York detective; there is no
great danger to be feared from either of these now.
On the other hand, never forget that you have powerful and unscrupulous enemies. Watch yourself.

Pop.

Lee put this in two envelopes, addressed the outer to Matthew
Rennert, and bought a stamp. He dropped his letter in the Green-
wich post office and gave his chauffeur the word to return to New
York.

CHAPTER TWENTY

WHEN LEE ENTERED his office next morning, both typewriters were clacking.

Fanny and Judy greeted him politely and went on with their work. The girls were still bearing themselves coolly toward their employer, and Lee, however exasperated he had felt, had not been able to get back at them, for while they sent him to Coventry they took care to do their work with extra care and thoroughness. In an unacknowledged war of this sort the male is at a disadvantage. Today, however, the end of the war was in sight, and Lee could afford to smile. To plague the girls, he affected to be in great spirits.

"Good morning, girls! Lovely day, isn't it? I felt so good I had to walk down."

Fanny and Judy smiled politely; said nothing. Lee saw them exchange a questioning glance; what cause has Pop to feel so gay? He went into his private office smiling inwardly.

When he had skimmed over his mail he called Fanny in. She brought her notebook. "No dictation this morning," he said. "I want you to do a little field work."

"Field work?" said Fanny, running up her eyebrows. "I didn't know you had a case on hand."

Lee said: "I want you to go up to a little café on Lexington Avenue in the neighborhood of 86th Street. The name is Hanley's."

Fanny's face didn't give anything away; she merely became wary. "What am I to do there?" she asked.

"Find, if you can, a waiter who was on duty at noon on Tuesday last."

"Do you know his name?"

"No. Do you?"

"I don't understand you," said Fanny coldly.

Lee went on with an innocent air. "It is important, you see, as a means of breaking down Jocker Stacey's testimony. I want to find out if there is a man at Hanley's—if more than one man, so much the better—who can go on the stand and swear that you and Al Yohe were served there at noon last Tuesday."

Fanny broke down then. "Who told you that Al and I were together last Tuesday?" she demanded.

"Al did."

"When did you see Al?"

"Had lunch with him yesterday."

Fanny stared in confusion.

"You went to Hanley's to take Al some money," Lee went on, "and I expect it will cause me a peck of trouble when it comes out in court."

Fanny saw that she had been fooled and frowned; then she perceived that the war was over and smiled. "Pop, you're a devil!" she said. "I'd pull your hair—if you had any!"

Lee had his laugh out then. In the front office Judy looked up, startled by the sound.

"What does it mean?" asked Fanny.

"It means that from now on this office is working night and day on the case of Alastair Yohe until he is cleared!"

Fanny's pretty face flushed red with pleasure. "Oh, Pop!" she cried, clasping her hands together. Notebook and pencil dropped to the floor. "Oh, Pop, I'm so glad! Oh, I could hug you for that!"

"Who's stopping you?" said Lee.

"Judy must know about this!" cried Fanny. "Judy! Judy! come in here!"

Judy ran in. She was the more emotional. When she was told, tears sprang in her big brown eyes. "Oh, Pop! Oh, Pop!"

"For God's sake, don't turn on the waterworks!" cried Lee. "Sit down! Smoke up! Let's have a little peace and comfort in the shop again!"

"This is like old times!" said Fanny, happily blowing smoke. "We can be happy in our work again!"

"It wasn't me spoiled it," said Lee. "By rights, I ought to fire both of you for the way you've been acting the past two weeks."

"But you were so stubborn, Pop!"

"I was not stubborn. I am a most reasonable man. I was only prudent."

"Now that we're all reunited," said Fanny, "do you mind if I telephone Tom Cottar? I've been mean to him lately. I'd like to tell him everything is all right."

"Go ahead," said Lee.

Redheaded Tom turned up in the outer office in record time. The stout fellow looked as if he had been put through the mill, and when he came, Lee called Judy as if he wished to dictate a letter and had her close the door between the two rooms. After giving the pair five minutes to effect an armistice, Lee opened the door and called them in. Tom looked made over; his homely face was beaming. As they settled themselves, Fanny said to Tom:

"Everything that is said in here is off the record."

"Ah, have I ever let you down yet?" said Tom, all ready to have his feelings hurt again.

"Skip it," said Lee equably. "We all trust each other."

As they discussed the case from different angles, Lee and Tom learned several things they had not known before; how little Charlotte had come to Fanny in the first place to implore her to use her influence in bringing Lee over to Al Yohe's side; how, later, all four of them, Al, Charlotte, Fanny and Judy, had plotted together to make it possible for Al himself to approach Lee.

"Very reprehensible conduct!" remarked Lee, taking a pinch of snuff.

Fanny flung an arm around his shoulders and gave him a squeeze.

In summarizing the situation Lee said: "We have two separate crimes to deal with; the first devilishly clever and well planned; the second, a clumsy murder carried out on impulse and immediately exposed. It is obvious they were not both conceived by the same brain. We can clear Al of the Philadelphia charge, but remember, he will be tried on the other first, and there is still work to be done on that."

Fanny was assigned to cover the route that Al had taken on the previous Tuesday to make sure of sufficient evidence to support his alibi. Tom was advised to dog Harry Brummel's steps and to interview him, if possible.

It was not likely that the crafty lawyer could be trapped into any dangerous admission; still, he did not know how much Lee and his friends knew, and he might let something fall that could be used to advantage.

"Kids, if we are able to show up that crooked attorney, we'd be public benefactors," said Lee.

Judy, to her disgust, was required to keep the office for the time being.

Later, her job was to win the confidence of Jocker Stacey's girl friend, Riqueta Seppi. Judy could play the part of an East Side girl to perfection.

"Before Jocker discovered what a gold mine there was in this case," said Lee, "he may have told the girl part of the truth. It is possible that Agnes Gartrey herself saw Jocker and, if so, the girl may be jealous. It would not be the first time that a great lady had stooped to a handsome young gangster. In any case, try playing on the girl's jealousy."

As to his own part, Lee said: "It is obvious that the final solution of the problem lies in the Gartrey apartment, and I'm going up there again."

They departed on their several errands. Lee did not telephone his coming in advance to Agnes Gartrey, for he had a wish to see what kind of reaction, if any, his unexpected arrival might have on her household.

Denman admitted him to the apartment. This young man's smooth, handsome face gave nothing away. In answer to Lee's inquiry, he asked:

"Are you expected, sir?"

"No," said Lee.

"Mrs. Gartrey has not been about yet, sir. I will have to ask if she can see you."

He conducted Lee into the salon. He left the doors open when he retired, and Lee made sure that he entered the corridor leading to the bedrooms.

In a minute or two, Denman returned saying: "Mrs. Gartrey will be happy to see you, sir, if you don't mind waiting a few minutes."

"Certainly," said Lee. To himself he added: I am still in favor!

Denman softly crossed the foyer on his rubber-shod feet and passed through the service door. The handsome young animal is well housebroken, thought Lee. After waiting a moment he noiselessly followed the servant.

The door into the service passage swung both ways and he went through it without making any sound. At the end of the passage there was a door into the pantry which usually stood open, and it was open now. Just within the opening, Lee flattened himself against the wall.

As he had expected, Denman was at the telephone switchboard. But Lee was not quick enough; the servant was almost finished dialing; Lee heard only the last two numbers, 8 and 9. Then Denman said softly: "Hello? Is this you? . . . Mappin is here."

Cheek! thought Lee. He heard half of a conversation:

"No, he wasn't expected, but Madam is going to see him. He's waiting in the salon. . . . I've tried that before and it's no good. Mappin is too suspicious. He always lowers his voice when he has anything important to say. . . . All right, I'll do that. . . . Good-by."

Lee slipped back through the swing door and regained his seat in the salon. This was decidedly interesting. He didn't know who Denman had called up, but he hoped that if he stuck around long enough the results of the conversation might appear.

While he waited, Lee looked around the magnificent room with its antique French furniture, Chinese porcelains and masterly paintings. There was a Persian rug covering the whole floor which must have cost a king's ransom. The paintings, he saw, were only copies of the great masters, though good ones. Evidently an expensive decorator had been given carte blanche in the apartment before the Gartreys moved in. The whole effect was opulent rather than tasteful. But quantities of fresh flowers lent grace to the room. Through open doors to the right, Lee looked into the music room upholstered in blue brocade. He could see a corner of the gold-encrusted grand piano standing between the windows. He wondered at the folly of a woman who could stake all this—against the death house.

Agnes Gartrey presently came floating toward him through the music room, clad in a seductive negligee. This was a dove-gray affair trimmed with bands of marabou. He had never seen her wear the same garment twice. Her face was smooth and smiling.

"Such a pleasure to see you, Mr. Mappin!"

"Should I apologize for coming at this hour?"

"You need never apologize to me! Let us go into the boudoir. I have a fire in there."

In the pink room they seated themselves and lighted cigarettes. Lee declined a drink.

"Too early, dear lady."

"What's the news?" she demanded with a strained eagerness she could not hide. "I hope you've come to tell me Al Yohe has been caught."

He shook his head.

"But surely the police have some clue to his whereabouts. His pictures are published every day in the newspapers. Everybody in the world knows what he looks like. . . ."

Lee spread out his hands.

Agnes arose with a jerk and started pacing. "This is disgraceful! Disgraceful! What's the matter with our police? Heaven knows they cost enough! One man against thousands. And what has happened to your great skill, Mr. Mappin?"

"Running down a fugitive is a little out of my line," said Lee deprecatingly.

"I cannot stand this suspense!" she cried, pressing knuckles to her temples. "I will never know peace of mind again until I have seen that wretch punished. The thought that he and the woman might eventually escape drives me mad!"

Lee wondered if the sleek Denman had his ear pressed against one of the doors. "Better lower your voice," he warned.

"You are right," she said, instantly obeying.

"Al and Charlotte cannot escape in the long run," said Lee.

"That's not good enough," Agnes sullenly retorted. "I'm tired of waiting for justice to overtake them. Obviously, somebody else is hiding them now. Why don't the police offer a reward for their capture? A reward big enough to tempt his fond friends?"

"The police have no fund for that purpose. A reward is usually offered by a private person."

Agnes came to a stop, staring. "I've a mind to offer a reward myself," she murmured.

Since Lee had already decided to bring Al Yohe in, this suggestion struck him as humorous. Why not encourage it? However, he kept a discreet silence.

"It must be a big reward," Agnes continued. "Five thousand— no, ten thousand."

Lee thought: How she tosses money around! He said dryly: "Surely ten thousand would be sufficient."

"All right," said Agnes, "I'll do it. It will square me with the public. They half believe that I know where Al Yohe is. More than once the newspapers have hinted that I am hiding him."

"But if you come forward as the donor of the reward," Lee objected, "Al Yohe will be warned that you have turned against him, and it will make him warier."

"That's right. . . . What do you advise?"

"Let the reward be advertised as from an anonymous donor. After Al Yohe is caught and lodged in jail, you can then come forward and identify yourself as the donor."

"Good!" she cried. "How thankful I am that I have you to advise me! Will you take care of the details? I'll write you a check now. To whom should I make it payable?"

"To me," said Lee dryly. "I'll deposit it and give my check to the Commissioner of Police."

Agnes instantly sat down at her desk. Handing the check to Lee, she said urgently: "Lose no time! Lose no time!"

"It will be advertised in the evening papers," said Lee.

"What brought you here this morning?" Agnes asked.

Lee parried the question. "My dear lady, you are shaking like a leaf! I recommend a spot of Scotch."

Agnes shrugged. "And you?" she said.

"I don't mind if I do."

She rang for a servant, and by this little maneuver Lee gained five minutes perhaps. Not until Denman had left the room for the second time did she repeat her question:

"What did you want to see me about?"

Lee was ready with the answer. "After I left you the other day, it occurred to me that there was a discrepancy in your story. . . ."

She broke in sharply: "You surely can't have any doubt as to Al Yohe's guilt?"

"Certainly not. But I don't want any holes to appear in the evidence against him. You told me that you saw him standing over poor Mr. Gartrey's body with the smoking gun in his hand. . . ."

"Well?"

"There were no fingerprints found on the gun."

Agnes changed color. "I'm glad you brought that up," she said quickly. "I forgot to mention that Al had a glove on his right hand when I saw him. Only the one glove."

"What color glove?"

"Oh, a brownish color. Looked soiled."

"Had you seen that glove before?"

"Of course not. He had it hidden."

"Hawkins said that Mr. Yohe's gloves were in the pocket of his topcoat when he hung it up."

"Surely. The other was a glove that Al had brought for that special purpose."

Lee had now been in the apartment for more than half an hour; nobody had come and Agnes had not been called to the telephone; he still had no clue to Denman's telephone conversation. To gain a little more time, he took Agnes over the whole story of the shooting again. She became impatient and suspicious, and in the end he had to take his leave unsatisfied.

CHAPTER TWENTY-ONE

DOWNSTAIRS, HE LEFT BY THE FRONT DOOR of the apartment house, turned the corner, and entered again by the service entrance on the side street. In the basement there was a corridor leading to a sort of waiting room. Here Lee was faced by the service elevator. Behind it rose the service stairs in a fireproof shaft. There were two youths on duty; one sat doing nothing; the other in the elevator car was reading the latest story of the Al Yohe case. Lee Mappin was known to both, and they stood to attention. He addressed the elevator boy.

"Were you on duty at the time Mr. Gartrey was shot?"

"Yes, Mr. Mappin."

"I'd like to ask you a question or two." Lee always prefaced such interviews with a generous tip. He slipped a bill to each boy and they pocketed it with grins. It transpired that the elevator boy was called Fred, and his mate was Bill. Lee continued: "The butler Hawkins testified that Al Yohe escaped down the service stairs. Did either of you boys see him?"

Fred answered: "No, sir. We didn't see him. According to the women, Al left Gartreys' by the front door, and went down to Mr. Deane's apartment on the second."

"Do you believe that story?"

Both young men grinned. "No, sir."

"Suppose, for the sake of argument, that Al did escape by the service stairs, would it have been possible for him to get out of the building without your seeing him?"

186

"It would be possible, sir," said Fred. "He could always place the elevator by the sound of the doors. I can't see the stairs from inside the car. As for Bill, here, he often has to answer the house telephone, and that's around the corner of the wall."

"The stairs are not much used, I take it."

"You might say that they was never used, sir. The stairs are only if the elevator service breaks down or in case of a fire."

Having started the boys' minds running in this direction, Lee casually put the real question that had brought him down to the basement. "I suppose both you fellows are acquainted with Denman."

"Sure," they both answered. Fred added with a reminiscent grin, "Denman is quite a fellow, quite a fellow!"

"How do you mean?" said Lee.

"He's a sport," said Fred. "I been out with him. When he's dressed you would never take him for a servant; he looks like a college boy and spends money like his old man was worth a million. He has class!"

"He was only second man at the Gartreys' until Hawkins left," said Lee. "A second man doesn't draw much."

"I don't know," said Fred. "Those rich folks will pay big for a good-looking fellow with a figure like Jack Denman. Some guys has all the luck! Jack always has money to spend."

"He was out of the house at the time Mr. Gartrey was shot," said Lee. "Do you remember him going out that day?"

"Sure, I remember him going out, because I thought afterwards it was lucky for him he was out. I remember bringing him down in the car shortly after three o'clock. He didn't go right out, but hung around fifteen, twenty minutes gassing with Bill and me." Fred turned to his mate. "Remember, Bill? He had a little bottle of prime whisky and gave us a drink. Gee! I can taste it yet! We all went back in the locker room and finished the bottle. It was only a little bottle."

Lee kept a wooden face. "Is there any way by which you can get from the service stairway to the front stairway?" he asked.

"No, sir. Except through the basement here, or over the roof."

Lee stroked his chin. Over the roof, he thought; sixteen flights of stairs, a stiff climb! But if a man was nerved by a deadly purpose, that wouldn't stop him.

"I get you!" said Fred excitedly. "You think maybe Al went up the service stairs to the roof, then down the front stairs to Mr. Deane's apartment! That's a new theory!"

"Something like that," said Lee, "but keep it to yourselves. . . . Will you take me up and let me see the roof?"

"Certainly, Mr. Mappin."

The elevator stopped at the sixteenth floor and Lee went up the last flight of stairs on foot. Fred accompanied him, full of curiosity. This house had been built before the setback style of architecture came into vogue and it had no terraces or penthouses. The roof presented nothing of interest; a huge water tank and the entrances to the two stairways, that was all. Fred explained that the roof was available to all the tenants in fine weather, but nobody used it except the servants, for the tenants were the sort of people who forsake New York as soon as the weather becomes pleasant. Lee crossed the roof to glance down the other stairway. Like the service stairway, it was of stone and steel construction, contained within a fireproof shaft.

"Are the doors to the roof ever locked?" he asked.

"No, sir; there's no need of it because you can't get on this roof from any other roof."

Lee looked all around in order to make sure of missing nothing. The apartment house across the side street was of newer construction and a little higher; it had a penthouse. On the terrace in the sun sat an old lady in a wheel chair, all bundled up against the cold. She was gazing at Lee with the liveliest curiosity and impatiently clapping her hands. The hand clapping brought a nurse or companion out of the house behind her. The old lady issued an order, apparently, and the nurse went back. Lee, his own curiosity aroused, waited to see what would happen. The nurse returned with a pair of binoculars which the old lady put to her eyes.

Lee smiled. What a stroke of luck if. . . . He waved to the old lady in good will, and she waved back. He said to Fred:

"It was two weeks ago today when Mr. Gartrey was shot. Do you remember if it was a fine day?"

"Yes, sir. We was having a long spell of pleasant weather then. I remember it by the funeral."

"Good!" said Lee.

They returned to the elevator.

Lee entered the fine apartment house across the street and presented his card to the functionary in charge of the hall. Lee had been written up so much of late, it was not necessary to explain himself. The functionary was greatly impressed.

"Yes, sir, Mr. Mappin, sir, this is an honor. Who would you be wishing to see, Mr. Mappin?"

"What is the name of the old lady, an invalid, who occupies the penthouse?"

"Mrs. Bradford, sir."

"I want to send up a note to her."

There was a desk in an alcove off the hall, and Lee wrote: "Would Mrs. Bradford be good enough to see Mr. Amos Lee Mappin for a few moments? They just exchanged greetings from roof to roof." He enclosed this in an envelope with his card and sent it upstairs.

The answer was not long in coming down: "Mrs. Bradford would be pleased to see Mr. Mappin."

Lee was left waiting for some minutes in the pleasant living room of the penthouse. The sun streamed in through a row of tall French windows giving on the terrace. When the old lady was wheeled in by her attendant, he saw the reason for the delay; she had undergone a complete change of costume in preparation for her visitor. She now wore a pretty silk dress with a lace shawl over her shoulders and a silken coverlet over her knees. She had a coquettish black bow in her white hair and a touch of rouge in her withered cheeks; her eyes were bright with anticipation. She carried a tortoise-shell fan—not that she needed a fan, but merely as a becoming stage property. She extended her hand with an air—undoubtedly she had been a great belle in her youth.

"How do you do, Mr. Mappin. It is an event for me to have a visitor—and especially such a distinguished visitor."

"The pleasure is mine, Mrs. Bradford," Lee said with his best bow.

When the wheel chair was placed to her satisfaction, she dismissed her attendant. She signed to Lee to seat himself close to her.

"It was very naughty of you, sir, to wave to me from the roof across the way!" She tapped his wrist with the closed fan and sadly shook her head.

"Ah, and it was much naughtier of me to wave back again! It brought back old times for a moment. Do you remember that story of de Maupassant's in which the little Comtesse nodded to a strange gentleman from her window and he came right upstairs? A dreadful story, and so true to life! But you waved first! However, when one is as old as I, there is, unfortunately, no danger!"

Lee said: "*L'esprit* never grows old, Mrs. Bradford."

She shook her fan at him. "You have a beguiling tongue, Mr. Mappin! . . . Seriously, the old have a thin time of it. People forget that they exist. I am crippled with arthritis, as you see. They carry me from my bed to my chair and from my chair back to my bed again. Is that living? Sunshine is supposed to be beneficial to me. I could go to Florida, but I will not live among other invalids. They have warped minds. So my son took this penthouse with a southern exposure and every fine day they wheel me out on the terrace, and there I sit, doing nothing, seeing nothing. I am too high up to see into the street. Before the weather grew cold, it used to amuse me to watch the servants spooning on the roof opposite, but nobody comes up there any more. So you can imagine how interested I was when you appeared on the roof a while ago. I must apologize for the rude way I stared at you."

"I was flattered by your interest," said Lee, "and here I am, you see!"

She tapped his wrist with the fan. Lee let her run on, perfectly willing to play the game of 1890 philandering with her because he could see that she was no fool. She knew that he had an object in coming, and in the end she asked him plainly what it was.

"It was the binoculars that gave me the idea," said Lee. "You are perhaps in a position to do me a very great service—and a service to others besides me."

"Tell me what it is, Mr. Mappin! I am consumed with curiosity!"

"This is Monday," said Lee. "I am thinking of another Monday two weeks ago. The sun was shining as it is today, but it was later than now, say shortly after three o'clock. Can you remember that afternoon?"

Mrs. Bradford spread out her hands. "All my days are so exactly alike! If there was something to fix that day in my mind . . . !"

"Another man on the roof across the way."

"Why yes, of course!" she cried. "That was the last person who appeared on the roof until I saw you today. He came out of one door, crossed the roof and went through the other door."

"Can you be sure it was Monday?"

"Let me see," she said; "even so small a thing makes a big difference in my afternoon. . . . Yes, that was the afternoon I broke a cup. My nurse brings me tea at four and I remember I was telling her about the man I saw when the cup slipped off the saucer and broke. Monday two weeks ago."

"Did you get a good look at the man?"

"I did. Through the binoculars."

"Would you recognize him if you saw him again?"

"I certainly would."

"Mrs. Bradford," said Lee, "is your condition such that you could appear in court to identify the man?"

The old lady clapped her hands on the arms of her chair and partly raised herself. Her eyes widened like a child's. "Go to court!" she cried, "Me? How wonderful! What a break in my dull life! I would like to see anybody stop me from going to court if I was wanted!"

"I would, of course, see that you were taken and brought home in comfort," said Lee.

"I'll go if they have to carry me on a stretcher, Mr. Mappin!"

AFTER HE HAD LEFT MRS. BRADFORD, Lee spent an hour darting from place to place in taxicabs. First to the Fulton National Bank to have Agnes Gartrey's check certified in case that unstable lady changed her mind; then to his own bank to deposit the check; to Police

Headquarters to hand his own check to Inspector Loasby and to give him the great news. To Loasby he said:

"You and I will go up to Greenwich tomorrow morning and fetch him down together—if a word of this gets out in advance, it will spoil everything."

"It will not get out through me!" said Loasby.

Lee then drove up to his own office. Fanny had come in, having satisfactorily performed her errand, and the two girls were having a belated lunch. Lee dictated a letter.

> Dear Johnny:
> Everything is shaping up well. A ten-thousand-dollar reward has been offered for your capture. This naturally will excite the Rennerts. They are poor people and it is not fair to put so heavy a strain on their loyalty. Tell Matt Rennert and his wife immediately (if you can get word to them before they read the papers, so much the better) that you have decided to give yourself up and that they may have the credit for it.
>
> Tell them that if they should try to take you in themselves, some smart guy would be sure to horn in on the reward. Inspector Loasby and I are coming up to fetch you at eleven o'clock tomorrow and they can then hand you over and take a receipt for you.
>
> Tell Charlotte that I have built up a pretty good case and there is no cause to worry.
>
> Yours, Pop.

Meanwhile, Lee had ordered a car with the driver he had used on the previous day. To the driver he said:

"This letter must be dropped in the Greenwich post-office before the mail goes out at four. You have a good hour and a half. Should you be delayed and miss the mail, carry the letter direct to Mount Pisgah and give it to somebody at the cottage inside the gate."

Soon after the man had departed, the extras were out on the streets, announcing the reward for information leading to the capture of Al Yohe.

It occurred to Lee that this would afford him an excuse to call again at the Gartrey apartment. Stuffing one of the papers in his pocket, he drove uptown.

Denman showed a little surprise upon seeing him so soon again. He showed Lee into the salon and went away to consult his mistress. Almost immediately he was back, saying:

"Mrs. Gartrey will see you, sir. Please follow me."

This did not suit Lee's plans at all. "You needn't trouble to show me, Denman," he said offhandedly. "I know the way."

"Very well, sir. Mrs. Gartrey is in the boudoir." Denman turned back toward the pantry while Lee started through the music room, keeping the tail of an eye on the servant. He lingered for a moment, affecting to examine a picture. The moment the service door swung to behind Denman, Lee ran across the foyer as fast as his short legs would carry him and pushed the door open again. He had pad and pencil ready. He was in time to hear Denman start dialing. Concentrating all his attention on the job, Lee made lines on his pad to suit . . . seven lines.

Denman got his connection at once. There was no greeting; the servant merely said: "Mappin is back again." Lee, waiting to hear no more, slipped back into the foyer. Here he came face to face with Agnes Gartrey, who had come looking for him. Her eyebrows went up to their highest. Lee, having got what he wanted, was not in the least abashed.

"Denman," he said mysteriously; "I have noticed that whenever I come here he always telephones the news to somebody. I was trying to find out who it was."

"And did you?" asked Agnes.

"No. No name was mentioned over the phone."

Agnes was disposed to be angry. "I've had enough of this. I will question Denman."

Lee did not greatly care—now—whether she did or not; however, he said:

"It would oblige me if you said nothing to him. Leave Denman to me and I'll catch him out yet."

"Do you suspect who it was?" she demanded.

Lee lied in his blandest fashion. "I have no idea."

Agnes, suspicious, angry, puzzled, scarcely knew how to take Lee. She said in an uncertain voice: "Will you come into the boudoir?"

"Thanks, no," said Lee. He pulled the newspaper out of his pocket. "I brought you this in order to show you that I had executed your commission."

Agnes merely glanced at the headline. "I have seen it."

Lee guessed that she already had reason to regret her precipitancy in offering the reward. "Well, then, we've nothing more to do except to wait for results," he said cheerfully. "Good-by, dear lady."

Agnes offered him a limp hand. Her glance was baleful.

In a taxicab, Lee figured out the telephone number from the lines on his pad. It ran thus: 12-6-6689. The first two numbers stood for the first letters of the exchange; the third number was the key number of the exchange; the last four digits represented the actual telephone number.

Back in his office he consulted a card listing all the exchanges and their key numbers, and it worked out thus: BEaver 6-6689. Lee smiled.

CHAPTER TWENTY-TWO

AT HALF PAST NINE NEXT MORNING, Lee Mappin and Inspector Loasby, accompanied by two plain-clothes men, were on their way to Greenwich in a discreet limousine which displayed no police insignia. Lee's hired car followed in order to provide Charlotte and the baby with a more private means of transportation back to town. It was a fine, still day, and the four men were in good spirits, particularly Loasby. The case which had threatened to wreck his career was as good as solved. During the long drive the conversation dealt with police work in general; the Al Yohe case was scarcely mentioned. Lee was not acquainted with Loasby's two men and, always fearful of a premature leak to the press, he did not care to expose his hand.

They were evidently expected at Mount Pisgah; Matt Rennert and his wife hastened to open the tall gates when they drew up before them. Lee's letter had been received in time. So far, so good. The Rennerts, simple, honest workers, were pale and slightly tremulous with excitement; they could scarcely believe in their good luck. They were invited to get into the second car and the two cars drove on through the woods and around the edge of the neglected lawn to the mansion.

Leaving the cars in the drive, the whole party walked around to the south front and passed through the main garden into the private enclosure. Lee smiled, seeing the baby carriage tucked in the sheltered corner of the cedars: nothing was to be allowed to interfere with young Lester's routine. Charlotte came running up. She was dressed for town but her face was drawn with anxiety.

195

"I'm so worried about Al!" she said.

"Where is he?" asked Lee sharply.

"Gone out."

"Gone out?"

Loasby's face turned grim. Al Yohe had slipped through his fingers so many times!

"Didn't he get my letter yesterday afternoon?" asked Lee sternly.

"Yes, Pop, but another letter supposed to be from you came this morning. It countermanded your previous instructions."

"I wrote no such letter!"

"I have it here," said Charlotte, opening her palm and revealing a crumpled paper. "Read it! Read it!"

Lee read the typewritten page:

Sunday night.

Dear Al:

Since I saw you today there have been some awkward developments. I can't stop to explain them now. I'll tell you when I see you. The police have been tipped off to your hide-out and you must make a quick getaway. I have found a new hide-out for you, absolutely safe. You will receive this about nine o'clock. Proceed immediately through the farm gates, past the farm buildings of Mount Pisgah, and along the farm road to the outer pasture. You will find a car waiting for you there. You can trust the chauffeur. I can't come myself because I'll be busy pulling wool over the eyes of the police. There's a gate from the pasture to a little-used public road. The chauffeur will bring you to me. Lose no time and don't worry about Charlotte and the kid. The police have nothing on her. Later on, I'll arrange to have her join you.

Yours in haste, L. M.

The initialed signature was penciled in a good imitation of Lee's hand.

"This is a fake!" cried Lee. "I don't address Al in that manner nor do I sign myself like that. Every word smells of deceit!"

"I know," said Charlotte piteously. "Al thought so, too."

"Then why did he go?"

"He thought he might be able to discover the identity of the real criminal and perhaps capture him."

"Oh, the young fool!" groaned Lee.

"He was armed," Charlotte continued. "He promised to be careful. He said he'd take a couple of the farm boys with him. I couldn't stop him."

"How long has he been gone?"

"More than an hour. I have been so . . ."

From far off in the still air came the sound of a shot. Charlotte caught her breath on a gasp. The whole group stood transfixed. There were two louder reports close together, another sharp one, and after a pause two more heavier reports. Charlotte's face turned paper white; she reeled on her feet and Lee caught her.

"Quick! to the car!" he cried to Loasby. "Follow the drive around the house and straight back to the farm gates!"

Lee handed the fainting girl over to the care of Mrs. Rennert and ran after the policemen. They piled into the car and let her out, turning the corner of the house on two wheels, speeding straight back between vegetable and fruit gardens. The farm gates stood open and they dashed through at seventy miles an hour. Outside, the well-cared-for fields of Pisgah spread wide before them; there were no humans in sight. They flew past the farm buildings without slackening speed and over a rough farm road beyond, springs leaping, body pounding on the chassis. Lee was grinding his teeth in mixed anger and apprehension. He had not realized before how deeply the scapegrace Al, with his beguiling smile and his gaiety, had crept into his affections—not to speak of Charlotte and the baby.

They banged across a little wooden bridge and climbed a long rise. Rounding a clump of woods, they came upon three figures walking in the road, and the driver ground to a stop with screaming brakes. Al Yohe, with a sheepish grin, was walking in the middle, a young farm laborer on either side of him. Lee was the first out of the car.

"Are you hurt?" he shouted.

"Not a scratch!" said Al.

Lee, conscious of a sudden weakness, sat down on the running board and wiped his face.

"Where's the man you came to meet?" demanded Loasby.

"Vamoosed," said Al, grinning wider.

After their big scare, the members of the rescue party felt a little sold. "Well . . . get in and let's go back," said Loasby gruffly.

The car turned around and they climbed in. The farm workers stood on the running board and dropped off when they came to the barn. Inside, Al told his story.

"On the way out I stopped off at the barn and persuaded these two fellows to go with me. I had an automatic and they took their shotguns. Not much good for two-legged game. We proceeded cautiously by the farm road. Couldn't see anything until after we had crossed the brook and climbed the hill beyond. The pasture is the last field on the farm. It's hidden by trees until you come to the fence. When we got there we could see a black sedan standing at the other side of the field, but there wasn't anybody in it, nor anywhere around, so far as we could see. There are woods to the east and the south of the pasture and we thought they might be hidden there, so we made a detour through the middle of the field where nobody could steal up on us. Luckily for me, there is a ditch running through the middle of the pasture.

"Suddenly we heard the crack of a shot from the car and a bullet pinged through my hat and carried it off. A near thing, that. We dropped flat and the boys let go with their cannons. I held my fire because I couldn't see anything. The bastard must have been crouching behind the engine hood, firing over the top. He fired again and I scrambled for the ditch and rolled into it. It was me he was shooting at. When he saw he couldn't reach me, he climbed in his car and drove across the pasture hell for leather, out through the gate and east on the public road. The boys banged away again, but their pellets wouldn't make a scratch at that distance. Stout fellows, those two. I must remember to give them a present. There was only one man in the car. Whoever he was, he played a lone hand. Damn good shot. What had he to gain by croaking me, Lee?"

Lee said: "He knows enough to realize that if you are arrested the whole truth is bound to come out and that it will spell his finish."

Al judged from Lee's expression that it would be wiser not to ask any more questions while there were so many listeners. "Who's got a cigarette?" he asked. "In my excitement, I left mine."

Lee offered his case. "You got off easier than you deserved," he said dryly.

There was a joyful reunion when they returned to the mansion. Charlotte, careless of the onlookers, flung herself into Al's arms.

"Oh, you frightened me so! You frightened me so!" she scolded.

Al soothed her. "I'm sorry, Charlie!" He glanced at Lee. "Seems like I made a fool of myself all round." The irrepressible grin broke through. "But how could I refuse a dare like that?"

The reunion was immediately followed by a tearful parting.

"Let's get going," said Loasby.

Al went with the police officers in the first car; Lee accompanied Charlotte and the baby in the second. Charlotte sternly called in her tears and talked about other things during the long drive to town. Her determination to be brave almost brought the tears to Lee's unaccustomed eyes. She weakened only once.

"Will they put him in a cell, Pop?"

"I'll have him out in a couple of days, Charlie."

"Will they let me see him?"

"Certainly, my dear."

Lee took her to her own flat on Park Avenue. Fanny Parran was waiting there. The two girls fell into each other's arms weeping, and Lee felt better. Charlotte would be all right now, he was sure, and he left them.

By two o'clock, Al was safely lodged in Police Headquarters without having been recognized by a single person on the way there. An hour or so later, newsboys in the streets of every city in the country were screaming the terrific news that Al Yohe had been arrested.

CHAPTER TWENTY-THREE

ON THE FOLLOWING MORNING Judy Bowles reported to Lee that she had succeeded in making friends with Jocker Stacey's girl, Riqueta Seppi. From the feeling evinced by the girl against Agnes Gartrey, Judy deduced that there had been meetings between Agnes and Jocker Stacey, but Judy did not believe that Riqueta could ever be induced or forced to tell the truth. The golden rewards dangled in front of Jocker and his girl were too potent.

Lee said: "It doesn't much matter now. If we can clear Al of the first charge, the second will fall of its own weight."

The case had now to be turned over to the District Attorney. Agnes Gartrey was the principal witness against the accused, and the District Attorney was so impressed with her wealth and social position that he announced, "in consideration of Mrs. Gartrey's recent bereavement," he would examine her in her own home on Wednesday afternoon. Inspector Loasby and Lee Mappin were invited to be present. The press, of course, was excluded. When this news was received in Lee's office, both girls looked at him longingly.

"I might take one of you as my secretary," said Lee, "but I would have no excuse for bringing both."

"Take Judy," said Fanny quickly.

"Take Fanny," said Judy.

"Flip a coin for it," said Lee.

Fanny won the toss.

The whole party arrived simultaneously at the Gartrey apartment. The District Attorney, a youngish man, very conscious of the importance of the occasion, brought two of his assistants and a male stenographer; Inspector Loasby had two of his men. All three of the police officers were in civilian clothes. Lee took Fanny. They were all received in the foyer by George Coler. He was almost as great a figure in the public eye as Mrs. Gartrey. He introduced himself to the officials as Mrs. Gartrey's business man and her closest friend. Coler had never appeared to better advantage. His air of grave friendliness was perfect. He showed the gentlemen into the salon and went away to fetch Agnes.

The scene appealed to Lee's sense of comedy. The curtains were drawn and lamps lighted; this was for the benefit of Agnes' complexion. Eight soberly clad men were sitting around on satin-covered chairs, all trying to look important and at their ease, and failing. From the D.A. down, they were a bit overwhelmed by the evidences of wealth and luxury that surrounded them. As usual, the big room was bedecked with quantities of roses, delphiniums, snapdragons, chrysanthemums. The D.A. produced a cigarette with a thoughtful air, tapping it on the back of his hand. But he had not nerve enough to light it and put it away, still thoughtful. He attempted to start a conversation with the Inspector, but it languished and died. As the silence lengthened out, their self-consciousness increased. Like a funeral, thought Lee—but whose funeral? Fanny had disappeared.

Agnes kept them waiting a good while in order to heighten the effect of her entrance. Finally she came through the music room, leaning on George Coler's arm. She had probably never looked handsomer. Made up to appear pale and romantic, she kept raising her beautiful eyes helplessly to Coler's face, and Lee bit his lip to keep from grinning. Her clinging costume of black and gray chiffon was exquisite. All the men sprang up at her entrance and obsequiously bent their necks. Agnes, perceiving the effect she had upon them, became slightly contemptuous. She was too stupid to comprehend the real danger of her situation, Lee thought, but Coler was aware of it. He was keeping a strong hold on himself.

Agnes, clinging to Coler's arm and glancing fondly in his face, said:

"Mr. District Attorney, is there any objection to having my friend, Mr. Coler, present? He has no evidence to give, but I should be so thankful to have his support."

"Certainly, Mrs. Gartrey."

Lee wondered what this public avowal of a fondness for Coler portended. The butterfly dartings of Agnes' mind were unpredictable. Coler, who loved her, ought to have been overjoyed by her present attitude, but if he was, he didn't show it.

Agnes dropped gracefully in a love seat on the District Attorney's right. All the men resumed their chairs. Coler drew up a chair behind Agnes. The District Attorney looked around.

"Is there anything you require?" asked Agnes languidly.

"A small table for my secretary, if you please." He pointed to a little table against the wall and the secretary moved toward it.

Agnes arrested him with a graceful gesture. "Don't trouble yourself, please." She looked at Coler and he pressed a button in the wall behind him.

Denman entered. "Remove the things from that table," said Agnes, "and place it before the District Attorney's secretary."

It was done. The manservant was visibly longing to remain in the room, but Agnes dismissed him. "Close the doors when you go out, and also the doors into the music room."

When the second pair of doors closed, she settled her bracelet and said: "Now, Mr. District Attorney."

He bowed. "Please tell the story in your own way, Mrs. Gartrey. I am distressed that I have to subject you to this ordeal, and I want to make it as easy for you as I can. Take your own time."

Agnes' eyelids flickered with contempt. She began languidly to tell the same story that she had told Lee, rounding it out with small added details here and there. Everybody listened with sympathetic attention. She told how she had seen Al standing over the body of her husband with the smoking gun in his hand; how he had dropped the gun and fled; she did not forget to mention this time that Al had a glove on his right hand. If this story stood up in court, a jury would have no choice but to send Al Yohe to the chair. However, this was not the courtroom and Lee quietly bided his time.

The District Attorney made no attempt to pin her down or to question any part of her story. There was no reminder that she had in the beginning told an entirely different story. Occasionally Agnes' eyes strayed to Lee's face, but Lee was taking care to look as bland as milk. Satisfied as she went on that she was creating a perfect effect, the hint of a satisfied smirk appeared around her beautiful lips. She is enjoying herself, God forgive her! thought Lee. When she had come to the end, Agnes said:

"As long as you are here, would you like to hear my maid's story? She was with me throughout that terrible afternoon."

"If you please, Mrs. Gartrey."

Denman was therefore summoned and sent to fetch Eliza Young. While they waited for Eliza, Agnes refreshed herself with a cigarette, but none of the men ventured to light up.

Eliza's large, pale face was damp with excitement and the pince-nez kept slipping down her nose. The presence of Lee in the room made her nervous. But nobody interrupted her; nobody questioned any part of her story, and she came through all right. She corroborated her mistress' story at every point.

After Eliza had been dismissed, the District Attorney arose to make a little speech. "I don't think we need trouble you any further, Mrs. Gartrey. Permit me to thank you for your co-operation and to compliment you on the absolute clearness of your story. May I also express my deepest sympathy . . ."

He was interrupted by a knock on the door. "Excuse me," said Agnes. "Come in!"

It was the golden-haired Fanny Parran. Everybody stared. Fanny said: "Excuse me, Mr. Mappin. Mrs. Bradford is here."

"Who is this person?" asked Agnes.

"My secretary," said Lee mildly.

"And who may Mrs. Bradford be?"

"That requires a word of explanation. Mrs. Bradford is a very old lady who lives across the street. She has some evidence to give in this case. It hasn't anything to do with Mrs. Gartrey's story, but as Mrs. Bradford is a cripple, I have taken the liberty of bringing her to the District Attorney in order to save her the fatigue of a journey downtown. Perhaps her evidence is of no importance, but I assume the District Attorney will have to listen to it sooner or later."

"It's all right with me," said the District Attorney, "if Mrs. Gartrey has no objection."

Agnes moved her shoulders pettishly. "I think I might have been consulted in advance. Is my house a railway station?" Everybody except Lee looked alarmed. "Oh, well," Agnes went on, "as long as she's here, bring her in."

Fanny wheeled Mrs. Bradford into the room in her chair. In a smart hat and a short fur jacket the old lady was very modish. Her eyes were starry with excitement. She waved her hand gaily in Lee's direction and bowed to Agnes as to an equal. Agnes stared at her rather rudely, but Mrs. Bradford was not at all put about by that. She took in everything and everybody in the room.

The District Attorney invited her to tell him what she knew about the Gartrey case and she launched forth on her story. She told him all about her arthritis; how good her son and his wife were to her; and how dull life was, nevertheless, for an invalid. The District Attorney had not Lee's patience. He began to fidget on his chair and finally signed to her to stop. He said to Lee sarcastically:

"Mr. Mappin, you are responsible for this witness. I can't see how her story applies to the case we are investigating. Perhaps you can bring it out—if there is any connection."

Mrs. Bradford looked affronted and then smiled at Lee. "It is so much easier to deal with a gentleman!" she murmured.

"Mrs. Bradford," said Lee, "where do you live?"

"In the penthouse of the apartment across the street, Mr. Mappin."

"From the terrace of the penthouse can you overlook the roof of this house?"

"Yes, sir. The roof of this house is about all I have to look at."

"I ask you to cast back in your memory to Monday afternoon two weeks ago, November 3rd."

All the listeners in the room pricked up their ears as he named the day Jules Gartrey was shot.

"Can you remember that afternoon?" asked Lee.

"Yes, sir. Perfectly."

"What happened to fix that particular afternoon in your mind?"

"I saw a man on the roof of this house. He came out of one door, crossed the roof and went through the other door."

The District Attorney intervened. "How can you be sure that it was that particular afternoon instead of another?"

"Because I broke a teacup that afternoon," said Mrs. Bradford coolly. "I happened to be telling my nurse about the man I had seen when the cup slipped from my hand."

Lee resumed his questioning. "Are you able to fix the hour at which you saw this man?"

"I can fix it almost exactly, Mr. Mappin. My nurse brings me my tea at four and it was about half an hour before she came that I saw the man. I remember using those words to my nurse: 'Half an hour ago I saw a man on the roof across the way.' So it was about half past three. The same nurse is with me. You can ask her if you distrust my memory."

"That will hardly be necessary," said the District Attorney stiffly.

"Mrs. Bradford," said Lee, "there are nine gentlemen in this room. I would like to have you look around and see if you can pick out the man you saw on the roof of this house at half past three on the afternoon of November 3rd."

"One moment," interrupted the District Attorney. "How could she possibly identify a man that she had only seen across the street?"

"I looked at him through my binoculars," said Mrs. Bradford sharply. "That brought him right close."

"Proceed, please."

The old lady, enjoying her moment in the limelight, looked slowly from one man to another. Each man became self-conscious in his turn. She smiled coquettishly at Lee. "It certainly wasn't you, Mr. Mappin."

"Eliminate me," said Lee.

After she had looked at them all, her glance returned to George Coler.

"The gentleman in the corner," she said, "I can't see him very well. The light is poor."

The District Attorney smiled as one who humors the vagaries of a very old person. "Would you mind standing, Mr. Coler?"

Coler stood up. His face was like a mask.

"That is the man," said Mrs. Bradford.

The silence of stupefaction fell on the room. Coler's face turned brick red and his eyes bulged. "It's a lie!" he burst out.

Mrs. Bradford drew herself up. "I beg your pardon, sir!"

Coler struggled hard to regain his poise. "I'm sorry," he said. "I did not mean to imply that you were making a misstatement, but only that you were mistaken." He tried to carry it off with a laugh. "On the afternoon in question I was engaged in my business as I am every afternoon. I have never been on the roof of this house. I have never been on any roof since I was a boy."

"You are the man I saw!" said Mrs. Bradford firmly.

Coler looked at Lee and laughed again. "This is a farce staged by the clever Mr. Mappin!"

It was an error in tactics, for all the policemen and the attorneys in the room were familiar with Lee's work in criminology. They began to think there was something in the old woman's story. Lee was looking at Agnes. Her air of complete astonishment satisfied him that she had never known the truth. She had really believed that Al Yohe shot her husband and had embroidered her evidence only to make certain of his conviction.

Fanny started to wheel Mrs. Bradford from the room. Lee shook hands with the old lady. "Thank you," he said gravely. "You have served justice today."

"Will I be called upon to testify in court?" she whispered eagerly.

"Without a doubt."

The District Attorney was in a state approaching consternation. "I don't understand," he said. "What does this mean, Mr. Mappin? Are you suggesting that Mr. Coler should be arrested for this crime?"

"Not at all," said Lee calmly. "Certainly not on such inconclusive evidence. Mr. Coler is one of the most prominent citizens of

New York. He's not going to run away. Should any explanations from him be required later, I'm sure he'll be glad to satisfy you at any time."

Coler was not deaf to the ironic intonations in Lee's voice, and his glance was poisonous. He laughed again. "This is the most preposterous thing I ever heard of!" With a glance at Agnes, he tried to draw her into his laughter, but Agnes was stony and dazed.

"Please take me to my room," she whispered.

They went out together.

The men got out of the apartment as best they could. Loasby whispered to Lee:

"Is it wise to let them go free?"

"What else can we do?" said Lee.

An hour later Lee and the District Attorney were sitting with Inspector Loasby in the latter's private office when word came over the teletype of a shocking accident in the neighborhood of Fort Lee. A Cadillac sedan had been driven at full speed over the edge of the Palisades, evidently with suicidal intent, and had smashed on the rocks below.

Shortly afterwards, word came that the two occupants of the sedan had been identified from papers on their persons as George Coler, President of Hasbrouck and Company, and Mrs. Jules Gartrey.

"What did I tell you!" cried Loasby.

"It was the cleanest way out," said Lee. "Far better than the poison of a long-drawn trial."

CHAPTER TWENTY-FOUR

"THE CIRCUMSTANCES WERE SUCH," Lee said to the District Attorney, "that Al Yohe believed Mrs. Gartrey had shot her husband and Mrs. Gartrey believed that Yohe had done it."

"How could that be, Mr. Mappin?"

"Mrs. Gartrey was in her dressing room. We must assume that she had left the door into the corridor open as a precaution. She heard the elevator door open, and ran out with some idea of preventing Gartrey from discovering that Al was in her boudoir. But the shot was fired before she reached him and she fell fainting in the corridor. A moment later, Yohe found her lying there. She must have come to as soon as Yohe ran back to the service entrance, and, finding him gone, drew the natural conclusion. When she heard the butler coming, she ran into the music room."

"Where was the lady's maid then?"

"She was still in the dressing room, paralyzed with terror, one may suppose. She didn't appear in the foyer until after her mistress came out of the music room."

"Mr. Mappin," asked the District Attorney, "when did you begin to suspect that George Coler was guilty?"

"It was a matter of slow development," said Lee. "In the beginning I was convinced, like everybody else, that Al Yohe was the murderer. It was not until after Al had forced himself into my presence and told me his story that I began to doubt."

"What put the doubt into your mind?"

"The fact that Al Yohe's story absolutely coincided with that of Hawkins, the butler. I was already satisfied that Hawkins was telling the truth. I then re-examined the stories told by the different inmates of the Gartrey household, and in some cases I questioned them myself. I questioned Mrs. Gartrey and the maid, Eliza Young, on several occasions. All this testimony satisfied me at length that neither Al Yohe nor Mrs. Gartrey could have done it.

"It was then necessary to find another culprit and for some days I was stumped. There was an effort to cast suspicion on the butler, Hawkins, but that wouldn't hold up for a moment. Eliza Young, too, was obviously incapable of such an act. All the testimony agreed that, saving these four, there was nobody near the spot when Mr. Gartrey was shot. The manservant, Denman, whose actions in other respects were suspicious, was in a watchmaker's shop when it happened. And how could any other person have got into a house so well guarded both front and rear by hall men and elevator operators? All these employees asserted that no unexplained person had entered the house previous to the murder.

"I was helped a good deal by a story told me by one who was in Mr. Gartrey's confidence. This person's name has never been mentioned in connection with the case, and I see no object to be gained by mentioning it now. The story gave me a picture of the situation that existed in the Gartrey household at the time of the murder. Mr. Gartrey was aware of his wife's infidelities. Indeed, she took little care to hide them, she was so sure that he would put up with anything rather than submit to the ordeal of a second ugly scandal in his domestic life. In this she was wrong, for Mr. Gartrey had made up his mind to divorce her. She had offered to go to Reno and divorce him without scandal in the customary manner, but had demanded so great a price that he refused to pay it. He had settled a very large sum on her at the time of their marriage. His suspicions settled on Al Yohe and, in order to conceal his hand, he befriended the young man. He even lent him a large sum of money on mortgage to decorate his night club. He had employed private detectives to watch his wife, but nothing came of that. He then paid one of his servants, this same Denman that I have spoken of, to call him up on the private phone at his office to inform him whenever Mrs. Gartrey received a gentleman visitor.

"When I asked myself: Who profited by Mr. Gartrey's death? the answer immediately presented itself—George Coler. Upon the death of Mr. Gartrey, Coler succeeded to the immense financial power that the older man had wielded in Wall Street. Furthermore, I presently discovered that Coler was in love with the beautiful Mrs. Gartrey. I then scented a devilish plot by which Coler had sought to remove *both* men who stood between him and his desire. But I had no evidence, no evidence. It was easy to establish that Coler was not in his office when Mr. Gartrey was shot, but how could he have got into the apartment house, guarded as it was at all times by hall men and elevator operators? Coler was well known to all these employees. At this point, a highly significant fact developed. *Nobody telephoned for Coler after the murder, yet he was one of the first to turn up at the apartment after it occurred.*

"Judging from what happened, Denman must have called up Mr. Gartrey shortly after three o'clock on November 3rd and told him that Al Yohe was in the apartment. Mr. Gartrey, greatly agitated, called for Coler, who was in his confidence. Coler's secretary reported that her employer had left shortly before. Note the word "left." If Coler had gone out she would naturally have said so. The word "left" signifies that she did not expect him back again. Mr. Gartrey must then have driven directly home. He arrived there at three-forty. He had no murder in his heart because he was not armed. All he was after was evidence.

"Note that Mr. Gartrey, for the first time in his life, did not warn the household of his coming by ringing the bell. It seemed as if his murderer must have been lying in wait for him just within his own door. But, if so, how had he got into the apartment? By the logic of circumstances I was forced to the conclusion that the murderer was not lying in wait for his victim; *they entered the apartment together.* If I was right about this, the murderer was certainly a man who was in Mr. Gartrey's confidence and this could be no other than Coler. But still no evidence. The boys downstairs all testified that Mr. Gartrey had come in alone.

"Well, if Coler had not come in with Mr. Gartrey, he must have been waiting for him somewhere inside the house. There was only one possible hiding place, the stairs. This stairway is contained within a fireproof shaft alongside the elevator. In a house of this type, the stairs are never used, and a man lurking there would be safe from discovery. On every floor at right angles to the elevator there is a fireproof door leading to the stairway. Since the stairway is supposed to serve as a fire escape, these doors are never locked. Each door has a little square pane of glass let in at eye level. It was therefore simple for Coler to wait behind the door watching for the coming of Mr. Gartrey. Coler would tell him that he had been watching on his behalf, or to prevent him from doing something reckless—or what you like. Mr. Gartrey trusted him. And after Coler had shot Gartrey, how easy to slip back into his hiding place on the stairs and watch there until the little elevator hall filled with excited people drawn by the report of the murder, all trying to get into the Gartrey apartment. Coler could mix with these people and none would be able to say later where he had come from.

"Still, I had no evidence that I could take into court. I had made the interesting discovery that though Mr. Gartrey was dead, Denman, the spy, was still reporting everything that happened in the house to somebody outside, by telephone. He did me the honor to take notice of all my comings. So, it appeared, he had been serving two masters. Had he telephoned to two men on the afternoon of the murder? Coler had a private phone on his desk. It was not until the day before yesterday that I discovered Denman was calling George Coler by his private number. The rest was easy. I found that shortly after three o'clock on November 3rd, Denman had seduced the two boys who were on duty at the service entrance away from their post, thus enabling Coler to gain the service stairway unseen. Coler had climbed the stairs to the roof and, crossing the roof, had descended the front stairs. Mrs. Bradford saw him on the roof and my case was complete, gentlemen."

"A very clever piece of deduction, Mr. Mappin," said the young District Attorney patronizingly.

Lee rubbed his upper lip.

Inspector Loasby, who knew Lee much better, said nothing, but only grasped Lee's hand and shook it solemnly.

"How did Coler get possession of Al Yohe's gun?" asked the District Attorney.

"For some weeks previous to the event, Coler had been assiduously cultivating Al Yohe's friendship. He was a frequent visitor to the young man's flat. The careless Al was often shut up in his dark room when people came, and Coler had ample opportunity to look for the gun."

"What about the Philadelphia murder?"

"A clumsy crime. The astute Coler had no part in that. It was a private venture of Mrs. Gartrey's, undertaken to save, as she thought, the man she loved. Coler was terribly upset when he learned of it. He was clever enough to see that it was likely to lead to disaster for both of them. It was undoubtedly Coler's idea to hang that murder on Al and to bring Harry Brummel into the case. Brummel will be able to wriggle out of it on the pretense of ignorance, but I'll get him some day!"

"What about the man who tried to shoot Al Yohe at Mount Pisgah?"

"Nobody got a good look at that man, but it was undoubtedly George Coler. I suppose he had followed me up there on Sunday and so discovered Al's hiding place. By that time he realized that the whole structure was coming down on his and Agnes' heads, and that Al's death was the only thing that would save them."

"And then the double suicide."

"I doubt if that was a double suicide," said Lee gravely. "The woman had not nerve enough to face death. Coler got her to enter his car on the pretext perhaps of escaping, and he drove over the cliff."

"Jocker Stacey's charge that Al Yohe hired him to kill Robert Hawkins is still in evidence," said the District Attorney.

"We needn't worry about that," said Lee. "Coler and Mrs. Gartrey are dead, and the enormous price offered Jocker for the lie will never be paid. There is no reason now why Jocker should not tell the truth."

"But without Harry Brummel to save him, Jocker must know that he will have to burn; a cold-blooded murder undertaken for pay. Suppose out of sheer cussedness he refuses to change his story?"

"Al Yohe is provided with an alibi," said Lee.

POSTSCRIPT

ALASTAIR YOHE WAS NOT REQUIRED to stand trial on either charge. Jocker Stacey recanted his first confession to the police and threw himself on the mercy of the court. He was, nevertheless, condemned to die. In his final confession, he named Alan Barry Deane as the man who had sought him out and had introduced him to Mrs. Gartrey. Deane had not been present during Jocker's interviews with the lady and was not liable to prosecution, since it could not be proved that he knew a murder was involved. However, it dealt a fatal blow to the elegant Mr. Deane's reputation and he disappeared from New York.

Al Yohe sold out of La Sourabaya and that scintillating establishment went the way of most of its kind and was presently extinguished. After a period of retirement from the public view, the Yohes turned up in Washington, where Al purchased a little hotel on Seventeenth Street in the thick of things and christened it the Charlotte. It gradually became known to the international gourmets that this was not just another hotel, but a place where superlative food was to be had—at a price. People then asked themselves why such a restaurant had not been opened in the nation's capital long ago.

Mr. Amos Lee Mappin had no inconsiderable part in making the Charlotte a success. He got into the habit of flying down to Washington about once a fortnight during the season to give a dinner. In New York Mr. Mappin's little dinners had long been famous, but they brought a new note into the oppressively formal

214

atmosphere of social Washington. Actually, the guests were not chosen for their names but for their personalities; Senators, Cabinet ministers, and Ambassadors had to take their chance with the unknown man. In attending one of Mr. Mappin's dinners you ground no social ax, you assumed no obligations; you went solely to enjoy yourself. It was quite an innovation.

Lee's chief sources of pleasure in his dinners at the Hotel Charlotte were that he was served by his friend, old François, and that the delicious Charlotte herself was placed opposite him at the table where he could look at her. Charlotte was an exception among the ladies present; she was not clever at all; but according to Lee the aura of sweetness surrounding her provided a sauce for his food rarer than any the chef could evolve.

HOW AMOS LEE MAPPIN WAS SNARED INTO AN INTERVIEW BY AN ENGAGING YOUNG REPORTER

A Letter

DARLING MARY:

I HAVE THE MOST WONDERFUL NEWS FOR YOU! I have a job as reporter on the *Blade*. On my first day at work I secured an interview with Amos Lee Mappin (through dumb luck) and my salary was doubled! Excuse it if you find me a little breathless. I enclose a clipping of the interview as it appeared this morning. Of course the rewrite man has bitched it some, but not too much. This is the official interview. Now I'm going to tell you what really happened.

To begin at the beginning; after my first interview with the city editor of the *Blade*, I returned yesterday at noon to hear the verdict and was hired on probation at twenty-five a week, starvation wages in New York. For my first assignment I was told to interview Amos Lee Mappin and get a line on his personal habits, methods of work, etc. It seems this is a kind of joke they play on each greenhorn that comes into the office. It's supposed to take down his conceit. But I didn't know that of course, and I set out to do or die.

Mr. Mappin has an office in an old building on lower Madison Avenue and I went there in the middle of the afternoon. He has two lovely secretaries, one blonde, one brunette. The little blonde one did the talking. She was perfectly businesslike of course, but there was a provoking twinkle in her eye too. The other girl addressed her as Fanny.

216

She said Mr. Mappin was out, but I knew by instinct that she was lying. There was an inner office with the door closed. She asked me what I wanted of him and I gave her my song and dance. Mr. Mappin never gave any interviews she said, except when he was engaged on a case that the public was entitled to know about. Since the Gartrey case has been settled there was nothing more to give out. Mr. Mappin was engaged in writing a book and could not be interrupted. This was positive and final. I spun it out as long as I could, hoping the inner door might open, but these girls were old hands at dealing with crashers and when the little one said as sweet as peaches: "You'll have to excuse us now," I had to beat it.

For a good two hours I walked up and down on the other side of the street watching the door. I knew what Mr. Mappin looked like from newspaper pictures, but he never came out. Shortly after five the two girls appeared and went home. I was pretty sure he was still there so I crossed the street and went up to his office. The door was locked now. There was a light in the back room so I just lighted my pipe and waited in the hall. In about half an hour he came out. Gosh! I had to work fast!

"Mr. Mappin," I said, "I'm a reporter on the *Blade*."

"Charmed!" he said sarcastically, "but you'll have to excuse me."

"I was hired today on probation," I said, "and instructed to interview you. If I don't get anything I'll be fired to-morrow."

"That will be just too bad," he said, starting down the stairs. But he had a sort of smiling look and I had a hunch to tell him about you and how we were going to be married as soon as I made good. All this while we were trotting downstairs side by side.

"Well!" he said when we got out in the street, "this is a desperate case!" He looked me over and said:

"You appear to be a good young egg though I'm probably mistaken. I don't know whether I'll give you an interview or not, but you may ride uptown with me."

So we got in a taxi. He told the man to drive up Fifth Avenue. I started asking him what I thought were intelligent questions, but he paid no attention. Instead he produced a snuffbox and springing the lid, offered me a pinch. That shut me up. Seems it's a trick of his to offer snuff to strangers just to see them look surprised. Nobody ever takes any. Then he started to talk without any prompting from me.

"It may take half an hour to get to Fifty-sixth Street this way but I wouldn't miss it. I have a passion for this city and this street. I recommend such an impersonal passion, young man, but of course at your age you can't see anything in it. One expects no return consequently there's no heart-break involved neither any possibility of satiety. It will last out one's life. Observe Altman's window-dressing. There is a creative spirit behind it. The most vital art of our day is to be found in window-dressing, but nobody takes it seriously because it's only to sell goods."

And so on all the way up the Avenue; a little lecture on the old library and the gigantic office building towering above it; the landmarks that have disappeared; Maillard's, Sherry's, Delmonico's and those that have survived; the St. Regis and the Gotham. He got off a little prose poem about the R.C.A. tower; "a gigantic sarcophagus raised to the sky." St. Patrick's cathedral, he said, was built five hundred years too late. Not a word about my interview until we drew up before the door of his apartment house on the East River. There, while sitting in the cab, he said with his eyes twinkling behind his glasses—you can't be sure whether he's pulling your leg or not:

"I have to protect myself because I am by nature indiscreet. I love to talk off the reservation and I have learned that it does not pay; there are too many ill-natured people in the world. But you look like a generous fellow, not yet corrupted by the town; if I give you your interview will you show me what you write before turning it in and promise not to add anything afterwards."

Of course I agreed to that.

"If you're so keen about the city," I said, "why must it corrupt me?"

"I'm crazy about it," he said, "but I am not kidded by it; it's a bad place for the young because of the furious, bitter struggle to get on in the world. The only thing that saved me was that I inherited a modest fortune."

I said: "I have no fortune, but if you would be my friend perhaps that will save me."

He was tickled. He clapped me on the shoulder saying:

"By God! I never received a prettier compliment! And from one of my own sex, too! Come on in and have a drink!"

I have described his apartment in my newspaper interview so I need not enlarge on it here. He has a cadaverous man-servant called Jermyn who idolizes him. When Mr. Mappin likes anybody he is always poking fun at him, that's how you know when you're making good with him. We sat in front of the fire with the best Scotch and soda I ever tasted and he said:

"Well, start the interview." Whereupon every idea flew out of my head. My first question was banal enough.

"Why have you never married, Mr. Mappin?" His eyes twinkled but he never cracked a smile.

"This is off the record, my boy. My inches are too few and my pounds too many. I recognized in the beginning that I would never make a figure of romance and I put it behind me. Men of my figure are usually attracted to Amazons of six feet or over and they do not respond to our devotion. I have my compensations, though. Men who are forever chasing after some woman or other can have no idea what interesting creatures they are when examined dispassionately."

My next approach was not much more sensible and he was frank to tell me so. I asked him to describe his methods of work and he said:

"How can I do that when each case presents a new set of problems? However, I will lend you a couple of my books and if you read the cases in which I have myself participated, you can see exactly how I proceeded. There is no magic in it. I will give you one piece of information that must be carefully guarded from the public."

"What's that?" I asked eagerly. He said with his grave face and shining glasses:

"I follow my hunches!" I suppose I showed in my face that I felt sold, because he laughed in his silent way, and poured me another drink.

When I asked him about his museum of crime that everybody talks about, he said:

"There's nothing to it. I have of course a file of notes, clippings, photographs and all printed or written matter pertaining to crime. Every one who does research must keep such a file. But material objects have no interest for me after I have finished with them. I am, to misquote Hokusai, the old man mad about psychology. What I am always after is, what makes people behave the way they do? However, I have a few objects that have been saved for one reason or another and I'll show you those."

He opened a cabinet in his living room.

"This odd little wooden barrel contains what is left of the cyanide that killed His Highness the Sultan of Shihkar when he was on his way to pay his respects to the President in Washington. You had better not unscrew the top. It was tossed out of a window of the Sultan's private car and picked up beside the Pennsylvania tracks next day. That was one of the strangest cases I ever confronted. It proved to me that after all the Eastern mind works in much the same fashion as the Western. I have kept the odd little barrel because I have never been able to establish how it came into the hands of the murderer. Every case leaves one or two such loose threads to tantalize the investigator.

"This," he went on, picking up a dainty little arrangement of human hair, "is the false mustache worn by the murderer of Gavin Dordress, the celebrated playwright, who was shot in his penthouse apartment a few years ago. The murderer, you may remember, reversing the usual process, shaved off his mustache to commit the crime and wore a false one afterwards to avoid detection. There is no reason for saving this. My man Jermyn happened to pick it up here in my living-room and stuck it in the cabinet."

The next object Mr. Mappin selected was a smooth gold knob.

"This once formed the head of a heavy ebony walking-stick. With this stick the famous Rene Doria was killed in his love nest in the Lancaster apartments—not killed exactly; he was struck down with the stick and shot through the head. A young man of extraordinary good looks, he masqueraded as an Italian count and

cut a wide swath in the nightclubs. He was about to marry one of
our greatest heiresses when he was killed. In reality he was the
son of a barber in Kansas City or some such place. I saved the knob
because I have reason to suspect that it was the instrument of several other murders, and I am hoping that some day I may be able
to fit the jig-saw puzzle together."

I asked Mr. Mappin if he had preserved any relics of the Walter
Ashley murder which created so much excitement at the time.

"Only the sheaf of letters," he said, "that the murderer wrote
to me before and after the crime, challenging me to bring it to light.
They have a quite unusual psychological value. That murder would
never have been discovered had it not been for the scoundrel's
vanity. He had to tell somebody how clever he was."

"Didn't he send you his victim's ear?" I asked.

"He did," said Mr. Mappin, "but I have not preserved that little
relic."

Mr. Mappin fetched the letters from his file and allowed me to
read them.

I had read them before in the newspapers, but it gave me a thrill
actually to have the originals in my hands.

You can piece out the rest of our talk from the newspaper
interview. I rushed away to my room and wrote the interview. Mr.
Mappin revised it and passed it the same night and I was able to
turn it in before the paper went to press. Did I enjoy my entrance
at the office—and how! The boss at first refused to believe that the
stuff was authentic. He called up Mappin to verify it. Then he gave
me the raise. I believe we could get along on fifty a week though it
would be close going in New York. But the point is that through
the kindness of this old gent I have established myself at the office
and things seem to be breaking right.

How about setting a date?

Yours ever,
Frank

COACHWHIP PUBLICATIONS

COACHWHIPBOOKS.COM

THE
MYSTERY
OF THE
FOLDED
PAPER

HULBERT
FOOTNER

ISBN 978-1-61646-255-8

COACHWHIP PUBLICATIONS

COACHWHIPBOOKS.COM

1

HULBERT FOOTNER
THE ADVENTURES OF
MADAME STOREY

ISBN 978-1-61646-236-9

COACHWHIP PUBLICATIONS

ALSO AVAILABLE

THE MUMMY
CASE MYSTERY

DERMOT
MORRAH

ISBN 978-1-61646-250-7

THE PHILOSOPHER'S
MURDER CASE

JACK R. CRAWFORD

ISBN 978-1-61646-251-5

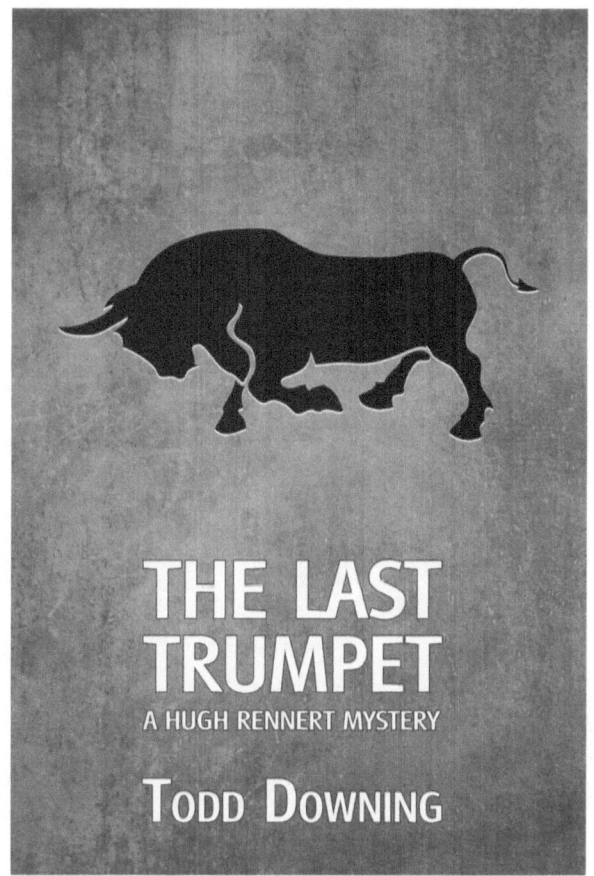

THE LAST
TRUMPET
A HUGH RENNERT MYSTERY

TODD DOWNING

ISBN 978-1-61646-152-2

COACHWHIP PUBLICATIONS

COACHWHIPBOOKS.COM

MURDER OF
THE HONEST BROKER

WILLOUGHBY SHARP

ISBN 978-1-61646-211-6

www.ingramcontent.com/pod-product-compliance
Lightning Source LLC
Chambersburg PA
CBHW031224260626
47169CB00007B/2178